MW01641697

TERRY & JORDAN

STENZELBARTON

Hell Happened

Zombies Vs Horsepower

Tia saw the men raise their weapons. She was a very bright woman and knew in an instant why they were aiming in her direction. “Oh shit,” she said to no one and looked in the rear view mirror. The zombies had just cleared the hole she’d made and were coming straight at her and the men who were on her crew.

“Like hell, you sons of bitches,” she hollered and threw the Escalade into reverse. The little woman, whose feet barely reached the floor, pulled on the steering wheel and stomped on the accelerator again.

The back window was shattered by the head of one of the zombies as she hit the two coming out first with the rear bumper. She felt the bodies being crushed beneath her truck, and shredded by four spinning tires as she gunned the SUV’s 400-horse powerplant.

She briefly recalled how it felt when she drove her old Durango too fast over speed bumps.

The Cadillac felt the same way driving over zombies.

Published by White Feather Press, LLC
www.whitefeatherpress.com

ISBN 978-1-61808-049-3

Printed in the United States of America

Cover design created by Terry Stenzelbarton

Reaffirming Faith in God, Family, and Country!

Acknowledgements

The idea for this novel came after a conversation I had with a fellow author following the sermon at the church we attend. We were talking about Star Trek novels and other ideas when Skip mentioned zombies. I didn't give it much thought until I was on my way home because I'd never written a zombie novel.

The storyline just exploded in my head while driving and singing to classic country songs on the radio. Yes, it's true, classic country songs gave me the kernel of an idea for a zombie novel.

I say exploded when I tell the story of where I got the idea, but I didn't have characters or an environment in which to put them. There were plot holes you could drive dump trucks through, no characters that needed redemption, no decent antagonist, no drama at all.

It was a narrative with no life. If it had been a horse, it would have been dog food by Monday morning.

Enter my son, Jordan. He and I usually spend Sunday afternoons foraging for food at the local stores, eating lunch at the ethnic restaurant and playing tennis with friends.

When I explained what I was thinking, he was more than willing to talk about zombies. What bothers him about typical zombies is they're dead. It was his idea to make the zombies included in the book not dead, but zombie-like. He and I talked for hours hammering out their attributes.

Jordan also listened to the story develop over the three weeks it took to write. He changed dialog and personalities of the people about who I wrote, changed the obstacles they faced to add realism and added the proper emotional responses.

But what Jordan did more for this book, and either of the other two I've written, was he pushed me when I locked up. I could stare at the words for hours and not see where to take the story. I'd read what I'd written to him and stop where I was stuck. From there, he'd bounce ideas off me until we came up with the story you're about to read.

Were it not for Jordan, it would not be the story it is.

Without my editor Kristen, however, this book wouldn't be as readable as it is. She spent a fortnight fixing my screw ups and poor grammar and she did it with a smile. I wish I'd used her as an editor on my other books and they might have done better. She is absolutely the very best.

Then there's Tia, the real person, not the Tia in the book. They are nothing alike, but I like the name so used it. She gave me the encouragement when I was tired and motivation when I slacked off. She's been my best friend for years and will get the second copy the publisher gives me.

Shout outs have to absolutely go to Russ, Cheryl, Kayla and Lisa, my dear friends who've been there for me through this ride. They heard I was again in my writing mode and cheered me on like the good people they are. To paraphrase Pastor Joel: if you want to know who I am, look at my friends. I'd say my friends are the best.

Last, but far from least, I have to say thanks to my Life Group, from whom I have freely stolen first names, not their personalities, just the names, for characters in the book. They put up with my attitude when I was tired, my anger when I was mad, and regularly overlook my failures.

Bless them all

Chapter One

"Dammit all to hell," Jerry cursed as he closed the main doors to his underground shelter with a slam. "What in God's name was Jeff thinking?" He slammed both bolts to their locked position, slapped his palm flat against the frame, then turned around and leaned against the heavy oak doors.

Jerry had not been having a good day and it was not looking to be a good night either.

Kellie knew it was not going to be a good night. She was grateful Jerry had not killed her when she and her little dog Molly had stumbled upon his shelter. He almost did when she came walking through his back field just before sunset three weeks earlier with her story of escaping a band of violent vigilantes. She'd come to know Jerry more by what he didn't say than what he expressed in words. She knew when he was angry he would and could use cursing as his outlet for frustration.

She knew he was pissed right now because she seldom heard him swear. Jerry read the bible regularly and he was a kind and gentle man of simple means and simple words and simple pleasures. He wasn't an angry man, so she just listened to him while he took off his work boots and jacket and muttered his displeasure at the turn of events. At 40 she'd had experience with violent men, including her ex-husband, and Jerry wasn't the type to be demonstrative, but when it came to cursing in frustration and anger, he could string together a line that was both entertaining and instructive.

Randy, who was used to his dad's occasional outbursts, also knew it was not going to be a good night. He loved his dad and knew him better than anyone alive. He knew his dad was angry because someone had done something really stupid if he was muttering like he was.

Randy knew it was best if he just stood quietly as his dad went on his little tirade. He made mental notes because his dad was really good at insulting people, and he might need some of the curses later.

Monica, the no-longer grossly overweight teen who had grown up two towns over, put her head in her hands and started to cry. She was, it turned out, a bit of a drama queen, as everyone in the shelter knew by now. She also knew Jerry was pissed.

Since he wasn't pissed at her, she needed to do something to get their attention back on her so she started crying.

No one cared. They had grown used to her crying.

Jerry and Randy had found Monica on their first sojourn away from their shelter and into the small city of Moody. She was eating Little Debbie snack cakes in one of the few quick-stop gas stations that hadn't been totally sacked and burned. How she'd survived on her own for so long was a surprise, but sometimes people just got lucky.

Jerry and his soft heart took her in, and she had gone from an obese, lazy whiner to a stout drama queen over the past three weeks. She hated her life, but Jerry was firm about rationing and insisted everyone try to eat healthy. The labor needed on the farm to keep everyone fed and safe was real work and if she wanted to keep being a part of it, she had to pitch in as well. She didn't like it, but there was no alternative. Jerry, the owner of the farm and the shelter in which she was living was fair, but he didn't enable her whining and laziness. Despite herself, she was becoming less of a bother and more of an asset, except for the need for attention.

Eddie, Randy's high-school friend who had survived the wave of death and collapse of civilization with nothing more than a "m'eh" attitude listened to Jerry's rant in silence. He knew, on very rare occasions, Jerry could spout a string of curses that left women crying and small children afraid of the dark. He sat and watched the leader of their group with his usual blank stare.

Truth be told, Eddie was from a younger generation who

figured some type of collapse of civilization would happen, so was not surprised that it did. The speed at which came, from start to the death of more than 99 percent of the human population of earth was less than two months. His mother had been one of the first to die and his dad had never been around, which left him not as shell-shocked as most people. His mother had been a whore who slept with anyone who would pay her some attention and he never really liked her although he did love his mom and would miss her.

Eddie liked Jerry, Randy's dad, and had spent a lot of time with them rather than his mother through high school and Jerry let him work on the farm to earn money.

He didn't care one way or the other if Jeff, the man about whom Jerry was currently cursing, never came back because the brutish former wrench head was a foul-mouthed bully who took every opportunity he could to talk trash about Jerry and the rest of the people who had taken refuge in Jerry's shelter.

Eddie didn't mind thinking that Jeff was being snacked on by some lucky zombies, or attacked by the vigilantes Kellie had told them about, but Eddie had made friends with Tony, the guy Jeff took on the scouting trip. Tony was a good kid and he and Randy made friends with the guy who was just a year younger, but a lot more adventuresome.

Tony had been found by Jeff and the two had been found by Jerry. He brought the two back to thc shelter.

In the days before being found, Jeff and Tony had lost a third person in their group to vigilantes so there had been some shared adversity between the two.

Mike, a former banking executive, and Terrill, a former homeless veteran, were already preparing the evening meal, and came into the foyer of the underground shelter to see what the commotion was all about. They, along with Kellie, were the most recent arrivals at the shelter Jerry had built and accounted for the entire human population of the shelter.

"What'd Jeff do now?" Mike asked, taking Jerry's AR-15 assault rifle and placing it in the gun safe that was always left open. Even though Jerry was nominally in charge, Mike always spoke in a manner which sounded like he was the leader.

His life was a history of management and being in charge. It had been difficult for him to transition from banking executive to survivalist, but he was making the effort, even if his way of speaking didn't always show it.

Mike and Terrill had been found a few weeks earlier. Jerry had a C.B. radio and a 30-foot lattice tower with antenna. Mike was a C.B. enthusiast who picked up Jerry's call out one night while scanning channels. While Mike was driving out of Birmingham, he found Terrill walking in the median of the interstate, looking lost and alone.

Jerry, having handed over the weapon and bandolier to Mike, was pulling off his light jacket and kicking off his boots while shaking his head. "That stupid fool was supposed to be back here an hour ago with the quads. I knew I shouldn't've have let them take the quads to Odenville," referring to both Jeff and Tony. Terrill wiped his hands on the white apron he wore and suggested Jerry tell everyone about it over the evening meal, which he'd just put on the table.

~ ~ ~

A war vet, Terrill was injured on his second tour of duty in Afghanistan from an improvised explosive device that killed his lieutenant and a specialist in the HUMVEE in which he was riding. They had been in the front seats, Terrill in back with the communications equipment. The explosion threw the vehicle 20 feet in the air and onto its side. Terrill blacked out for a moment and when he came to, he screamed.

Terrill lost both his right leg below the knee and the hearing in his right ear. He had scars on his right arm and hand and burn marks on his face. He also lost his want to be in the military and took a medical discharge.

Three years after his discharge, he was drinking his monthly allotment from the government and living on the streets of Harrisburg, about 12 miles southeast of Odenville. He was sleeping any place he could find that was out of the weather. He couldn't, or wouldn't hold a job because he no longer cared about being alive. He just wanted to drink away the memories of the lieutenant's brains dripping onto his lap while he waited to be extricated from the damaged vehicle.

He had to drink a lot. He became quite good at it.

When people started dying all around the city of Harrisburg, he stole as much alcohol as he could and walked out of the city, pushing a shopping cart filled with various spirits and several guns. He didn't think it was fair that so many others died a relatively painless death while he continued to suffer a painful life. He was too weak-willed to commit suicide, but he wasn't going to let someone else take his life from him either. He had more drinking to finish before he went through the pearly gates.

Terrill was walking along I-20 when Mike in his Escalade drove by. Mike almost drove on without stopping for the dirty, heavily-bearded man who was walking along the side of the road with a cart half filled with bottles and guns. Mike saw the military boots and camo pants and took the risk, stopping several hundred feet down the road from Terrill, just in case.

Zombies didn't drive, but Terrill knew vigilantes did, so he approached the luxury SUV carefully. He may have been homeless for a while, he may be a drunk at the time, but he was also a former soldier and he was armed with an M9 9mm pistol holstered under his dirty ACU (Army Combat Uniform) jacket. From 50 feet apart they introduced themselves.

Terrill took Mike up on his offer to make contact with Jerry. It would at least get him further away from the big city and the vigilantes and the zombies. Where Mike picked up Terrill was only about 10 miles from Moody, Alabama, and the outskirts of where Jerry had built his survival shelter into the back of a hill behind his farm.

There was suspicion from both of the people in the Escalade and they rode mostly in silence, but being alone for Mike was worse than being with someone who was silent. They made several wrong turns before finding the right farm. The last couple miles Terrill was able to help Mike by using the C.B. while Mike navigated around wrecked vehicles. It had been more than a week since Terrill had spoken at all and using commo equipment brought back bad memories, but Mike needed all his attention on the road.

They pulled into the long drive. They'd almost missed it,

what with the trees that were still in full bloom and Jerry had disguised it a little more to keep others from finding it easily. The dirt drive led up to a farmhouse. There was a barn and garage built into a hill and several outbuildings. The house looked vacant, the barn a little run down and yard and pasture were overgrown. There were some cattle in the distance grazing.

They stopped the SUV in the parking area and climbed out of their vehicle. Jerry called out from the barn, asking if either was armed. Both said they weren't, but Jerry didn't believe the soldier and called him on it.

Mike hadn't known Terrill was packing the 9mm. He raised his eyebrows at the former soldier.

When Terrill pulled out the handgun, Jerry asked him to put it on the hood of the SUV before he came out of hiding. He had to be sure it was safe to come out, and he didn't expose himself to the men without someone to cover him. Randy and Monica were both hiding in the farm house with rifles and Eddie was in the loft of the oldest barn with a 12 gauge shot gun loaded with buckshot.

Jerry walked out of his hiding space still carrying his AR-15, but kept it aimed at the ground. He introduced himself and asked a few directed questions to Mike and Terrill before relaxing. The real icebreaker was the cold beer Terrill offered him. Jerry was not a heavy drinker, but he did like a cold beer. That act of generosity was enough for Jerry to allow Terrill to put his handgun back in its holster and invited the men to meet with the others who had been in hiding.

The three men walked up the path that led behind the barns and around the hill to the shelter followed by the three younger adults who kept their guns loaded, but un-cocked. Mike said he could drive the SUV out of sight, but Jerry asked him to leave it where it was for now until he was sure he could trust these two men.

There was being friendly, then there was being reckless and Jerry made sure they were not too much of either.

~ ~ ~

Jerry had survived the fall of the government and the

world, and he did it without losing his son, which not many people could say. He was alive and fed and had a reasonably secure shelter, not because he had ever believed the world would come to an end, but because he was bored with his life. It just worked out that he had made a self-sufficient shelter.

Jerry was a divorced, moderately-successful soybean farmer. He grew up on his parent's farm not far from Moody, Alabama and took it over when his dad died in a tractor accident just before Jerry's 18th birthday. His mom passed on a few years later and everyone attested she'd died of a broken heart even though they found a lot of empty wine bottles and pills in her room.

The basic shelter was built several years earlier after his wife had divorced him, leaving him lonely and pissed. It had started with just digging a big hole in the side of the hill in which he thought he'd bury yard waste. Using his International Harvester tractor and its front end loader, the more he dug, the better he felt.

Jerry liked digging the hole and driving his tractor. The dirt he dug out, he piled as high as his tractor could pile it to form a parapet around the entrance to the hole he dug. He had no real plan, but he realized if the city tax assessor had discovered his hole, his estate taxes would go up, so he spent some serious time camouflaging the entrance.

Jerry wasn't a survivalist, but he did know how to survive, and over the weeks as the hole became enlarged, Jerry would often ask himself why he was digging it. Sometimes he would spend the entire weekend just digging deeper into the hill and enlarging the hole he dug and think about what he was digging and how he could improve upon it. Every few feet he'd add rail road ties to shore it up and keep it from caving in on him and his tractor.

Randy, his 22-year-old son and video game aficionado, would sometimes come out and check on his dad. He was no farmer and if the end of civilization had not encroached upon his life, he probably would have continued going to community college until he was forced to get a job at a local store in Moody, working as a stocker or cashier and hoping one day to rise to assistant manager. Randy was not a motivated young man, but he loved his dad and his dad loved him, even if they didn't understand each other and had far different work ethics.

Jerry's daughter, two years younger than Randy, had gone off to the military the day she turned 18. The farm life was not for her. She needed adventure. She had been an athlete in high school, but not outstanding at anything. She'd inherited her dad's independence and he'd applauded her choice, which was the final wedge that had driven his wife away.

Jerry hadn't heard from his daughter since the virus killed off nearly everyone in the world and the phone and internet had gone down, but he thought of her every day and hoped she'd inherited his and his son's resistance to the virus and was still alive. Someday he hoped to find out one way or the other.

The hole started becoming a survival shelter after Jerry watched some end-of-the-world documentary on late-night cable television. That was a year before the national news started warning people of a new flu being reported. It had interested him and for the next few months, Jerry slowly built a cramped nine-room shelter under the hill in the hole behind his house. As a farmer he had plenty of lumber around from an older barn he'd torn down which he used for walls and floors. There were still 50 bags of concrete left over from the new garage he'd built the previous spring to sturdy up the shelter. He also had the time on his hands which he had to put to work.

He stocked the shelter's cellar with hundreds of MREs he purchased off the internet, bulk vegetables and canned goods he bought wholesale, installed his own custom-built air filter and water purifier with parts bought off eBay and all L.E.D. lighting because he thought it looked nice. He wasn't stocking it in case the world collapsed; he stocked it in case another hurricane shut everything down like Katrina had done.

There was a bathroom and shower with a good drain field far from the shelter, an efficiency kitchen that had a freezer for the fish caught, and animals hunted, and a two-burner electric stove, stainless steel sink and a refrigerator Jerry had at one time filled with Budweiser beer, bar-be-cue sauce, mustard and assorted soft drinks.

~ ~ ~

Once civilization started falling, he'd also moved in some furniture he had taken out of the farm house. He knew that place would draw attention while the entrance to the shelter was hidden behind the hill.

After the government fell, he moved his weapon's safe from the office in the old barn to his new office in the shelter for protection and because Jerry knew Alabama Power Company would not be able to provide power to his home and farm now that everyone who worked there was dead or a near-dead body still walking around just searching for human flesh to eat. The farm house without electricity was a liability.

Electricity for his shelter was provided by a waterwheel generator he built out of parts from an old Massey Ferguson tractor and a generator he picked up from Sears in Birmingham. A tributary from the river that fed Lake Joyce ran through his property and was reliable for the generator. He also had two small wind generators on the peak of the hill. For a back up he also had a Honda 6500 watt gas generator.

A year after he'd started the shelter, and just a week before the first victims started dying enough to be mentioned on the national news, Jerry had finished installing the 150-gallon water tank and a Keltech tankless water heater. The shelter was as complete as Jerry thought he'd carry the plan.

He hadn't set out to create an apocalypse shelter, it just evolved to become one because of boredom and something to keep him busy when he wasn't working in the fields of his farm or tending the 22 Holsteins he and his boy milked twice a day.

His son Randy told him one late night as he came into the farmhouse they shared that it seemed his dad had become obsessed with the shelter and suggested his dad get out and around people more. Randy was a good boy who cared deeply for his dad, but sometimes, Jerry thought, the little brat could be meddlesome.

Jerry had taken his son's advice and went to the Lions Club that weekend. He still had a lifetime membership at the club. There he met up with his long-time friend Remi and they ditched the club for a little bar hopping like in the days of old. Jerry hadn't gone out to meet a woman, still stinging from his wife leaving him years earlier, but meet someone he did. Her name was Sissy, and like Jerry she was divorced and still a little bitter from her divorce. Remi had also introduced him to a woman named Mary and promptly took off for the dance floor with the woman leaving him and Sissy at the table.

After too many uncomfortable silent seconds, Sissy and Jerry were able to start up a conversation. They talked most of the evening while Mary and Remi danced most of the night, which seemed to please everyone. At the end of the evening as the bar lights came up, Sissy and Jerry exchanged email addresses and phone numbers.

Now she was probably, like most of the people of the United States and all over the world, dead or wishing she was dead. They'd exchanged a couple of emails and he'd called her the Wednesday following their first meeting to arrange a real date. That Friday, however, the government issued a statement about the death totals from the "virus" that had been hardly been given a more than passing mention in the news. The government spoke of world-wide numbers and warned that people should avoid public places. Schools, colleges, churches, football games, all public events and the like were all ordered closed or cancelled.

Jerry and Sissy put off their date as they went about their own preparations for surviving the "virus." Sissy, who lived in an apartment in a suburb of Birmingham and was living paycheck to paycheck, needed to get food in her apartment before the stores either closed or ran out. When he tried to call her that Friday night, he got her answering machine.

Jerry, who tried to be self-sufficient as possible, also went into town for foods he didn't have in stock already, but the stores were already being raided for everything and he was only able to get a few items he really needed like wheat flour and lard. Hoarding and vandalism was already starting. The internet went down the following Monday, followed by the electricity and telephone service and all of the public utilities that most people depended on. Public utilities were now a thing of the past.

The government fell fast.

Local television, now mostly just network feeds of dead bodies in the major cities, was hosted by anyone who wanted to be on camera. The local personalities were all dead or gone and the studios had been left running until the power went out.

Using a diesel generator, civil defense and local Alabama National Guard units took over the stations to give the news that the end of the world had happened. Even that stopped as soldiers and civilian died en masses.

That was when Jerry and Randy moved all their belongings out of the house and into the shelter. He moved the 300-gallon diesel fuel tank that he used to store fuel for his two tractors, the skid steer and his truck, and which was still about half full, back behind the hill and hid it in some brush. The 100-gallon gas tank he had for the generator which could run the barn lights he moved to a place near the diesel tank, but not so close as someone who found one, would find the other.

The world died while Jerry and Randy prepared for what was to come. They both thought they too would die, but when they didn't, when they heard some others were surviving, very damn few, but some, they put serious and thoughtful effort into making surviving on their own possible.

On the radio, when they could pick up a station with someone talking and not a loop of the civil defense instructions, they heard that very few others survived.

They also heard some of those who survived became the worst nightmare of humankind. Some people were mutated into a flesh eating, super strong and violently aggressive "zombies." Even though they had never been dead, this label stuck.

It was bad. Real bad.

The world died around them and each night, after closing and locking the shelter, the two would talk about what was next for them. Neither had an idea.

Eddie showed up soon after the fall. He never left.

Unreliable, but still believable, stories on the radio told of small encampments being attacked in the night by the savage not-deads. It was a glimpse into the outside world for the shelter's inhabitants.

A mutated virus laid waste to the populations around the world. It might have come from some highly-organized terrorist cell, maybe some scientist who'd made a mistake, some nation that didn't know what it was unleashing upon the world, or from the never-before-seen meteor shower that had peppered the earth for three days not long before the outbreak.

The speed at which it infected the populations around the world was staggering, but the after effects were even worse.

People died. Billions died.

It started in different countries around the world at about the same time. Newscasts down played it at first, but when people by the tens of thousands began dying, people of every race, of every faith, on every continent, it couldn't be down played any longer. Most of the population on earth was dead less than two weeks after the first reported death. There was no vaccine, no explanation, and no chance at isolating the virus.

The word "Armageddon" and phrases like "The End of Time" were tossed around by television commentators. Church attendance was at an all-time high.

None of it changed what was to come.

More than 99 percent of the world's population died within two days of becoming infected. There were stories of people lasting three days, but they too died so no one cared that someone survived a few hours longer than their loved one.

From the first known and documented victim to the wholesale deaths of tens or hundreds of millions in a single day, less than a month had passed.

The victims coughed and sweated for a day or so, said their good-byes then died. It wasn't a painful or horrifying death like in the movies, just a few coughs, a body temperature of 100 degrees plus or minus, then the brain just shut off and the person dropped dead.

Cats had also died, everything from the African Golden to the European Wildcat, from the wildest jungle cat to the most domesticated house cat, all had fallen to the virus. Other species that were known to have died were bats, horses and, much to everyone's great relief, the common mosquito. These were just the known species to have died, others might have but all the scientists who could have looked into the death of a species were all dead. Some species of birds died, while others survived and the same went for some snakes, but not others. It was a mystery no one left alive was able to figure out.

Of the fraction of a percent of humans who survived, someone figured about 50 percent of those became "zombies." They were not really zombies because they were alive, and they were more intelligent than movie zombies. The not-dead hid from the light of day and avoided bright lights and flames.

No one knew why.

There was no one left to investigate why the zombies didn't die. There was no one left to investigate why they would want to eat human flesh. There was no one left to do anything except survive as best they could.

The not-dead humans did not eat cows or pigs or dogs that had survived their owner's demise. The zombies only went after live humans, or, recently dead humans, which was pretty gross to watch. They feasted on the flesh with gusto, sometimes even before the victim was dead.

Oddly, they also didn't eat other not-dead humans. No one knew why and without scientists to explain their reasoning, it just remained a mystery.

The not-deads didn't use guns or bows and arrows or knives or any weapon. They used strength and speed and teeth to de-flesh a good human.

The humans left alive found out early that killing a zombie was not as easy as just shooting them with a shotgun. The damn things seemed to have no feeling in their extremities. You could put a bullet in their arms and legs and the zombies would continue to attack.

A shot in the torso of a zombie wasn't a guaranteed kill as some found out too late. People had witnessed more than one zombie eating a fresh kill and the consumed flesh would just fall out the open hole in the gunshot zombie.

Killing a zombie was only achieved with a good shot to the brain stem or by putting enough rounds into its body that blood loss or detached nerves put the zombie down. They were not an easy kill, but they weren't a major issue if uninfected humans barricaded themselves in to a secure location before sunset and stayed out of buildings they were not sure were clear of the zombies.

Something in the virus with which the zombies had been infected gave them superior visual ability in very low light and darkness, and a sense of smell that could pick up the scent of human miles away. They were super strong and while not stupid, they were not geniuses either. They would work together to break into strongholds to get at the humans inside.

Jerry had come across one other stronghold that had been raided by the zombies not far from his own farm.

It hadn't been pretty. It hadn't been clean. He hadn't gone back.

~ ~ ~

Now Jerry sat at the table with the other remaining six people who were living in his shelter. He didn't demand to sit at the head of the table; it was just the way things had evolved. His son and Eddie sat to his right, followed by an empty chair where Tony usually sat. Kellie sat at the other end of the table with Monica and Terrill on her right with an empty chair beside him where Jeff usually sat and Mike filled the last chair.

As usual, Monica dug in to the food before everyone had fully sat down and adjusted their chairs. It was a decent meal of large-mouth bass caught by Randy, Eddie and Tony early that morning, baked potatoes from the larder, some fresh asparagus Kellie had picked and a bundt cake with a sugar icing made by the former soldier Terrill. There was cold milk fresh from the 20 cows Jerry kept in the barn.

They filled their plates in silence except for the clatter of serving utensils on the steel serving dishes.

It was Jerry who eventually broke the silence as to why he was so angry.

"Jeff and Tony went Odenville to scout out a place that was supposed to have more ammunition and some heavier weapons," Jerry explained. They had nearly used up the ammunition for the AR-15 Jerry always carried with him. They had another 30 rounds for the Browning 12 gage and 50 for the Remington 700. Randy's weapon of choice was a Ruger Model 77 .30/06 with a 3x8 low-light scope. "I didn't want to send them, but they've been cooped up here for two weeks and they wanted to get away and do something beside work the gardens and build this place up.

"I shouldn't have let them go, but Jeff was becoming a pain in the ass and I thought he might do us some good," Jerry said between mouthfuls. "I told them to take the quads and stay off the main roads, and I know I said to be back by six. Tony went along because I know I can trust him to be smart and he gets along better with Jeff than anyone else."

Kellie was the first to voice a positive spin. "Maybe they ran into some trouble and had to hide out. I'm sure they'll show up. If not tonight, then in the morning. You know they are both smart enough to find shelter before dark."

"Dammit, I should have sent them with the truck with the radio in it so if they had trouble they could have called us," Jerry said with recrimination.

"Jerry, you don't know that would have been safer. The next time we go foraging, we'll see if we can't find some of those long distance walkie-talkies," Kellie said.

"We're not survivalists and we're all doing the best we can in the worst possible situation."

"Yeah, well," Jerry allowed, "like you said, we never had to do this kind of stuff before and the only reason I'm in charge is because I accidentally made this place." He used his chin to point around the small dining area. "I was thinking of retiring here in 15 or 20 years and watch the sun set for the rest of my life.

"I didn't think I'd be making life and death decisions for other people and just hoping to make it through a day to make it to tomorrow."

"We're all in the same boat, Jerry. I used to be a teacher of special needs children, and every day I asked myself if this was all they would become," Kellie said. "And now all of them are dead and nothing I did in my life has meant anything.

"I spent four days walking with Molly," she said referring to her multi-breed little mutt, "and would have walked until I died or until someone killed me because I was ready to die. Everyone in my life was gone. Every mistake I made didn't mean anything anymore. I was a clean slate when I came across your field," Kellie went on, distracting Jerry from his sulking thoughts. "We're all new at this and you're doing the best job anyone could ask of you."

"Thanks," he grumbled, not really mollified, but amendable to her words.

"Yeah dad," Randy added after a few seconds of silence. "What she said."

Randy had never been an articulate kid. He wasn't the smartest kid in school and failed a few classes, forcing him to take summer school twice. He'd never been very talkative unless it was something to do with video games. He was a large boy, topping his six-foot-tall dad by two inches and 60 pounds.

The seven of them ate in silence for a while longer. Usually there was some banter around the table, but tonight the joy of being alive was muted. Tony had fit in pretty well with the group, he played with electronics, and while Jeff was a pain in the ass with counter-views on seemingly everything, he was a good mechanic and now the two of them were missing.

"Well, the sun has gone down so no one is going out tonight," Jerry finally said as he cut into the bundt cake. "But what we can do is put up a lookout for them."

Jerry, when building the shelter, had spent a lot of time working on how the air would move around the enclosure. He had the main living area, kitchen, dining and bathroom on the main floor and a stairway down to a cellar where there was a storage area with the washer and dryer, central air and filtering set up. He also had a few other essentials for keeping his hole in the ground warm and dry.

Jerry hadn't started out to build a fortress, he started just to dig a hole and that turned into a shelter. The shelter was meant for himself and no one else.

~ ~ ~

Everything underground was a slap in the face to any aesthetic architect. The place had no square corners. It was haphazardly put together by someone who had a rough idea and just kept building on it and changing as he went along. Every wall was insulated from the ground with #15 felt, some waterproofing tar and concrete, but the concrete varied in thickness and, where it wasn't covered by barn wood or plywood, the finish of the concrete was damned ugly.

The walls that were covered by wood, the wood that had been salvaged off the old barn, and were of varying degrees of age and quality. The lighting throughout was all strings of LED lights which, in Jerry's mind, gave the place a cheery appeal and saved on electricity.

Jerry had built this place for himself and had not expected the end of the world as he knew it to be bringing him visitors. The visitors who did come, the ones now at the table with him, didn't complain. There were worse places they could be.

A spiral staircase, made from welded plow parts and leftover steel, led upward to three more small rooms which had been turned into sleeping areas now that Jerry wasn't going to be using them for his hobbies or for storing stuff. They all had inflatable beds with a pillow, sheets and blankets. There were Rubbermaid storage totes for clothes instead of dressers and a radio in each room. The radio antenna was alligator clipped to a wire that went outside and brought in pretty good reception.

Jerry and Randy had slept in one room, Kellie and Monica in another, Mike, Tony and Eddie in the third. Jeff had bunked down on the couch and Terrill felt most comfortable sleeping in the cellar. It was crowded, but no one was complaining about being out of the Alabama weather every night.

Above those three bedrooms, at the top of the staircase, were the air ducts for the return of warm air to the cellar and introduction of outside air when the inside air got stuffy. Up there Jerry had put an escape hatch for no other reason that he didn't want there to be just one opening to his shelter. It wasn't easy to get to and was covered with a manhole cover he'd picked up at an auction, so it wasn't easy to open either.

From the outside, the cover was hidden by shrubbery and only the most serious searcher or luckiest wanderer could have stumbled across it.

~ ~ ~

Jerry suggested that if Jeff and Tony did come back after dark, they'd probably be in a hurry. "I want someone sitting out through that hatch all night. We'll do it in shifts," he said. Kellie got up and retrieved the deck of cards from the living room. She'd guessed that everyone was going to whine about whichever order Jerry chose, so drawing cards was the fairest way. Jerry gave her a wink that said he would have suggested something similar to her idea. His favorite was drawing toothpicks.

She spread them out on the table and everyone scrambled for a card.

Monica drew the three of hearts, Mike the five of spades. They'd take the first two shifts. Randy and Eddie both drew sevens and instead of arguing they said they'd both sit the watch together which would be in the middle of the night. Terrill drew the nine of spades and he'd be relieved by Kellie who drew the 10 of clubs. She'd wake Jerry for the morning shift because of his King of hearts.

To Jerry, it seemed the card draw worked out well because he was always an early riser and no one else complained because maybe everyone was hoping Jeff and Tony would make it back yet tonight, meaning they wouldn't have to pull their shift.

That decision made, everyone finished off the food on their plates, leaving enough leftovers for the wayward two just in case, and took their plates and silverware to the kitchen. It was Jerry's turn to wash dishes, Kellie's turn to dry and stack. The others finished up any house cleaning chores they had.

Terrill vacuum-sealed the leftovers and put them in the freezer. He knew the adage of wasting not.

Monica had climbed the spiral staircase and Jerry could hear her grunting while lifting the manhole cover. He thought about going up to help her, but Mike put his hand out and whispered "She can do it. Let her do it," then gave a little nod.

Several grunts later, the hatch opened and Jerry could look all the way up and out to the stars above his hole in the hill.

Monica looked down at him, sitting on the rim of the exit after squeezing her teenaged fat ass through the hatchway. Even from 30 feet below he could sense the accomplishment in her smile. Maybe for the first time in her life she was proud of herself for accomplishing something...even if it was just opening a hatch cover.

Jerry waved and went to finish the dishes.

Randy and Eddie had already put the night's movie in the DVD and turned on the TV, but Jerry was pretty sure no one was going to watch the movie tonight. The boys plopped down on a pair of beanbag chairs and pulled out the hand held electronic games. They'd worked hard today and he was sure they'd not play long before going to bed.

Mike picked up his Galaxy Tablet to read from, Terrill a book to read, while Kellie and Jerry finished the dishes and cleaned the table and kitchen. There was little talk at all.

With the night's chores done, Kellie said she was retiring because she'd have to be up early for her watch. She bade everyone a good night. She even climbed all the way to the top of the shelter to say good night to Monica.

Jerry took the towels to the cellar and threw them in the dryer with a load of laundry Kellie had started earlier. He grabbed a pair of 10x42mm Trailblazer binoculars for the lookouts to use. Coming out of the cellar, he was thinking of what Jeff and Tony must be going through and it made him shiver a little. He knew he had to do something.

"Boys," he said to Randy and Eddie, "make sure you get some sleep tonight before your shift on watch."

"Okay, dad," and "Sure thing, boss," came the acknowledgements from the boys. He then climbed the spiral staircase, not for the first time thinking he should have put more effort into making the stairs wider and easier to climb. He passed by Kellie's door and heard her humming a Reba song and it made him smile.

Finishing his climb, Monica moved her big legs out of the way so he could exit through the hatch. He excused himself as he climbed through and stood atop his hill, his shelter, his world.

He looked up to see the stars. Without mercury and sodium vapor lights glaring around his farm, the view of the sky was unusually clear. Stars were sharper than anytime he could remember as a child and he never tired of looking upward.

He could see Venus, the bright, shiny blue planet, a hand's breadth above the horizon, unblinking but brighter than anything in the sky. The moon, which would be near full tonight had yet to come across the horizon and the sun which had set hours ago had left it as dark as it could get without cloud cover.

Knowing what to watch for, he could see satellites and the International Space Station go overhead. Standing in silence, he wondered what the men and women who had been stranded up there were thinking. They knew earth was dead and that no one down here could reach them. No one left had the knowledge to send anything into space.

"The poor bastards," he whispered while looking upward.

He'd almost forgotten the binoculars around his neck. He took them off and handed them to Monica. "I brought these up for you guys. They're pretty good, but not at night. But if you see lights in the distance, you'll be able to get a good look before they get close."

"What do you think happened to them, Mr. Saunders? You think they'll be okay?" Monica asked before he headed back down. He'd asked her to call him "Jerry" like everyone else, but she insisted on calling him Mr. Saunders.

"I don't know, Monica," he said, carefully saying what would least bother this sensitive young lady. "Jeff is a good man with street smarts and Tony is tough for a guy his size.

"I'm sure they probably just ran into some trouble and they'll show up tomorrow if they don't show up here yet tonight." This seemed to calm her worries and she took the binoculars and looked around then up at the stars. "I never saw the stars like this when I was growing up. They're beautiful," she said with a little bit of awe in her voice.

"Well, if you start feeling tired, make sure you climb up

and down the stairway some," he instructed. "Keep an eye out and if you see or hear anything, make sure to lock the hatch on your way down and wake up everyone."

"Yes, sir," she said, still looking through to binoculars.

"Wake up Randy in two hours. You'll probably have to shake him some because he's a heavy sleeper, and make sure he gets out of bed, because he will fall back asleep on you."

"Okay. I will. Good night," she said as he climbed back down the hatchway and down the spiral staircase. Kellie had stopped humming as he passed by her door and he hoped she had pleasant dreams.

Reaching the main floor, the boys were still playing their games and the two older men were reading. Jerry picked up the remote for the TV to turn on the movie but his heart wasn't into it. He turned the remote over in his hands and popped the batteries out and then put them back in. After a few minutes of thought he just blurted it out. "Tomorrow, we're going to take the truck and go looking for Jeff and Tony."

There, he said it. The decision was made.

It hadn't been a good evening and despite making the decision to search in the morning, he didn't foresee it being a good night to sleep.

Chapter Two

Jerry rolled over and looked at the clock. The time read 20 minutes after five in the morning. He knew Kellie would be down to wake him up in about 25 minutes like he'd asked, so he decided to get up now and save her the trouble. He wasn't sleeping very well anyhow. He threw off the covers and pulled on the same jeans he'd worn yesterday. He skipped putting on socks and just slipped his feet into the same worn corduroy slippers he'd worn for the past three years.

He pulled on a clean tee shirt and a red flannel shirt and made sure he turned off the alarm before he left the room. He had set the alarm everyday for the past 10 or 15 years, but could only remember a handful of times where he hadn't awakened before it went off. For a moment he wondered if keeping track of time even mattered anymore. With most of the world dead, did it really matter if it was 6 a.m. or 6:15? He ran his fingers through his hair and decided it wasn't worth thinking about.

It was very quiet in the shelter this early in the morning. He'd noticed how without all the modern conveniences running like he'd had in the farmhouse the silence could almost be a sound itself. He was able to hear the whisper quiet blower from the air circulator in the cellar and the very gentle hum of the refrigerator in the kitchen. But other than those two pieces of equipment, there was a wonderful silence in the shelter.

He padded down the stairs to the bathroom where he did his morning constitutional and brushed his teeth. He would shave and put all clean clothes on later this morning, but right now, he just wasn't in the mood and he didn't want to wake the others. He also wanted to know if anyone had seen anything, though he knew someone would have woken him if there'd been news.

Wiping his face with the towel he looked at himself in the mirror. "When did I start making life and death decisions?" he asked himself, not for the first time, as he looked into his own eyes. They stared back without an answer.

For much of his life, the biggest worries he had was if the farm was going to make a profit, or what could he have done different to keep Andrea, his ex-wife, from leaving him to grow old all alone. He'd never had an exciting life; just a day-to-day running of a farm, hiring helpers to assist him in the busy months and letting them go at the end of the season. He'd made some friends, but only one or two close ones, and they were all dead thanks to the virus that had spared his son and him, and a few others.

Whenever he looked into the mirror now, he saw a man who was in way over his head and way over his experience. He didn't see a survivalist, just a farmer who was trying to make the most of what was.

He hung the towel back on the rack and left his reflection to ponder. He had other things to worry about. As he remembered his ex-wife saying so many times that he just wasn't an introspective man or a very deep thinker.

Andrea had divorced Jerry six months after his daughter had joined the Army. She hated the "military machine" and by extension, began to hate Jerry. One morning he came in from the field and there was a note saying she still loved him, just wasn't "in love" with him anymore.

They'd had fights in the past, disagreements that lasted days and weeks, but Jerry thought they'd done pretty well raising two kids. They'd been married in their mid-20s and had almost 20 years together when the dam broke and she left him.

Try as he might, Jerry couldn't convince Andrea to come back home. She filed divorce papers, took her share of their savings and moved to Seattle to be with her high school sweetheart.

It'd pissed Jerry off and he lost 28 pounds from not caring if he ate or not, and the farm had suffered some as well.

Randy and Jerry's friends from Horizon Church where he worshipped got him through the hell. It was a slow process, but Jerry eventually found a way to make it through another day without wanting to just curl up and die.

Just thinking back to those times caused a flicker of pain in Jerry's chest, but not the thudding like he'd had three years earlier. It was the past. She was also probably dead. So probably was her high school sweetheart.

Kellie heard him coming and offered her hand as he climbed through the hatch. "Good morning," she said quietly. He took her hand and lifted himself up. Someone had brought a chair up sometime during the night and Kellie had been sitting in it.

"Good morning. No one showed up?" She'd had the fore thought to also make coffee. She had a mug beside her and offered him some which he took gratefully. "Nope. Randy and Eddie said they thought they heard some shots that were really far off, but they weren't sure. No one saw anything," she told him.

Jerry sat down on the grass and picked up the binoculars. It was still more than an hour before sunrise, but the eastern horizon was already getting light enough to see five or 10 miles distant. He saw nothing moving.

They sat in silence for a few minutes.

Jerry wasn't sure why Kellie hadn't gone back to bed. She could still get in a couple more hours sleep before everyone started waking up and making too much noise for anyone to sleep. Maybe she didn't want to go back down before her shift was really over.

"You don't have to stay, Kellie. Go down and get some sleep if you can," he told her, not as an order, but a suggestion. He pulled a piece of grass and flicked it in the air. It was a cool Alabama morning with a light breeze coming in from the gulf, and the air was moist, but not uncomfortable.

"I'm not tired, Jerry," she said as she sat back in the chair and leaned it back on two legs against a Slippery Elm sapling. "It's peaceful up here and I want to watch the sun come up. If you're tired, you can go back to bed," she offered.

"Nah," he said absently. "You know me. I'm always up early. It's that dang farmer's blood in me."

"I am learning a lot about you, Jerry."

Jerry, who'd only been half listening to Kellie, took a moment to realize she was saying more than her words. He stopped scanning through the binoculars and looked over at her. "Huh?"

~ ~ ~

Kellie smiled at the farmer and watched as he hesitated a moment, thinking of something to say. When he didn't come up with anything, he went back to looking through the binoculars.

Jerry was so much like the men she avoided so often in her past. He was a simple man, a man of the earth. He had dirty hands, calloused from hard work and scarred from injury. His face was open and honest, but his nose was already showing veins from too much time in the sun. His eyes were plain green and neither piercing nor expressive. His hairline had already recessed most the way up his head and he had a bald spot that his dirty work hat usually covered.

There were so many things about Jerry she never found attractive before the fall of the world. She'd always been drawn to the "pretty boy" or the "bad boy" type of man who had money to spend. Her ex-husband was of the type. He had been tall, handsome, a full head of dark hair, muscles that were defined from his time in the gym, athletic, well-dressed and a smile that drove the other female teachers, and two of the male teachers, at her school absolutely green with jealousy. Her friends congratulated her on such a handsome husband, and often told her how lucky she was to have snagged such a kind and caring man.

The new earrings she wore, the lovely necklace, the expensive bracelet, the car, were all gifts from her ex-husband. He was a successful investment broker who made good money and while she didn't need to work, she enjoyed her job.

She was the envy of the other teachers.

The earrings were an apology for the slap that left a hand print for several days and had to be covered with make-up.

The necklace was an apology for throwing a can of beer at her hard enough to leave a bump on the back of her head. The bracelet was his way of saying he was sorry for pulling her hair so hard and bruising her forehead.

The car…that was when she found out he'd been cheating on her with one of the many women with whom he worked.

Seven years of marriage went down the drain. She felt she was lucky they'd never had children, even though she loved kids, but Warren had been infertile. It was something she knew going into the marriage and they'd talked of adopting.

When he first started hitting and abusing her she attributed it to his anger at not being able to have children. His brothers had all sired children, but he never would. The plans they'd discussed about adoption never materialized.

She was happy about that decision.

While she had wanted children, as a teacher, she was able to enjoy them while still having freedom to enjoy the unencumbered life of not having them at home. She thought it was the perfect life that she'd won.

But the violence got worse the longer they were married.

Early in the marriage, it was the sulking and silence from him when Kellie had done something of which he didn't approve. Then he started getting more demonstrative. He hollered at her more and she still recalled to this day the first time he hit her. He said it had been an accident in which he hadn't meant to really hit her; it was that she'd made him so angry he just lashed out.

He convinced her with presents and candlelight dinners and that handsome smile that he really didn't mean it. She forgave him.

Some months after that, he had another accident during an argument over her purchase of a little puppy. She knew it was her fault for buying the little guy without asking him, but he was so cute and Kellie always had loved little dogs. She thought for sure Warren would love the little Pug she named "Rip Van Wrinkles."

Warren was pissed for a long time and complained about every hair he found in their usually well-kept house. If the dog had an accident, Warren would go on about it for hours and sometimes days. If the dog barked or growled, Warren found a reason to complain. One time when Wrinkles was caught on the bed, Warren pulled the blankets off, dog and all, and threw them at Kellie, telling her to keep the damn dog off the bed or else.

When Kellie had had enough and told him "fine, I'll take him to the pound in the morning and you won't have to put up with him," Warren lost his temper and kicked at and missed the friendly little dog, which scampered out of the way and ran to hide under the kitchen table.

Kellie went to get the frightened dog to calm his fears before he had an accident when Warren, still upset from missing the dog with his foot, threw his beer at the dog and accidentally hit Kellie in the back of the head. He said he was sorry that she'd gotten in the way of his throw.

The heart-shaped necklace with the ¼ carat diamond was accompanied by a dozen long-stem roses sent to her classroom was his apology, but Wrinkles had already been taken to the pound. She forgave Warren, again rationalizing that it was her fault for getting the puppy in the first place.

The bracelet was his apology from when he grabbed her hair and was pulling her into the kitchen to show her how the coffee maker she'd left on by accident had boiled the coffee dry, leaving a burned smell in the kitchen and a cracked carafe. She'd just gotten home from school and he had a beer in his hand when she walked through the door. She was barely able to yelp when he swaggered up to her, a smile on his face, the smile which melted women's hearts.

Instead of kissing her like she thought he was going to, Warren grabbed her hair and hollered right in her ear "are you trying to burn our house down you stupid cow?" He was already pulling her to the kitchen while she was trying to ask him what he was talking about. He had grabbed her hair hard and she felt it being pulled out when she was bashed into the hardwood archway which separated the kitchen from the dining area. Her left temple struck the hardwood frame and left her dizzy as Warren screamed about the coffee maker and the smell and the carafe, which he threw into the sink, shattering it.

It was later that night, after Warren had fallen asleep that Kellie had left him for the first time. She went to her sister Jennie's house and cried herself to sleep in her sister's bed with her sister beside her, just like when they were kids. Jennie's husband, Rich, who was a dear man, had offered up his room and wife. He slept in their sons' room with their three boys while Jennie and Kellie talked through most of the night.

Jennie counseled Kellie to get away, to get a divorce and never go back and offered her home, small as it was, as a place for Kellie to stay until she got things figured out.

Kellie finally fell asleep.

Kellie stayed with her sister for three days, calling the school to say she was sick the next morning, a Friday and the entire weekend. On Monday she went back to school. Jennie sent her husband to Kellie's house to get a change of clothes and some personal belongings.

Warren wasn't there when Rich made the clothing run, which was good with him. Rich and Warren never really got along, even when Kellie and Warren weren't fighting. Also, Warren was huge and Rich was a portly, gentle man. In a fight, Rich would get his ass kicked six ways before he could put his dukes up to defend himself.

Kellie said she was going to contact a lawyer after school, but she was intercepted by Warren with two dozen long stem roses in the parking lot, and made sure Kellie's friends all saw him there.

Kellie always left the school with two or three of her friends.

She was so predictable and Warren knew it.

Kellie might have told her friends they had been fighting, but he was sure she hadn't told them he had hit her. That wasn't the way Kellie was. All of Kellie's friends would see the roses, would see tuxedo he was wearing, would notice the heart-shaped flower pedals he'd arranged on her car. They'd all be envious of the way Warren apologized with gifts and old fashion romanticism.

Kellie would listen to his apology and know her friends would be eavesdropping or watching from their own cars. Kellie wouldn't make a scene because it wasn't her way. They'd all see how Kellie had a man so big, so wealthy, so powerful, bend down to one knee to apologize for some wrong he had done. The other women would go home to their husbands and say things like "why can't you be more like Warren?"

If they only knew what Warren's personality was really like behind the façade he made public, they would thank God their husbands weren't like Warren.

Kellie did contact an attorney, but not that night. That night she really tried to believe him when he said he'd never hurt her again and how he had been upset by losing some big account and every other excuse he could throw in. It was the first time he had admitted that it wasn't her fault that he'd hurt her.

She really tried to believe him when tears rolled down his face. She contacted an attorney when less than a year later she found a pair of women's panties in the center console of her husband's Lexus. They had been going out to dinner that evening when Warren was pulled over for speeding, again. She reached for the registration and insurance papers in the console only to be surprised by something Victoria Secret had sent someone else. Warren might have been able to explain them as a gift he was hiding to give to her later on, except the note that was bobby-pinned to the panties was in someone else's hand writing and read "Warren, anytime you get lonely again, I'm ready!' and signed by Suzy with a phone number underneath.

Kellie hid the incriminating evidence while Warren was out of the car talking with the officer.

He talked the female officer out of issuing a ticket and Kellie listened to him as he gloated how he had used his charm to get out of a ticket…again.

She pretended nothing was wrong through dinner because she refused to make a scene in public and listened while Warren told of his exploits at work and how another big account had come to him. All through his ramblings, Kellie kept the face of the adoring wife and Warren ate it up.

But inside, she seethed at the disgusting bastard.

Back home, Warren took a shower in preparation for a night of loving with his wife and while he did, she put the panties on the bed sans the note which she kept, packed as many things as she could into a suitcase and left.

A new Toyota Sequoia was delivered a week later to her sister's house, where Kellie was staying until she could get an apartment. It came with a large red bow. Inside were a heartfelt apology and the title for the car in her name.

She kept the car after the divorce and gave her three-year-old Volvo to her sister and brother-in-law. He was going to fight it in court, but Kellie had kept enough proof, and didn't ask for more than her share of their joint belongings, that in the end he signed the divorce papers and called her a worthless whore.

~ ~ ~

As Jerry scanned the fields and distant roads, he couldn't tell that Kellie wasn't waiting for the sunrise, but instead she was recalling their first encounter. She had been afraid of him when they had first met in the field behind his shelter.

Her world had fallen apart in more ways than just her personal life. She had been a news junkie and when the first reports of flu that was killing people broke, she followed every story, read every article she could find in newspapers and the internet.

She'd teach during the day, but in the evening her TV was on CNN or MSNBC or Fox News, laptop on the corner table of the sectional in her living room and her dog Molly by her side. To her, it seemed like an avalanche, like the ones she and Warren had seen outside of their rented chalet in Vail, except it wasn't snow destroying everything in its path, it was the flu.

It hit home for her when her sister's kids all died within 14 hours of each other. Rich was by their sides and took his own life when the youngest child finally slipped into that long good night. Jennie, who had planned to be with her family when the end game finally played out, never arrived because of wrecked vehicles on the roads and bad planning. She'd been a flight attendant and in the wrong city when the airlines were shut down for good. She was driving home when her end came.

When Kellie arrived at her sister's small house, everything was in order and her brother-in-law and three nephews were lying together in the same room where she'd cried her eyes out to her sister less than a year before.

Her sanity slipped away for days as she cried and screamed and yelled at God for the hell He hath wrought. She got in her car, followed by her dog Molly who she barely even noticed, and drove away. She didn't want to destroy the last peaceful scene of what had been her family.

Kellie crashed the car on a dirt road outside of the city. She came around a corner too fast and the tears in her eyes, or memories and rage in her mind, made her miss seeing the two cars that had met head on and were in the middle of the road.

The quickness at which she made the decision to accelerate and die right there or hit the brakes and try to avoid the accident scene could have been measure in 10ths of a heartbeat.

She accelerated.

Molly, sensing something, jumped on the floor board from her passenger seat.

She hit the wrecked cars at 42 miles per hour.

The screaming shriek of tearing metal, the hood slamming into the windshield shattering it, the driver's side front tire exploding and the sound of tires sliding on the hard-packed dirt road were all drowned out by the sounds of eight air-bags deploying.

She sat in the driver's seat for two full minutes.

She was stunned by what she'd just done.

She couldn't even die right, she thought to herself.

Molly climbed up from the floor and sat on her lap. Her mutt face stared at her.

She'd wrecked the car.

She didn't die.

What was wrong with her life that she wouldn't die?

Molly licked her face once and sat back down on her lap.

Finally getting some grip on whom she was and where she was, she looked down into Molly's big black eyes. Her black whiskers had dust on them, the brown wiry fur on her ears had gotten damp from some liquid pouring out of the dash, and her little black nose was smudged with some powder from the airbag that'd deployed on the passenger side of the car.

But Molly was happy to see her.

Kellie hugged her dog, the precious and loyal friend she'd received from her sister after the divorce, and extricated herself from the car. She hadn't been injured, but the car was wrecked.

She started walking in no particular direction and Molly sometimes followed and sometimes led.

The first night she slept in a house she'd come across that didn't have dead bodies in it. The second night she slept in a Winnebago that was parked in a driveway.

By the third night she was well away from the city. She could have driven any car of her choice, but she had no where to go so she and Molly just continued to walk aimlessly. When Molly got hungry, she'd find her some food. When she was thirsty, streams and garden hoses made her happy.

The third night she slept in the foyer of a vacant manufacturing building that was vacant. She would later look back on that night as her luckiest since the fall of the world. The not-deads, the mutated humans Kellie had not encountered yet, often took refuge from the sunlight in such buildings.

In the early morning hours, something had frightened Molly to where she jumped on Kellie, waking her. Molly had heard voices from, what Kellie would later find out to be, a vigilant hunting party.

Peering through the blinds, she could see the flashlights of a half-dozen men. They were vulgar and dirty, armed with various weapons. There were no women with them. She watched as the men started to circle the building in which she had taken refuge, and listened to hear if they were going to break in, or they were like her and just looking for a place to sleep.

The broken window also allowed her to hear the men talking. She came to the quick conclusion there was no way she would allow men like these to take her alive. They walked with a swagger, carrying guns and smoking cigarettes. They had the look of thugs, of ruffians and men who would do unspeakable horrors without regard for anyone's life but their own.

Grabbing up Molly, she found a door that opened deeper into the little factory in which she'd been sleeping. She found a cleaning closet that had a door that locked on the inside. She hid like a frightened little girl. Tears and sobs that might betray her were kept in check.

For five hours she and Molly hid out. She heard the men enter the building and Kellie took pills she'd liberated from a pharmacy from her pocket, ready to swallow them all if they found her. A single gun shot echoed in the building and it made her jump. Molly started to growl, but Kellie's hand placed over her nose quieted the little dog.

Then there was silence. It sounded like the men left, but Kellie remained in the closet for at least an hour to be sure they were gone. She was careful to stretch her stiff muscles before she finally worked up the nerve to unlock the door and look out.

Slowly she made sure there was no one still lurking.

From the light streaming through the opaque windows, the sun had risen and she could see the men who had been here had shot at a community board with pictures of what had probably been the company's annual picnic.

No one was on the factory floor and she didn't see anyone from her vantage point. Since she had been sleeping on the foyer's couch, if the men were still in the building, she figured they'd have taken up residence in the offices with the comfortable furniture and carpeted floors.

Still holding Molly, she crept to the door under the exit sign on the side wall of the factory floor. The door had "fire exit" on it so she was pretty certain she could push it open and head into the woods.

Holding tightly to Molly she tried to push it gently open. A loud click from the latching mechanism announced that the door was unlocked, and the door opened. She slipped through quietly and then allowed the door to close as gently as she could without having a handle on the outside on which to hold.

There was a heavy wooded area behind the small factory and she kept along the side of the building as long as she could, ducking below the one window she passed. She looked around the corner of the end of the building and seeing no one she ran to the tree line. Molly jumped out of her arms as they ran through the woods.

Molly led the way and Kellie followed her. She never knew if the men were still in the building. She never stopped to find out. She'd had her fill of violent men and there was no way she would let herself be taken by them. She put the pills back into her pocket and slowed to a walk behind Molly. She didn't know how lucky she'd gotten, but, in a startling revelation, she realized she wasn't ready to die.

She was walking through a field of soybeans later that afternoon when a man waved to her from a quarter a mile away. Hearing a real voice startled her and she was afraid. Molly growled and looked in the man's direction, but didn't leave her side.

The man, backed by a younger man and an elderly black gentleman, approached her slowly and carefully, making it clear to her they were armed, but not threatening her.

In the middle of the dozen-acre field, there was no place for her to hide. She berated herself for not staying near the wood line, but it was a cool day for Alabama and the sun was hidden by clouds, making her walk almost enjoyable. The field was not over grown with weeds and thickets and it made walking easy.

Kellie found a comfortable place to sit with her dog and wait for the men to approach. She reached into her pocket and collected up the pills she stored there for the end. If they killed her outright, so be it, but she wasn't going to be used as a sex slave or punching bag.

The pills in her hand, she waited for the three men to approach her.

Molly, never leaving her side, watched the men get closer, alternately with watching Kellie to see what her owner wanted her to do.

When the men were about 20 paces from her, the leader, a clean-shaven, middle-aged man with a tanned face, a dirty NASCAR baseball hat with the #48 on it, a white tee shirt and faded, but clean jeans stopped the trio. He had what looked to be a military weapon in his hand, but he was holding it by the handle, not like he was ready to shoot someone.

The younger man on his left side looked a lot like the leader, but much heavier and softer. He had a rifle, but it was slung on his back. Kellie thought the man about 17 or 18 years old and not like the men from earlier in the morning. He was smiling at something his dad, she guessed, was saying and his hands were in his shorts' pockets. He didn't look like a young man who was out for raping and pillaging.

The other man looked even more out of place. He was a handsome elderly black gentleman that only the south can produce. His hair had streaks of grey and he wore, which really stood out in the bean field, expensive dress shoes, a pair of what looked to be well-tailored dress pants, a powder blue shirt with creases and a vest that was probably made by Armani. He looked more like he belonged in a boardroom with 20 people following his every instruction. He had the air of wisdom and confidence about him, but also projecting strength and control even though he didn't appear to have a weapon.

"Out for a walk today, ma'am?" the leader of the trio asked as they came to a stop. He had that accent only a true Alabama-native had. He tipped his hat to her as any proper southern gentleman would do, but also kept his hand on the rifle he carried.

Just hours earlier she has been so frightened she almost lost control of her bodily functions.

But here, in the middle of a field, facing what could even be considered a worse threat, she didn't feel fear.

"I…I…I'm lost," she stammered. It came out like she was a frightened little girl. "I'm hungry."

Putting his hat back on after wiping his forehead, the leader told her who he was. "Well, I'm Jerry. This is my son Randy," he said pointing with his head to the youngest of the trio, "and this is Mr. Fournier, but he prefers we call him Mike. "We have some food back at our place if you want to share some. It's pretty good eats and will fill your belly.

"As for you being lost," he took his hat off again and started pointing, "Odenville is that way, Leeds is that way, Harrisburg is over that way and if you're headed to Birmingham, go that way until you hit the highway and follow it."

She thought it odd he didn't ask her where she was going or what she hoped to find when she got there. He was doing everything he could to make sure she didn't feel threatened. He slung his rifle over his shoulder. "We're headed back to our shelter now if you want to follow, just don't try anything funny agin us, and you'll be safe." She stood up from where she'd been sitting and picked Molly up.

And promptly started crying.

The three men stood there like she'd hit them with an electric bolt from heaven. It was Mike who finally walked toward her first. "It's okay ma'am," he said in a smooth and comforting baritone. "No one here is going to hurt you. You're safe with us and Jerry and his boy here have a good safe place." He put his arm comfortingly over her shoulder, the way a father does to his crying daughter, and her sobs became stronger and tears gushed down her face.

She didn't know why, but she knew she was, at least for now, safe from the hell and fear she'd been living with. The pills dropped from her hands and Mike didn't stoop to pick them up. Instead he re-assured her that she was safe and was welcome to break bread with them.

The four of them walked back to the shelter, Jerry and Randy in the lead, followed by Mike and Kellie. Molly yipped once or twice, but seemed happy around the group once Kellie's tears had stopped flowing and she could walk without being supported.

~ ~ ~

It had been three weeks and Kellie never continued her walk. She was welcomed to stay and she slept peacefully for the first time since before the fall.

Now here she was, sitting in a chair leaned against a sapling in a way she'd criticized her students for doing, watching a man who was seemingly oblivious of her adoration and admiration.

"We have to go after them," Jerry finally said, not looking at the woman who was looking at him. He was usually uncomfortable around women, especially ones who were being as forward as Kellie was right now.

"It would be the right thing to do," she responded. "At least try to find out what happened to them."

Jerry picked up another blade of grass. Instead of tossing it into the air this time, he put it in his mouth. "Yeah. If we don't try, we'll kick ourselves and I won't sleep well ever again."

The sun took that moment to cross over the horizon.

They watched it grow in beautiful silence until it was the full sun.

The silence was shattered when they heard a bowl hit the floor down the shaft and Monica's voice. "Aww, son of a bitch."

"That'll wake everyone," Kellie said. Monica had one of those voices which carried. "Let's go down and get something to eat and tell everyone what you're going to do."

Jerry took one last look around through the binoculars and followed her down.

Thirty minutes later, table cleared of breakfast dishes, the group went over the plan of action for the day. Jerry had listened to everyone's thoughts and opinions and adjusted his own plans to, if not bow to their requests, at least allow them to feel like their opinions mattered, which they did.

Randy voiced his displeasure about being left behind because Tony was his friend, but Jerry insisted that if anything went wrong, someone needed to be able to keep the farm running.

Kellie, Monica and Mike would also stay at the farm.

Eddie was probably the best shot with a rifle, and Jerry wanted Terrill along because of his military training. The young man might be a wounded warrior with training in communications and not infantry tactics, but he was a military man. Monica would monitor the base CB with Mike, while

Kellie and Eddie would do the chores with whoever wasn't monitoring the radio. There was plenty to keep everyone busy.

Jerry outlined the timetable he planned on using. With the internet down, he was depending on the TomTom in his truck to search around Odenville.

Times had really changed since he had gotten his license more than 30 years ago. Back then if he'd wanted to go somewhere he'd never been, he used a map. Now even finding a map would be difficult because GPS devices and the internet made them just about useless over the past few years.

Jeff hadn't been real clear on where the gun store was. He'd just said it was on the southwest side of Odenville, off I-74 South.

Jerry planned on driving circuitous routes north of Moody, take back roads to get south of Branchville and search the south side of Odenville for signs of Jeff and Tony. He wouldn't drive on the main road through either town because Jeff said the main roads would be watched by any competent vigilante group.

He'd maintain radio contact with the base, giving them a call every half hour. He figured taking their time and being careful would be safer than driving headlong into trouble.

Eddie got up and pulled his favorite rifle from the safe, the Remington 700 with the variable scope and 24-inch barrel. He picked up a dozen extra rounds. He wouldn't load the weapon until he was outside, a rule set by Jerry.

Jerry, of course, liked the Colt AR-15. He'd bought it a few years back from a friend who needed some bail money. It came with three 20-round clips, a tactical sling and a 4x20 scope. It was light, easy to carry and previously not legal, but Jerry didn't think it mattered anymore.

Eddie handed Terrill the M1911 and two magazines. It was the closest thing they had to the 9mm the vet had used in the Army. Terrill's job would be manning the radio and guarding the 2004 Ford F-350 Crew Cab if Eddie and Jerry had to investigate a building.

Jerry stood up from the table and everyone followed suit. He gave his son a quick hug and some last minute instructions about making sure chores got finished. He then looked him straight in the eye and ordered him to not send out a rescue party if contact was lost, but set up the best defense he could and keep the farm running. He self-imposed a time limit of six hours to search for Jeff and Tony.

With the truck fueled, the spare tire and CB checked, he, Eddie and Terrill drove away. Kellie put her arm over Randy's shoulder, difficult because she was six inches shorter than the young man and said "Your dad is quite a guy."

Randy just nodded.

~ ~ ~

A little more than an hour later, the three searchers had worked their way to a few miles southwest of Odenville. They had taken every back road they could find and the GPS, which still operated like it had before the fall, kept recalculating the directions.

Terrill had called the base twice and received Monica's response that things were still good.

Eddie and Terrill used binoculars as Jerry drove slowly down dirt roads. He was looking for any sign of the quads or tracks they might have left. Since the fall of the world, there were no road graders or enough traffic to obscure tracks, but neither were there crews to repair roads or remove debris.

Driving on some nameless road that paralleled I-74, Eddie's left hand flung out and slapped Jerry, who was concentrating on avoiding a washout. Jerry hit the brakes and the truck skidded to a halt from seven miles-per-hour.

"Look there," he said, pointing to a house across a field.

Jerry pulled out his own set of binoculars, a powerful set he'd picked up while foraging for supplies a few weeks back. He scanned the general direction of where Eddie was pointing.

"Yup. Good eyes, boy. Those're our quads. But I don't see anyone." Still scanning the area, Eddie said he didn't see anyone either. They were pretty close to the town so maybe Jeff and Tony had left the quads there and walked to the gun shop Jeff had said was in the area.

After several minutes of watching, no one saw any movement. Terrill called the base and told them the quads had been found. Monica asked questions no one was ready to answer so Terrill just told her to stand by.

"Let's move the truck up there to hide it," Jerry said, pointing to the trees ahead. "Then Eddie and I will go look around.

"Terrill, here's my binoculars. You keep us in sight," he said handing over his big glasses. "I wish we had a walkie-talkie, but we'll make do with what we have."

"What do I do if you guys get into trouble?" Terrill asked. Jerry stopped the truck in the trees. He didn't have an answer. As they unloaded from the truck, all he could say to the veteran was "use your best guess. I don't really know."

Jerry and Eddie, both used to hunting, skirted the tree line, staying in the shadows as they approached the quads. Neither of them saw anyone near the machines, but they weren't taking any chances.

The two men came to a clearing and had to cross a two-lane highway to get to the quads. Jerry said he'd go first. When he got to the quads he'd make sure no one was around and then signal Eddie to join him.

The plan was executed flawlessly.

The quads were from the farm, and they still had gas in them. Jerry hesitated to start them for fear that someone might be in the surrounding buildings, so he instructed Eddie to push the smaller one over to the trees they'd just been in. Once he was safely hidden, Jerry would move the bigger quad.

That plan was also executed perfectly.

The truck was another 500 yards away, so they took turns moving the quads back to the truck, 100 yards at a time, then stop and make sure there was no threat. First one would move forward, then hunch down and cover the second one.

Sweating and tired, the two men were greeted in whispers by Terrill, who limped out to meet them. The three men worked to get the quads loaded and strapped down in the truck bed, before answering Terrill's unasked question.

"We didn't see anyone, but the tracks look like they went in the direction of the main street," he told Terrill, then repeated it to Mike who was now monitoring the CB at the base.

"So, what are you going to do, Jerry?" Mike asked.

"I don't know, Mike. It looks to be deserted around here. Maybe we should at least go see if they did go to the food market."

"Do you really think that's where they went?"

"I don't know Odenville that well, but I do know the food market is on the main street. If they came this far, you know how Jeff was always wanting to get some grits. He might have talked Tony into trying to get some. One thing's for dang sure, there ain't no gun shop here abouts." Jerry didn't like being lied to and his voice told the story of the hell he was going to give Jeff if they got themselves into trouble over grits.

"It sounds like you've already decided and Kellie said to be careful," Mike told him over the radio.

"Thanks, Mike, we will. Out." he then put the microphone in its holder on the dash. He looked at Eddie who was still sweating from his workout with the quads and Terrill, who was leaning on the passenger door.

After a minute of playing with the GPS on the dash, he'd made his decision. "Terrill, can you drive?" A valid question because Terrill had an artificial leg below the knee on his right side. Jerry had never asked and had never seen him drive.

"Yes, sir," he said. "I can't feel the gas pedal with my foot, but I can tell if I am accelerating or braking. I got my license too if you want to see it." Jerry smiled at the vet. He might have a beard and look like a disheveled homeless person, but his wit was sharp and he was always respectful, no matter the situation.

"Good, good. No I don't need to see your license, I'll believe you. But if you get pulled over by the state police while driving, it's good to know you have it with you.

"Here's what I want to do," he said pointing to the GPS' layout of roads on the display. "Eddie and I are going to go back along this tree line again, but this time we're not going to cross the road. We're going to work our way up along the tree line until we can see the market."

Both the men nodded, starting to see the plan.

"When we get out of sight, I want you to move the truck up

to the other side of the trees. We'll be able to hear you move. I want you to hide the truck as best you can, but put it somewhere so you can see where we're going."

Terrill nodded. He'd been in this area before and was sure he could find a place to hide the truck and where he'd be able to see the other two. "Eddie and I'll go have a look around. Maybe we can find a clue as to where our boys went. If we can't, and if it is safe and no one is still here, we'll grab some stuff from the food mart and head back home."

Both men nodded.

"You okay with this, Eddie?"

"Sure, boss. You know me. This is like a live video game."

"Yeah, but here you only get one life, you can't hit reset, and you don't get to pause the game," Jerry said seriously. Danged boy never would take anything seriously.

"Most video games I play are like that already," Eddie responded with a small smile. Jerry cuffed him in the back of the head for being a wiseass.

Twenty minutes later, Jerry and Eddie heard the truck start up. They'd moved quickly along the tree line and along side the road toward the main drag though town. They'd seen no one. When they heard the truck start, they moved deeper into the woods and hustled to the end of the tree line where they could get a good look at any movement that might have been stirred up by the truck.

They heard the truck shut off, but didn't see where until Terrill limped out of the woods about 400 yards to their left. When he saw that the two had seen him, he moved back into the brush.

Looking down the main street, they saw obvious signs someone had been in the area. Widows were broken out of the building across the road to their left, and its doors had been smashed in, but it wasn't the wanton destruction they'd seen in Branchville. That little village had been nearly burned to the ground. They could see from their vantage point, a once-lit sign that said "Fr…" but had been shattered by gunfire. Jerry knew that was the food store. He whispered for Eddie to follow him as the moved closer and hid under a billboard sign that had fallen into disrepair. Houses off to their left had burned to the ground, but they could see the food mart was still standing.

"What's that?" Jerry asked pointing to one of the parking lot light poles at the food mart.

Eddie looked through his binoculars until he found what he was looking for.

"Aww, for the love of all that sucks about this bullshit life. That looks like two guys tied up to the pole."

Jerry hated when Eddie used that type of language, but if it was Jeff and Tony, and they were dead, he could understand why Eddie'd be upset.

"Can you tell if they're alive?" he asked, quieter than before because he knew that someone had tied those two up and were probably still around and probably watching. And if they were tied up, that meant vigilantes because the not-deads would rather eat human flesh than tie it to a light pole.

"Can't tell, boss. It looks like our guys. They're not moving and we're still too far away. Maybe if we creep closer to that road there?"

There was a narrow strip of black top between their billboard and the food mart which Eddie motioned to.

"Wait, first let's go tell Terrill what we've seen. He might have a better idea and we can tell the base what we're going to do."

Eddie, still looking through the binoculars, said "Okay, boss. But they haven't moved and I don't see anything moving in the store." Jerry led the way, keeping low and moving slowly. Weeds had flourished since the fall of the world and they made concealment easier.

It took almost 15 minutes of crouch walking to reach where Terrill had parked the truck. They'd actually snuck past him, them not seeing the truck and Terrill not seeing them. It wasn't until Jerry realized they'd gone too far because he'd run out of trees, that they'd backtracked and found the truck. Terrill had missed seeing them because nature had called him at the right time to miss them sneaking by.

Jerry, on a spot he'd cleared on the ground, drew a layout

and explained to Terrill what they'd seen. They talked about plans until they came up with the one they were going to use. Eddie said he hadn't seen anyone in the store and Terrill suggested making sure the other buildings with a view to the parking lot were checked out as well. Eddie hadn't thought to check the building to the east of the store or the one across the road that hadn't been burned completely to the ground.

Jerry called the farm and Randy answered.

Jerry outlined the situation and told him what they were going to do. All Randy said was "Roger, dad. Good luck and try to keep Eddie from shooting himself in his own ass." Jerry didn't think this was a time for levity, but his son was always ready to lighten the mood. Eddie was listening and when he smiled at his friend's remark, Jerry figured a little humor might help ease the stress of what Eddie had seen through his binoculars.

~ ~ ~

Jerry never understood how or why his son and Eddie, a rail-thin, carrot-top with geeky black-rimmed glasses became friends. Eddie had been a snappy dresser for being from a poor family, where Randy dressed in his farm clothes for everything but when he attended church. While they both liked playing video games, Eddie was more into games like Call of Duty and Modern Warfare while Randy played more of the first-person adventure games.

For whatever common ground they had found, one day Randy had brought Eddie home for dinner when the boy's mom had gone off somewhere. The boy became a part of the family and helped out for a few extra bucks Jerry could offer him. He worked hard and paid attention to what he was doing and didn't hurt himself. He was a good influence on his son, and Jerry just started treating him like a second son.

~ ~ ~

The three men took a five minute break, drank some water and relieved themselves. They made sure they had everything they were going to need to go check on the men in the parking lot and with a nod to Terrill, who'd gotten back into the driver's seat of the truck. Jerry and Eddie went back to the billboard sign to wait.

They heard the truck start up and leave, heading back the other way down the two lane highway away from town. Jerry and Eddie moved up beside the road separating them from the food mart's parking lot. This time, as close as they were, Eddie could tell the men, at least one of them, was alive.

Leaning close to Jerry he whispered "Tony, on the left has moved his legs. He's not the way I saw him sitting last time. That must be Jeff on the right, but he ain't moved."

"Good. Maybe they're both still alive and Jeff is just sleeping. Now we wait for Terrill."

Terrill had taken the truck away from town as quietly as the big diesel truck could. A mile down the road he slowed and watched his rear view mirror to make sure he wasn't being followed. After 10 minutes, he turned the truck around and accelerated to better than 70 miles per hour.

There was a long straight road going into town, and they agreed that they'd need the truck if they were going to rescue the two men, so Terrill drove into town with the engine off, coasting the truck the last quarter mile, past the white wood fence he'd seen headed out of town, and into a parking lot across the street from the food market that Jerry had described. The truck rolled quietly to a stop and Jerry and Eddie both had their rifles up, ready to defend Terrill.

Everyone waited.

The minutes passed and no one moved.

Sweat dripped from Jerry face. He hoped whoever had left Jeff and Tony tied up had left the area until evening, or better yet, for good, but he wasn't taking any chances. Jerry and Eddie scanned the food mart and the building to the east.

He saw Terrill slip out from the truck and look through the big binoculars while staying mostly hidden. Terrill also scanned the area before giving the hand signal which told the two men laying in the weeds the coast appeared clear.

Jerry looked over at Eddie. "Okay, I'm going to cover you as you cross the road and hide in that ditch," he said pointing at the corner of the parking lot nearest the highway. "When you're there and ready, you'll cover me as I go see how those guys are tied up.

"If I can cut 'em loose, I will and you'll give Terrill the signal to get the truck over here pronto and you'll cover the both of us as we load both the men up.

"If I can't get them loose, we'll get back across the road and come up with another plan."

"Got it, boss," was all Eddie said. They'd gone over this plan already and he knew what had to be done. Playing video games all his life, he'd killed thousands of video graphic people and zombies. He kept telling himself, that's what Jerry was asking him to do now, but in this case, they really would probably shoot back at him and like Jerry said, there is only one life in this game.

"Good boy. Go when you're ready."

With one last good look through his binoculars, Eddie rose to his knees, slung the binoculars behind him, grabbed his rifle with both hands and dashed across the road. Jerry watched the front of the store while Terrill watched the other buildings. He missed seeing what would have been a perfect slide into second base, had Eddie played baseball.

Nothing moved in the store and Jerry waited a good two minutes after Eddie gave him the signal that he hadn't seen anything either. Swallowing, his throat was dry and he wished for a drink of water, but knowing he'd left his canteen belt with the truck, Jerry knew he had to go now.

He admitted to himself he was scared. Someone had tied those men up and he had no idea where they were at. He did know they weren't zombies. He knew there were humans, probably watching them, ready to shoot and use him and Eddie as bait for the zombies.

"Damn," he said quietly, then just as sincerely asked God to watch over him as he carried out his own stupid idea. He wasn't as fast as Eddie had been, but he knew both Eddie and Terrill were watching his back and covering him.

He moved down the ditch before crossing the road so he would be on the side of the store where there were no windows. He looked toward the parking lot and could see Eddie was scanning left to right and not watching him. That was just what he'd asked the kid to do.

Jerry got to the corner of the store and was only about 15 feet from the men. He slung his rifle over his back and unsheathed the eight-inch hunting knife. This was his signal to Eddie that he was ready to approach the men in the parking lot. Eddie nodded and gave Terrill the signal that Jerry was about to approach the men in the open.

Eddie scanned two more times before giving the go ahead and Jerry crouched as he ran to the men.

Tony raised his head as Jerry approached and tried to say something, but Jerry shushed him. They were trussed up with speaker wire and Jerry's knife had trouble cutting through.

"They're over there," Tony rasped through dry lips. "We're bait for the zom…gren…on…eff" was all he got out before the first shot was fired. The shot hit the pavement a foot from where Jerry was kneeling.

"Oh shit," was all Jerry could say as he struggled with all the wiring that bound the men to the pole.

He heard Eddie's rifle fire and a window shatter in the building on the left side of the store. He didn't look up because he was afraid of cutting the guys' wrists he was trying to free. Another shot from Eddie broke the silence and two more shots came from the building. This time they were aiming at Eddie and not Jerry, which was both good and bad.

He heard his truck start up and knew it'd be here in less than 15 seconds.

Three more shots came from the building and Eddie returned each shot with one of his own as Terrill screeched into the parking lot as fast as the big truck could maneuver. He slid the truck between Jerry and the building from where the shots were coming, slamming on the brakes as he was shifting it into park before jumping out to help Jerry load the two men.

The unmoving Jeff was freed first so Terrill could grab him while Jerry worked on freeing Tony.

"Oh, Christ," Terrill exclaimed as he pulled Jeff's jacket. He immediately let go, instead grabbed at the fragmentation grenade that fell out of Jeff's shirt. Jerry didn't see it and didn't look up. He was focused on cutting through the last wire holding Tony to the post.

Jerry never saw the grenade or the last act of heroism by the former soldier.

~ ~ ~

Terrill's life ended six seconds after the pin popped off the grenade inside of Jeff's jacket, but it stretched out long enough for Terrill to feel like he was redeeming himself for the life he'd lived.

In those six seconds, Terrill's life did flash before him.

He'd been a coward in elementary school, beaten up and picked on by others because he was small, weak and passive. In high school he had few friends and played no sports because he had always been afraid of losing or getting hurt. When he joined the Army after high school, he hoped they'd teach him to get over his fears and help instill in him the courage he never had.

He became a communications specialist and found he was not like a lot of other soldiers who were a little afraid, but ready to fight. It was what they were trained to do and he heard others talk about how they were ready to be deployed and see some action.

Terrill joined their bravado talk even though inside he knew he was a lot afraid.

His first tour as a private, he was assigned to a signal company and spent most of his time fixing radios. It was boring, but not life threatening. After 12 months he was rotated back stateside. Six months later he was scheduled to be deployed again with his battalion.

He was assigned to a transportation unit and worked for the unit's commander, Lt. (P) Luther Morgan, as radio operator. Where ever Lt. Morgan went in the field, Terrill was there with the radio.

Lt. Morgan was a West Point graduate on the fast track for promotions and was currently on his third tour in Afghanistan. He'd already served as a platoon leader for an infantry unit twice, and was waiting for his captain's bars to be awarded. The IED which killed him exploded and the HUMVEE flipped 270 degrees landing on the passenger side. The lieutenant, outside whose door the device exploded, was dead before the truck landed. His upper body landed in Terrill's lap.

Morgan's captain's bars were awarded posthumously.

The specialist driving the HUMVEE died hours later from shrapnel wounds.

Terrill was stunned, but never lost consciousness. He felt a lot of pain in his right leg when it was crushed, and he knew he was partially deaf. He couldn't move because of the equipment crushing him and he cried and prayed and screamed for help as soldiers from his unit struggled to cut him and the others out of the HUMVEE, all while taking fire from insurgents. The fire from the explosion burned his right side with an intense pain like none Terrill had ever felt before.

He cried in the hospital and refused the medal offered him by the officer who visited him at Walter Reed. He just wanted to hide from the fear he always felt.

He started drinking after he left the hospital. He couldn't hold the most menial job because he was drowning in the bottle. His family tried to help, they tried to get him to seek professional help, offered him money and a place to stay, but Terrill just wanted to be away from everyone. He was arrested several times for public intoxication and once for defecating in public.

Then the real end of the world came.

The coward in Terrill hoped he would die soon, but the man in Terrill lived on while those around him died. In the days and weeks after the fall, he saw others who died at the hands of vigilantes or the not-deads, but Terrill kept on living.

When Mike stopped on the highway, Terrill made the choice then that he was not ready to die. For some reason, he believed, God kept him alive for some purpose. He still drank, and he kept to himself all the horrors he'd seen, but Jerry was a nice guy, never pried into his past, offered him respite from the hell with which he lived and made him feel like he was part of something greater.

Jerry even gave him a bible, one of the small ones with just the New Testament and Proverbs, when Terrill was seen reading from one Jerry kept in the living room. He never said a word, just handed Terrill the bible and went back to what he was doing.

Terrill kept the bible with him always and read it when he felt the need. He remembered a passage from John 14:1, and it was the last thing he thought before the grenade extinguished his life: "Let not your hearts be troubled. Believe in God; believe also in me."

~ ~ ~

Terrill grabbed the grenade, pulled it deep into his curling up body, putting the light pole between himself and Jerry and Tony, and his life ended.

The concussion from the blast stunned Jerry, but between the concrete which held and protected the light pole from cars, and Terrill's heroic sacrifice he was able to get Tony in the truck.

There was still sporadic gunfire from Eddie and the building as he reached for Jeff.

Jeff's head lolled to one side and Jerry knew that the neck was obviously broken. Jeff's life had been shortened long before he'd been discovered by Jerry. He left the former auto mechanic where he was and jumped in the truck. It was still running thanks to Terrill and Jerry was able to drive it up to Eddie. He heard two hits on the truck, but they hadn't hit anything important and the truck kept on running. Eddie dove into the bed of the truck before it had even stopped and hollered at Jerry to "Go! Go! Go!"

Jerry matted the accelerator, tears rolling freely down his face at the sacrifice Terrill had made for them.

"Get a good seat up there, soldier," he said as the truck raced out of town. "You deserve the best."

Chapter Three

Jerry drove the truck away from Odenville at a speed which was not fast enough to outrun the memories, but fast enough that if anyone was following them, they'd play hell catching up.

Eddie, having jumped in the back, hung onto one of the quads with one hand and his rifle with the other. He was watching out for anyone following them as well.

Jerry stayed on the highway to put as much distance between them and anyone following from the store. He drove faster than he had since high school and kept a firm grip on the wheel. He paid very close attention to what was ahead of him. There weren't many vehicles left abandoned on the road, but there were enough and Jerry didn't want hit any of them. If someone was following, Jerry was sure Eddie would let him know by shooting first.

After several minutes he slowed to a more reasonable rate of speed and cresting a hill he saw a dirt road off to the right. He slowed quickly and made a wide turn so as not to raise any dust. He hoped Eddie was hanging on tightly to the quad in back. He drove slowly until the highway was out of sight and he pulled over and shut the truck off.

The silence was nearly absolute, except for a few birds complaining about having their territory infringed upon. He quietly got out of the truck and listened. He heard vehicles in the distance so he grabbed his rifle from the front of the truck as Eddie jumped out of the back and stood behind him. Both had their rifles at their shoulder, ready to shoot, but the vehicles never slowed at the dirt road and soon they were far enough away that both men lowered their weapon.

They looked at each other.

The smile Eddie had perpetually worn was gone. He'd

been the only one who had a perfect view of Terrill's sacrifice and it had changed him...aged him.

For Jerry, it had been a trial he'd never expected having to face, but he'd done it without thinking about it too much, though he knew he'd play it over in his head for the rest of his life.

No words needed to be said and neither of them really wanted to talk about it anyway. They turned their attention to Tony in the back seat. Jerry opened the rear door on the crew cab. Tony, who Jerry had unceremoniously manhandled into the truck, was lying on the back seat, feet on the floor and arms hiding his eyes from the light.

Tony's clothes were dirty and sweat dried. From the stains and smell, it looked like the boy had been tied up there overnight. He was obviously in a lot of pain.

There was dried blood from his nose on his face, and more in his blonde hair. He had taken a beating, and it was plain to see bruises on his face and arms. His right ankle was at an odd angle, but Jerry didn't know how to set it and he knew Eddie didn't either.

"How you feeling, Tony," Jerry asked gently.

Not moving his arms, he rasped "Not good, Jerry. I feel real bad. They beat us up real good."

"We're going to get you home, Tonedeaf," Eddie added, using his friend's made up nickname. "Don't you worry," It was Eddie and Jerry who worried when Tony leaned over and threw up on the floor. There was blood in it.

"Sorry," he barely whispered. Jerry grabbed a red handkerchief to wipe the young man's face and Eddie held the canteen up to his lips.

"No sweat, Tony. Just take a sip of this. There you go, not too much," Jerry said to him. "I'll clean it up after we get you home. That's what we're going to do right now, as fast as we safely can." Eddie took the hint and went around the other side of the truck. Jerry shut the door, careful to not shut Tony's foot in it. The way the foot was angled, it might very well be broken.

Jerry climbed in to the driver's seat and started up the

truck. Once they were on their way he indicated the CB and told Eddie to tell the shelter that they were on their way back with Tony.

"Don't give them any details except that we got Tony," Jerry told his son's friend. "Tell them we'll be there in less than an hour and coming in the same way Kellie had." Eddie knew Jerry was going to drive the long way around and enter through the back gate of Jerry's farm. It would take longer, but it kept them off the main roads, away from anyone who might be looking for them and Jerry would drive right up to the entrance of the shelter. If someone were listening on the CB to their conversation, they'd be looking for someplace an hour away instead 20 minutes from where they were now.

Jerry drove in silence and Eddie sat quietly with his thoughts. Tony moaned, but there was nothing Jerry or Eddie could do to help him except get him back to the shelter.

He arrived at the back gate which was off a dirt road and well hidden by over growth. Jerry pulled out the key from the ashtray. He hadn't been here in months and Eddie had to move some brush out of the way. The chain was rusted, but the lock had been coated with grease to protect it from the weather. Eddie opened the gate and after Jerry had pulled through he closed and re-locked it before climbing back in the truck.

Eddie gave the microphone three clicks then waited. Then he gave three clicks more and received a two click response. It was their way of telling the shelter they were a couple minutes away without sending any information over the air.

Kellie, Monica and Mike were waiting for them as they drove up to the partially hidden entrance. Jerry hardly got the truck in park before Monica had the back door open while Kellie opened Eddie's door and hugged him.

Mike opened the driver's door behind Jerry to help Monica with Tony while Jerry walked around the other side to help. Before he could ask, Kellie told him Randy was on the antenna making sure no one had followed them at a distance.

Jerry told her the bad news. "Terrill didn't make it," he said as gently as he could. "I'll tell you about it after we get Tony settled.

"Eddie, how 'bout you take the truck down to the barn and clean it out for me, while I help here."

"Okay, boss," he said, but not with the lightness he usually had. Jerry figured the young man could use some time to himself. Maybe in a little while he'd send Randy down and the two could talk without the adults around.

Mike had gone into the shelter and brought out the long folding table to use as a stretcher. Jerry kicked himself for not thinking ahead. He and Mike helped Monica get Tony onto the makeshift stretcher and then the both of them grabbed each end while the women made sure he didn't fall off as they took him inside. As they were carrying him, Jerry saw Tony's foot and was now sure the ankle was broken.

Kellie opened the door to the shelter and Jerry was glad that he'd put in the double doors instead of just the single 36-inch door. They were able to get Tony through the door and onto the saw horses the table usually sat on.

Jerry was again out of his element. He knew how to sew up cuts, stop bloody noses, cure headaches, sore muscles and bruises, but he'd never set a broken bone except for fingers and noses. He didn't know any of these people well enough to know if they did either.

He thought it would be Kellie, who had been a teacher, who would have stepped forward and taken over, but instead it was Monica who was shoving people out of the way. "I need the first aid kit, some bandages, hot water, ice packs and some quiet," she said pushing Mike out of the way and looking into Tony's eyes. "He threw up in the truck and there was blood in it," was all Jerry could think to add.

Kellie and Mike went to get the supplies Monica wanted.

Looking up at Jerry she said in a tone that was not the drama queen attention whore he'd come to know. "Stop standing there. You're making me nervous. Go find me a flashlight. And if you have them, two small funnels and a plastic hose about this long," she said holding her hands about 15 inches apart.

Jerry went to find what she'd asked for, having no idea why she wanted them. The flashlight he had in the cellar, as well as a couple of the cheap plastic funnels he had left over from when he tried reloading bullets. He went down the steps and overheard Monica asking Kellie if she had any rubbing alcohol.

In the cellar he found the flashlight and the funnels. The only hose he could find was an old garden hose he used to drain the hot water heater. He used his knife to cut off a piece about as long as Monica asked.

By the time he got back up stairs, Monica had Tony's shirt off and was gently probing him for injuries. Kellie had gotten ice packs made and Mike had hot water and a blanket ready.

"Oh good," she said taking the flashlight from Jerry. "Now everyone get out of here until I call you. I have a lot to remember."

Jerry, Mike and Kellie went into the living room and sat, not talking and trying not to watch Monica. She looked in Tony's eyes with the flashlight, then in his ears with a child's plastic magnifying glass someone had found. She also looked up Tony's nose then opened Tony's mouth as gently as she could.

She turned the flashlight off and picked up the two funnels. She forced the hose on the small end of each and used it as a make-shift stethoscope. Where she'd learned that little trick, Jerry hoped to learn some day, but it seemed she knew what she was doing.

The ingenuity of the girl sparked some words from Jerry. "There's a lot about that girl I didn't know. Who is she? MacGyver's illegitimate daughter?" Kellie smiled and Mike snorted.

"She does look like she knows what she's doing, though," Kellie added.

Placing the stethoscope first on his chest, then his stomach she listened. "Mike, I need you." He got up and hurried over. She told him in a low voice what she wanted and Mike rolled Tony gently onto his side while Monica placed one of the funnels on several places on his back while listening to the other end. She nodded to Mike and he gently laid him back down flat on the table.

"His heart is beating strong," she said. "That's a good sign."

Then she called Jerry and Kellie in to help hold Tony down.

"I'm going to set this bone while he's still out of it. We don't have any anesthesia here and if we did it while he was awake, he'd probably pass out again," she said. "I'll eventually need a splint for it when we get it straight, but want to get the swelling down before we put it on.

"He's lucky, if you can find any luck about this. I think it's a simple break and not a compound fracture. Looks like someone stomped on his leg above the ankle. It feels like a simple break and setting it now, even if it is wrong, has got to be better than having it off kilter like it is.

"Mike, push gently down on his shoulders because this is going to hurt. Yes, I see the bruises, but they are superficial and nothing is broken up there.

"Kellie, use that towel under his head and hold down on his forehead. He might have a concussion, but there doesn't appear to be any bones broken in his head. There are two bumps, so be careful.

"Jerry, lie across his legs and hold him as still as you can. I hope I remember how to do this. Everyone take your place," she ordered, a quiver in her voice betraying the confidence she had been showing. Mike and Kellie had to work around each other to get in position Jerry just leaned over the prone Tony and held on tight. Tony, not fully unconscious tried to move some, but the three held him still.

Jerry started to look away from what Monica was going to do before deciding this procedure might be something he'd have to do in the future so didn't look away.

He watched as she firmly grasped the foot and the heel, her arms crossed. "Here we go," she said as she pulled and twisted the foot. He could hear snapping or cracking but when she was finished, the foot was facing straight up, like the other foot and the blue color seemed to be changing to red. Tony moaned and murmured something, but never came fully awake.

"Good job," Jerry told her.

"He's not out of the woods. I think I set it right, but we don't have an X-ray machine or an MRI. There might be bone fragments, torn ligaments, any number of things still wrong with that ankle, but at least now it is facing the right way, and it felt like it set."

She ran her hand across the top of the foot and felt for a pulse in the ankle. "It feels warmer already and I can feel the pulse better. "For the next 24 hours, let's put him on the couch with the leg elevated and alternate hot and cold to bring the swelling down. Day after tomorrow the swelling should be down enough and we'll splint it."

"What about the blood he was spitting up?" Jerry asked.

"Yeah, I heard what you said about that and was worried he had a perforated stomach or some other internal injuries. But when I looked and listened to his chest and belly area it sounded clear. There's some congestion in his chest, some rasping, but I don't know what to do about that and think maybe nothing is the best treatment until he comes out of it. He'd been punched in the stomach, but it didn't look like critical hits...like he was hit, but not real hard.

"The blood he spit up was from the blood he swallowed when his teeth were knocked out or from his bloody nose. He's lost two teeth on the left side and it looks like he bit his tongue pretty bad. His cheeks are torn up some and from the bruising it looks like someone punched him in the face."

"How long do you think he'll be out of it?"

"I don't know, Jerry," Monica said, sounding a little exasperated from his questions. "He needs to be hydrated, but we don't have that kind of stuff here. He needs to wake up before we give him water. I've done all I can do unless you got any ideas."

Jerry had none and shook his head. She returned to cleaning Tony's body. The smell was terrible and Jerry could tell he was no longer needed so he went to find Randy. It had been a rough day and right now, now that Tony was in good hands, Jerry wanted nothing more than to hug his son. When Monica was ready to move Tony from the stretcher to the couch, she'd call him.

He found his son just climbing down from the antenna, wearing leather gloves and a safety harness. Jerry remembered the first time he'd shown his son how to use the safety equipment and how afraid the boy had been. Now here he was three years later, showing some initiative and forethought before climbing up the 30-foot antenna.

Randy didn't see his dad approach so started unbuckling the harness after taking off his gloves. Jerry waited until the harness was off before saying anything.

"Well done, son."

Randy quickly turned around at the sound of the voice. He and his dad had never been demonstrative, but right then, at that moment in time, with no one else around to see them, Randy wanted nothing more than to hug his dad and have his dad hug him.

"You did good, boy," Jerry said as his son's arms wrapped around him. "I knew you could do it."

"Dad, I was so scared," his son said, voice cracking a little. "For Tony and Jeff, for Eddie and Terrill, but I don't know what I'd do if you'd gotten hurt or killed."

Randy was still a big kid, Jerry realized. At 22-years-old, he was immature and had led a sheltered life, even though he grew up on a farm. Jerry often thought he'd not done a very good job raising the boy like he'd been raised. He wasn't a strict parent like Jerry's father had been and allowed his son to find his own path. Looking back, he saw where he made a lot of mistakes, missed a lot of opportunities, failed to teach his son a lot of things.

But at this moment in time, feeling the big bear hug from his "little boy" who stood two inches taller and weighed 60 pounds more, Jerry felt more pride in his son than ever before in his life.

"You did good, son," he said again, feeling the pressure of his son's two strong arms. "Now I can't breathe." Randy released his dad and the two looked at each other. There was relief in both men's eyes.

"So dad, what happened?"

"I'll tell you, but let's wait until I can get everyone together. Go get Eddie and Mike from the barn. They should have the truck cleaned out soon so give them a hand if they need it.

"We have some planning to do because the shit hit the fan today and I think we need to re-think what we've got going here. Have everyone back up to the shelter," he looked at his watch, "in an hour."

Randy picked up his harness and headed over the hill to get Eddie and Mike.

Jerry walked over to where the chair was still sitting from this morning, where he and Kellie had watched the sunrise. He sat down and thought about the day's events and his decision to allow Jeff and Tony to go look for more weapons, then his decision to take Terrill and Eddie to find out what happened to the other two. It seemed everything had happened with spur of the moment decisions, without thinking them through, and now Jeff and Terrill were both dead and Tony was injured.

Maybe he wasn't the one who should be in charge of his shelter. Maybe he shouldn't be the one making decisions. Maybe he should just take care of his farm the best he could and let someone else be in charge of making life and death decisions.

The doubts ran through his mind as he sat in the chair, watching the sun pass through the trees and shadows cross over the farm he'd been working for more than 30 years. His life had been simple before the fall. He paid his taxes, paid his bills, went into debt and struggled to get back out every year, watched TV and woke up every morning knowing what work he had to get done before going back to his house in the evening.

With the fall of the world, everything was different. Now his decision to get a loan for a new tractor, something he'd agonized over for weeks last spring, seemed insignificant compared to what was being asked of him now.

Jerry wasn't a man who wanted to make decisions for anyone other than himself and his family.

~ ~ ~

In the first days of the catastrophic death tolls world-wide, it had been just Jerry, his son and Eddie on the farm. Eddie showed up the day after his mom died because he had no where else to go.

They watched the news reports until network and local television stations went off the air. With the ending of public utilities, they used the power provided by water wheel and two wind turbines to power the shelter. They also worked the farm and twice made trips to get supplies. There had still been people around, very damn few, but civilization as they knew it was done.

They found out what they could, and saw what was happening in their community and around the world so they isolated themselves to the farm. The radio Jerry pulled out of the barn, he put in the living room for the three to listen to at night after the supper dishes were cleaned and put away and the day's work was done.

Most stations were off the air, but there were still a few they could pick up on the AM band. This is where they heard of stories of the not-deads who were eating human flesh. They heard of the vigilantes who were taking over cities, raping and plundering what was left. Millions of dead were rotting in big cities, billions world-wide were left unburied. When the three heard that statistic from some nameless radio announcer, they shuddered. Their mind couldn't comprehend the enormity of billions. They couldn't even really grasp what a million dead would be like.

Jerry's farm was 20 miles from Birmingham, a city with a population of 225,000 people. If the announcer was correct, or even close to what he said, there'd be maybe 200 people left alive, like Jerry, Randy and Eddie, and another 200 of the not-dead zombies.

The three agreed to stay away from the big cities, not only because of the dangers, but the dead bodies would be rotting in the Alabama heat and diseases would be running rampant. Not just the disease that had killed the world, but others from the decaying bodies. There was no longer any organized government or policing force and the announcer said it clearly before he signed off. "It's every man for himself."

~ ~ ~

Jerry was pulled out of his reverie when heard voices and looked down the hill and saw Randy, Eddie and Mike walking up the path that led from the barn to the house. Jerry looked at his watch and saw almost an hour had passed since he'd first sat down to contemplate the past 24 hours and last few weeks.

Instead of climbing down through the hatch, he walked down the hill to walk the rest of the way with the others. He had never been a "people person" but right now he wanted to be with his son, his son's friend, and the very wise former bank executive.

Randy waved to his dad and Eddie, whose smile looked rather ragged, acknowledged his arrival. Mike, who was a bit winded from the walk up the path broke the silence. "You got some real good boys here, Jerry."

"Thanks," he said as he walked with the little group. "How you doing, Eddie?"

Eddie, one hand in his pocket, probably playing with the one dollar coin he always seemed to have, hesitated before speaking, something he rarely did. "It's not like a video game that's for damn sure."

"He hasn't told us what happened, but we got the truck cleaned out and fueled it back up, and unloaded the quads," Mike said as the silence stretched on for a few paces. "We only have about 100 gallons of diesel fuel left and about 75 of gasoline. We might want to think of finding a way to make our own fuel soon or else start salvaging some. Which means some way to move it and some place to store it."

Jerry nodded. Again Mike was thinking ahead. Jerry hadn't thought of making their own fuel, thinking they could get it from the hundreds of cars and trucks and semis sitting around abandoned on the highways, but after today, the less they traveled, the better it might be to stay out of the way of the vigilantes. It was something else he had to think about now.

Again he thought that maybe he should put Mike in charge. The man was a natural leader.

Entering through the front door, they saw Tony on the

couch already. He was awake now, talking quietly with Monica. She had laid him out and made a sling which she safety pinned to the back of the couch to keep his right ankle elevated. There was a glass of water half empty beside them.

Kellie was in the kitchen. From the smell, she'd made something for them all to eat. Jerry hadn't realized it, but more than seven hours had passed since they left this morning and he and Eddie hadn't eaten anything.

She brought three bowls of soup in for them, one for Eddie and Jerry and the other for Tony. "Sorry if it doesn't tastes real good. I just opened the cans and put it over heat. I'll never be the cook Terrill was."

"Thanks, Kellie," Jerry said. "I'm sure it will be fine."

With the mention of Terrill's name, Jerry began to relate what had happened that day. He didn't inflate his or Eddie's role, and neither did he shy away from saying how afraid they'd been. When he told of how Terrill had died, he choked back tears. When he finished, he dipped his spoon into the soup and ate more. No one asked him any questions and Eddie didn't offer any more to the story.

Tony, having finished his soup, handed the bowl to Monica. Jerry noticed that Monica had taped up three of his fingers on his left hand and cleaned and bandaged all his wounds. He's had all his clothes removed and was covered from the chest down by one of the blankets Kellie had found for her. It must have come from the cellar because it wasn't one he had seen before. It had probably been one of Terrill's which made using it wholly appropriate.

Tony cleared his throat and ran his tongue over the spot where some of his teeth were now missing. He was a very different person than the 21-year-old, weed-smoking, wild kid he'd been two days ago.

His story told why.

"Me and Jeff wanted to just get away from here for a few hours and have some fun," he began. "We know Mr. Saunders didn't allow smoking of any kind, so Jeff came up with the story of the gun shop he'd heard about. We knew he would let us go if we said something about it enough.

"We thought he'd let us take the truck, but when he told us we could take his quads we were, like, 'cool – cross country.'

"We drove to Odenville because Branchville was all burned up. Jeff used to work at a bodyshop in Odenville and he said he knew of a place where we could probably get some more weed. We stopped a couple of times to smoke and we were feeling pretty good." The language made Jerry cringe, but he didn't want to interrupt Tony.

"We parked the quads behind some building because we saw a truck on the highway and heard some shooting. We were half-baked and we really weren't thinking clearly. Jeff said he was hungry for something besides the shit," he stopped there and thought for a moment, "the food Terrill had been making for us. He said he wanted raw hotdogs, cookie dough and taco-flavored chips."

"We saw the store where you found us and we watched it for a while. It had big front windows and we figured those would keep the zombies from being there. We didn't see anyone around and the truck that we'd seen before was long gone we'd guessed because we didn't hear it.

"Jeff said he was sure there was no one around and the store didn't look like it had been ransacked. He didn't see any dead bodies around so we snuck around the side of the building, thinking of going through the back door like burglars. For some reason I thought it was funny as hell at the time and Jeff kept telling me to shut the…kept telling me to shut up, but I kept laughing."

He stopped his narrative and took another drink of water before continuing. His longish hair was still matted to his head, but Monica had cleaned his face. There were obvious bruises from being hit.

"The back door was open and we looked inside. It was dark, but not too dark to see that it was stacked with boxes of shit. Jeff went batshit and said he had found heaven. We got inside and started ripping open boxes when we heard the zombies.

"If you never seen zombies, be glad. I hope I never see them again and if I do, I'm going to put every bullet I have into them except my last, which I'll put through my own head.

"They grunt when they move and are faster than they look. They have great big black eyeballs and their skin looks like it is stretched really tight and let me tell you, they are scarier than anything you ever saw on TV.

"We heard them and we both dropped the boxes we were cutting open and ran for the door, 'cause, you know, they don't like the light and we sure as hell weren't going to be able to fight them in the dark.

"Just as we ran out the back door, someone slammed it behind us and these guys tackled us and beat the shit out of us. Jeff took the worst of it and he was swearing and screaming about killing the guys who caught us.

"I wasn't much of a threat. One guy punched me in the face and I went down. He put his knee on my gut and beat me up until I quit struggling, which didn't take very long.

"Jeff did better than me, but there were four guys and some chick that jumped him. He was still high a little and they really had to fight to get him to stay down. They kicked him in the nuts and the gut and one of the guys hit him with the butt of a rifle.

"Then they start tying us up. It was the chick's idea, a huge black lady, to tie us up. They took us over to that building where Eddie shot at them this morning. They kept us tied up all night, trying to decide what to do with us. There were nine or 10 guys and two women in the building.

"Half of them wanted to kill us right way and the others wanted to just let us go. Jeff made up some story about me being his queer and that we'd come from Birmingham looking for other people. They never asked about you guys or our quads.

"The lady in charge, Sasha was her name I think, came up with the idea of tying us to the light post out front of the store this morning. She told us that they'd lost two women and a man trying to get food from there and the zombies kept killing anyone who tried.

"She figured if we were tied out front, the damn zombies would come out tonight for us and they'd rig us to blow up and kill all of them outside the store.

"That's when Jeff went crazy. He was struggling so hard to get away because he didn't want to be bait for any damn zombies. I tried to help us get free, but in the struggles he broke my fingers and the wires tore at my wrists and neck. He was thrashing and struggling and just losing his mind. One guy tried to put a wire around Jeff's neck and Jeff kicked him with both feet and that guy probably won't ever piss without hurting again.

"That's when some big guy named Alberto or something jumped on Jeff. He broke his neck. I was so scared I pissed myself as they dragged us out and tied us up. I tried to get away, but when I fell, Alberto kicked me in the ankle and after that, I couldn't even stand. I cried until I had no tears left. I didn't want to die being eaten by the zombies and I begged them to kill me but they just laughed at me.

"I was screaming at them to not leave me there, that they only needed one body to draw the zombies out and anything else I could think of to get them to come back and not leave me alone with a dead body.

"I don't remember what I said but someone came back and slapped me in the face several times and my head hit the concrete. That was the last thing I remember clearly before you guys showed up.

"You know the rest."

No one said anything. They all sat there, not in shock at the story, but because there were still people who were so cruel and heartless to use other people as bait. Tony hadn't hidden his mistakes. He admitted that what they had done had gotten Jeff killed in a brutal way.

Tony laid his head down on the pillow Monica had given him. There was a haunted sadness about him. He knew he was lucky the people who had captured him had not killed him too; lucky that Jerry and his band of people were friendly and concerned with his safety and had not left him out there to be eaten alive by the monsters of everyone's nightmares.

Kellie, Monica and Mike were all shedding tears. Monica put her hand gently on Tony's head. Everyone sat in silence for a long time while they digested what Tony had told them.

It was a long afternoon that stretched into a long evening for everyone.

~ ~ ~

It was Randy who broke up the silence. He needed to milk the cows. He gathered up Eddie to help feed them. Mike picked up the bowls and took them to the kitchen.

"I'll be out in the garden," Jerry told them and Kellie followed him. The garden was on the back side of the hill, the same side as the entrance, but far enough away to be out of sight, out of mind, and hidden from view from anyone on the road which passed in front of the farm. Jerry had planted it in the spring with tomatoes and sweet corn, cucumbers and beans and some other vegetables. It had been just a Saturday morning project, and when he put it in he had intentions of keeping it up because he did like fresh vegetables, just like every other year, the garden had been forgotten about and started to get over grown with weeds.

Only after the fall did he really begin putting effort into maintaining the garden. Now it wasn't just a fad, now the vegetables grown here would help feed him and the people under his roof.

Most of the garden had been cleared of the biggest weeds and the plants were growing pretty well. Jerry started in the middle and Kellie joined him on the other side of the plants so they were working side by side.

They didn't speak for most of the row. Kellie watched how Jerry pulled the weeds out of the ground to take maximum amount of root with the weed. She tried to mimic his technique, but had to settle with ripping the top off most weeds. Her hand had never had to do manual labor, but she had learned over the past few weeks to do just that. She didn't have the calluses Jerry had, but there was now dirt under her very short and unpainted fingernails.

They finished the first row and threw the weeds they'd pulled into a pile and started on the next.

"You okay?" she asked him as they started down the row.

Jerry had several different replies he thought about, from

say "yeah, I'm okay" to "dumbass got what he deserved" but couldn't say any of them. He was conflicted and didn't know what he was supposed to be thinking. "I don't know, Kellie," he finally answered. "Are any of us ever going to be okay?"

He really didn't think the former special education teacher was going to answer. They finished up another row of weeding and started on a third. "Jerry," Kellie said, stopping weeding for a moment and sat back on her haunches like a kid might do. "What you did was the bravest thing I have ever heard of.

"I don't have the answers to the question of if we'll ever be okay, but what you and Eddie did, what Terrill did, and how you got Mike and Monica to back you up, was what makes me think that no matter what happens tomorrow, or in all of whatever tomorrows we have left, that right here, in our little world, things are going to be okay."

Jerry stopped weeding and stood up. The sun had reached the point in the sky that he knew it was getting close to supper time. He looked down at Kellie who was still squatting. She wasn't looking at him, rather looking at the ground where they had been pulling weeds.

He looked around him. He had soybean fields, some corn and some hay fields that all needed attention from him. He had only a hundred or so gallons of diesel fuel for his tractors and now, an injured man who would be little help on the farm for the next eight to 12 weeks and six other people who depended on him in some way, including his son. Add to that he had now pissed off some vigilante thugs who would like nothing more than to find out who had rescued their bait.

Things were actually worse for him than they were this morning.

But what he realized, with the words that Kellie had brought into focus for him, was that he wanted to survive and help his son, and these other people survive.

He was tired of reacting and decided right there in the garden that he was going to be a lot more pro-active. He'd always depended on himself to get things done. He depended on his son to a lesser extent, but after seeing how his son had manned-up and took initiative, he had more confidence in the boy.

Jerry knew life was going to get worse before it got better and he damn well wasn't going to hide in the garden every time something bad happened. He was going to stop letting things happen then react to them, he was going to think about more than tomorrow or the next day, he was going to plan for the winter months and the following year.

He wanted these people who had trusted him today to do more than survive. He wanted them to thrive.

Kellie was still playing with a weed at her feet.

Jerry kicked some dirt at her hand.

She looked up at him and smiled. "The old 'toe-in-the-dirt-aww-shucks' routine?"

He had no idea to what she was referring.

"Let's go get some supper. I'm starving," he said, instead of pretending he knew what the toe in the dirt comment meant.

She started to get up and he offered her his hand. She took it and they walked along their separate rows, like he was escorting her, until the end of the row. Molly, who had been sunning herself at the end of the rows in which they were working, lifted her head. Her tongue hung to the side as she panted in the heat. She had a happy look on her face.

Neither knew which of them let go first, but their hands separated and they brushed themselves off.

Tony was sleeping when they entered the shelter, Randy was coming down the spiral staircase and Jerry could see he'd locked he hatch. Eddie must have been the one in the shower because Mike was in the kitchen already making the evening meal and Monica was napping in the chair beside Tony.

When Eddie had finished, Jerry suggested Kellie get the shower next. All of them knew that showers and cleanliness was important when in such close quarters. Everyone showered almost every day and laundry was done daily. Jerry and Randy were the only ones with plenty of clothes so the others had to wash what little they had often.

"Supper'll be ready in about 10 minutes," Mike said from the kitchen. Kellie hurried to the shower to finish before supper. Mike and Randy washed their hands and face in the kitchen sink and then sat plates on the table.

The running water or Mike's announcement woke Monica but not Tony. She reached over and checked his breathing and pulse gently, without waking him. Jerry could see her counting the thrum of his pulse while looking at her watch. She then carefully uncovered his right foot and saw that it was no longer blue but a healthy red and the swelling was noticeably lessened.

This was the side of her he'd never seen. She had been sitting on the curb of a gas station eating a stack of snack cakes she'd scavenged. Jerry and Randy hadn't frightened her when they pulled up. They figured she's lost her mind a little.

They talked with her for a short time while she ate and told her about their place. She was overweight, bordering obese, and the men knew she'd not last long if they left her where she was. They didn't force her to come with them, but she almost didn't volunteer. That'd been more than three weeks ago. She was still overweight, but her clothes were no longer tight on her and she was obviously losing weight with the work she had to do every day, and the lack of candy and sweets.

There was still her drama they had to contend with, but even that was becoming less of an issue with everyone knowing everything about what was happening. There was no drama she could manufacture that was more incredible than what had transpired on this day.

She obviously had some medical training, though she spoke almost nothing of her past except how much she missed her doting parents. Jerry was glad she was with them today because he couldn't have done what she did for Tony and he was sure no one else could have.

Kellie came out of the shower in her bra and a pair of Randy's swimming shorts, modesty having had to have been suspended with the lack of clothes. She had a towel wrapped around her head and her dirty clothes in her hand. Jerry tossed her one of his clean shirts he'd brought up from the cellar.

"Let's eat," Mike said, turning off the burner and bringing the large pot off the stove. Everyone sat down at the table, but had moved around so there were no empty seats between anyone. Jerry guessed they didn't want to be reminded that they'd lost two of their own in the last 48 hours and another was injured on the couch.

Supper was a stew Mike had put together. There were large chunks of meat, potatoes, tomatoes, onions and celery and it tasted pretty good to Jerry. It was flavorful and had just a bit of spicy without being overpowering. It hit the hunger spot he had. He told Mike as much and the old man smiled. "After my wife died a few years back, I had to feed myself. She had been a great cook and I missed eating her food. Restaurants couldn't do it justice, so I started learning how to make a few of the meals she used to make." Pointing to the stew, "This was one of her best dishes."

"I like it too," Eddie said. "Me, too" and "Nicely done" came from others at the table. Mike seemed to inflate as he was able to share something of his wife, to whom he'd been married for 45 years, with these new friends. "I'll be sure to let Shirley know," he said.

There was small talk at the table about the garden and the fuel and the people they'd encountered today but nothing in-depth and too serious. There was no talk of what part Jerry and Eddie had played. It was by unspoken agreement that their actions were a verboten topic unless they brought it up and neither did.

After supper was over, the leftovers sealed up and put in the freezer except for a bowl Monica took in for Tony who was waking up, Jerry and Randy did the dishes so they could talk by themselves. Mike found a new book to read, Eddie put in a movie for himself, Monica and Tony, and Kellie went to her room to brush out her hair.

Jerry told Randy about what Kellie had said in the garden and bounced a few ideas off his son. Randy listened and nodded at some, thought seriously about others, disagreed with a couple outright. By the time dished were cleaned and put away, Jerry had decided what he was going to present to the group and he knew Randy, while not agreeing with everything, had been able to refine some of his ideas.

He asked Kellie to come down when she finished and join the rest of them in the living room. Tony was looking much better for his ordeal and sitting mostly upright. The kid had taken a beating, however his eyes were no longer glassy and vacant but alive with the will to live. Kellie sat in one of the chair's she'd brought in from the dining area and allowed Molly to jump up on her lap.

Mike put his book down and Eddie paused the movie and everyone looked expectantly at Jerry as he sat down in his favorite chair he'd taken from the farmhouse.

"We have got to get better prepared," he said without preamble. "It sucks that we lost Jeff and Terrill, may they rest in peace, but we did because we've been thinking about this wrong…no, I've been thinking about this wrong.

"I've been thinking ever since the world's people died, Randy and I would just live out our lives here and pick up whoever came along and make them a friend and slowly build this into a little compound of people who survived.

"Today we found out not everyone wants what I pictured.

"Tomorrow morning we will change the way we think about the people left alive. We're going to protect our shelter here better, going to find some supplies we really need, find ways to better communicate when we're out and make sure the vigilantes think twice before screwing with us. We made some enemies today and they probably will come after us.

"If they do, I want us prepared. So here's what I want to do. Tomorrow, four of us are going out to forage for supplies and this is what I think we need most," Jerry said, starting to hold up fingers.

"One – medical supplies. And I don't mean just first aid kits. We need drugs and stuff that we can't even imagine right now. Monica will be in charge of that because I think she has the most medical knowledge of all of us. The women also need stuff that women need," no one laughed although Jerry expected Eddie to, "so one of our priorities will be a pharmacy.

"Two – walkie-talkies of some sort so everyone can have one. We need to be able to communicate in some other way than just the CB. We need to find an electronics store. Randy will be in charge of that. He'll also be looking for batteries for as long as we can find them. Duracell said their batteries last seven years on the shelf, but we can't depend on that so we need to get what we can while we can. If he can find rechargeable batteries, we need to get as many as we can.

"Three – Survival books. Monica showed us today how little most of us know of survival. We don't have internet anymore, but we can all read. Mike, I'd like you to keep this mind.

"One other thing Mike, you seem to be the smartest of all of us, I'd like you to think of yourself as the general manager of our group. If you see something we need or see something we're doing wrong or whatever, I want you to speak up. And don't think you're going to be ratting out Randy to me if you see him wasting gas, because Randy and I have already talked about it."

"You want me to be your lieutenant, is what I hear you saying," Mike clarified.

"Yes. And it's because you obviously have 40 years more experience than Randy."

"I was a lieutenant in the Marines and I think I can remember how to do that," he said, giving them all another piece of his history. Jerry realized he'd thought the old bank executive was a soft, pampered man. Now he found out the man used to be a Marine and he knew from the TV show NCIS that a Marine was always a Marine. He'd underestimated the man and the man had let him so as not to undercut Jerry's authority.

Putting fingers back up, Jerry continued. "Fourth – weapons, more than we have, but nothing we don't know how to use. We found out today that there are people with hand grenades and they aren't afraid to use them. Mike, I hope you'll help us in that respect as well.

"Fifth – scavenging, we need to do a better job of it. Today we let opportunities pass where we could have picked up stuff at no risk to ourselves and we didn't. When we see something we can use, we need to get it. If we see something we need, we get it because if we don't and we need it we're going to kick ourselves for being stupid. And if we don't get it, someone else, like those sons of bitches today, will. We need to all start being smarter and that means me as well.

"Kellie, I'd like you to take control of the house and what's in it and figure out what we need most so we don't start looking for stuff we don't need right away, like how we need more clothes for everyone, but not more beer, even though one would taste good right now."

Kellie's eyebrows shot up. "Me? Why me?"

"Because you're the most organized of all of us, even more than Mike. I need someone who is smart and organized to make sure we're not wasting resources chasing after stuff we don't need. Also, everyone here knows you have the least amount of experience in survival, but you do know something about organization," he explained in such a way so the woman was not insulted. He wasn't being sexist by asking her to organize the shelter, he was just using the people he had in a way that helped the whole group.

"Will I get to be called Lieutenant Kellie?" she asked with a wink to Mike and to lighten up what could have been a tense moment.

Before Jerry could respond it was Eddie who spoke up. "Hey, yeah, Lt. Stone, though. You go by your last name. I like that." Mimicking her higher pitched voice he added, "Lt. Stone has the bridge. Bring all weapons to bear and let's go kick some alien assholes." The little bit of comedic relief was welcomed by everyone. Eddie had changed a lot today, but the core of him was still the little wiseass with the smart mouth.

Bringing everyone back to the purpose of the meeting Jerry put up one last finger. The last item, but possibly one of the most important is fuel. We're running out and we need some. Every time we're out, we're going to have to look for fuel. Randy will be in charge of making sure all the vehicles are always full and ready to go when we need them. Nothing would be as bad as having to pump 20 gallons of diesel into the truck by hand while someone else is waiting for back up 10 miles down the road."

He looked around the room at everyone. "That's what I have, anyone want to say anything?"

Eddie opened his mouth and Randy stopped him. He knew his friend well enough to know when he was about to make some inappropriate smart ass remark. "Shut up, Eddie." Eddie smiled and closed his mouth.

It was Mike who spoke the sage advice. "You've given us a lot to think about, Jerry. I like your ideas, personally, but before we talk about it more, why don't we all take the rest of the evening to think about it and in the morning we'll hash out any issues we have."

Everyone seemed to agree with Mike's idea so Jerry stood up from his chair. "Good thinking, Mike. I'm a little tired and need a shower."

Tony spoke up before Jerry could leave the room. "Thanks again, Jerry. I won't let you down again."

Jerry looked at the man. "You didn't let me down, Tony. We all make some poor decisions and Jeff made some, you made some and I made some. All we can do is move on from here."

With his good hand, Tony reached out from under the blanket and offered it to Jerry. Jerry took it gently and shook it solemnly the released it. "I need that shower then I'm off to bed. I'll see you all at breakfast."

~ ~ ~

When he got to his room, he started stripping off his dirty clothes and tossed them into the white basket he kept in the corner. Tomorrow he'd collect up all of Jeff's stuff that was in the room and clear a spot so Mike could move into this room.

Tomorrow things were going change, but the smell of his own sweat was enough for him to think more about right now than tomorrow. He put on the old robe he'd been given by his ex-wife eight or nine years earlier and went back down stairs, showered and brushed his teeth and put on clean shorts and tee shirt. Just before he retired for the evening, he tussled his son's hair and told him good night and checked on Tony.

Monica would stay beside him tonight and there was nothing anyone could say to dissuade her.

In his room, he pulled a book from the shelf, a good science fiction novel that'd help him lose himself in someone else's narrative before sleep. He was tired of thinking about today and even though he knew he'd never forget what happened, or stop second guessing himself, he knew he needed to sleep because he'd put forth some real plans for tomorrow and they were going to depend on him.

He hung up the robe on the back of the door to his room and climbed into the single bed, propped himself up so he could read comfortably. He just started the first paragraph when there was a knock at the door.

He assumed it was either Randy or Mike with a question. He was surprised it was Kellie.

Jerry was over 50 and had survived raising two kids, including a daughter whose teenage years were a roller coaster of emotions. His marriage had fallen apart, like half the other marriages in the USA and he survived that as well. By all accounts, as lives in the United States went, Jerry's had been typical, without a lot of drama or stress. He had flirted with bankruptcy, but selling one quarter of his farm to a developer who had planned on building a housing development kept him solvent.

It had been difficult for him when his dad died, but he carried on in the stoic way his dad would have wanted. His mom passing three years later had been difficult as well, but his friends and relatives helped him through that too.

When he met Andrea and fell in love, life was good. Then their kids were born, Randy followed two years later by Amanda. They grew up and graduated high school. Randy went to the community college part time and helped on the farm and played video games. Amanda went into the Army to be a helicopter mechanic. Jerry thought about her every day and never stopped believing she'd survived the virus.

Six months after Amanda had joined the Army, Andrea was gone and six months after that, the divorce was final. Jerry's life moved on.

By anyone's measure, Jerry's life had been boring. He didn't participate in politics or sports, he attended church regularly, but not the bible study programs. He watched TV and farmed his fields, milked his cows every morning and every evening, tended the fields during the day and drank beer at the local Lions Club once in a while.

He wasn't a handsome man, barely reaching six foot in height, his hair was leaving him quickly, his eyebrows a mix of brown and a strand to two of grey, an unspectacular jaw line, teeth that were just a little crooked and one was chipped. Despite working the farm his entire life, he never developed into a muscular man, taking after his mother rather than his dad. He was slender and had a wiry strength, but wasn't a brute of a man.

He'd tried dating after Andrea divorced him and failed miserably so he quit trying. He didn't have the inclination nor wanted to expend the effort. The drama was too much for the man who was used to an orderly, simple and drama-free life. He could live without hearing about some woman's problems with her ex and her children and her job and her boss and her mother and her car and her etcetera, etcetera. The first date he had after Andrea had divorced him killed any desire for him to date again.

Were it not for Remi, his Cajun friend from high school, he'd've never met Sissy the week before the fall of the world and he probably would have gone to the grave having not given more than just a passing thought to enjoying the companionship of a woman again. He'd thought of her often in the weeks that followed, but knew she had died from the virus. The flame that had been rekindled died again.

When he first saw Kellie and her dog in his field, he thought she was probably insane. He, Randy and Mike were careful when approaching her. She was dirty with hallowed cheeks and had scratches on her hands and face; her clothes were torn, shoes muddy, hair a mess and had eyes that looked as if they'd died already.

Her voice however, was firm, if a little shaky and he could tell she was very close to breaking down. They told her she was welcome to come with them to shelter. Her dog growled a little but she shushed the little mutt she called Molly. It had taken 10 minutes to convince her they were not going to hurt her. He thinks the dog was the key when he knelt down and

Molly timidly came up to him and licked his outstretched hand.

Kellie agreed to follow them back to the shelter, still obviously scared. She started crying in gushes and leaned on the gentle Mike. Mike was the one who comforted her led her back to the shelter and Jerry called for Monica. Monica came out and led Kellie inside. She heated some soup and biscuits Terrill had made that morning while Kellie composed herself.

She ate and watched the men and Monica carefully, looking for anything that might be a ruse. There was none. She finished eating and fell asleep, a peaceful sleep right there on the table. Monica woke her after an hour, suggested she take a shower and then showed her the extra inflatable bed in her room that was hers for as long as she wanted it.

Monica took Molly outside and fed the mutt some leftovers while Kellie showered. The little dog was hungry and finished them before Kellie finally felt she'd gotten all the dirt off. She came out wearing a pair of Jerry's jeans, held onto her narrow hips by an old belt, and one of Randy's tee shirts. It wasn't much, but she wore it without complaint.

Over the next week she got to know the people in the house and they got to know her and the struggles she had getting to where they found her. She was a dainty woman who had obviously led an easy life up until the fall. She spoke with an educated voice and used words Jerry could tell she'd learned from a good school and college. She told them her version of what had happened to the world and it paralleled what they had heard and experienced.

Randy filled her in on how fortunate she'd been the previous night, sleeping in the factory building, and not having met any of the not-dead zombies. She stared at him in disbelief, but Mike and Jerry confirmed the young man wasn't kidding. She'd not encountered any zombies, and after what Jerry and Randy said, she could go the rest of her life without meeting them.

She chipped in with the chores and found a way to fit in with the vastly different personalities and people.

After hearing Jerry talk tonight, explaining to them his vision and willingness to lead, Kellie felt she was where she belonged for the first time in years. She missed her sister and her family terribly, she missed her school kids and her friends, but of all the bad things that had happened, she was glad she was here with these people. It made the sorrow and pain less tormenting to her dreams.

Chapter Four

Jerry had climbed into bed with a book, intent on reading until his mind was full of sci-fi and not reality. It was cool, but not cold, in his room so he pulled the single blanket up and put on his reading glasses.

Then there was a knock at his door. "Can I come in?" she asked, peeking through the door. She wanted to tell him how much it meant to her to feel like part of something so special.

"Sure," he said pulling the blanket up to cover more of himself. He laid the book down and took his glasses off. "What's up? Something wrong?"

"No, not wrong," she said, staying by the door. "I don't want to be a bother, just wanted to let you know how much confidence you instill in those people."

"You're not a bother, Kellie," he said. "And thank you. They are really good people and don't need me to give them confidence." She really liked his self-deprecating manner. He was never too proud and always willing to listen to others. She again counted herself fortunate to have stumbled upon this man and this shelter.

"May I sit down?" she asked. It was probably the first time a woman had ever been so forward to him. She knew what this must look like to him, but he hadn't made any move which might even be vaguely considered inappropriate or threatening to her. She felt safe with him.

Jerry stuttered something that sounded like "please" and moved his feet to the side of the narrow bed.

She took the offered seat and she sat with her hands clasped together in her lap. She looked uncomfortable to Jerry, like she wanted to say something but didn't know if he'd under stand what she was going to say.

"What is it, Kellie?"

There was a long pause. Jerry was never the type push someone into talking about something they didn't want to.

"Terrill was a tortured soul," Kellie began. "He told me what happened to him in Afghanistan and it was terrible. He was always afraid growing up and he joined the Army to try to get the confidence to not be afraid. When his Army truck was blown up, he was afraid again and he just wanted to get away from the Army and the heroes there who faced terror every day.

The death of Terrill weighed heavily on Jerry. He replayed it in his mind at least a hundred times already.

"He started drinking to forget the horrors he saw and when the end of the world came, he thought he wouldn't have to be afraid anymore, but the vigilantes and the zombies continued to make him afraid every day and every night. At one point he tried to drink himself to death, but he stopped before he did. He was too afraid to even die.

"When he came here, after he came to know you and your son and the others, for the first time in his life he wasn't afraid all the time. When you asked him his opinion on the wisdom of going to look for Tony and Jeff, Terrill felt you listened to him. It made him feel like a part of something…something important. He told me this the night before you guys left.

She paused for a minute to stifle back the tears she was fighting. "I don't know because I wasn't there, but I think Terrill's sacrifice today was his way of facing the terrors and the fears he'd been carrying with him all his life.

"I think because he died saving you and Tony, you're going to be afraid to make difficult decisions and you'll second guess yourself. You might even start thinking of quitting and let someone else do it so you don't have to."

Jerry's eyebrows went up high on his forehead because he'd been thinking just that, back when she and Jerry were talking in the garden and then again earlier today. She was perceptive if nothing else.

"Big decisions will always weigh heavy on you and I hope they always do because then you'll never take someone's life for granted.

"But I hope you never become afraid to lead like you did tonight. I don't pretend to know what tomorrow or the next day will be like, but I know I wouldn't want to have anyone but you to follow."

Jerry's rubbed his face and then his head. He didn't know what to say or if he should say anything at all. He was blushing like a teen after a first kiss.

"I just thought you should know how much you mean to everyone."

"Uh," Jerry stuttered. "Thanks."

She got up from the foot of his bed and kissed him. It was a kiss that was more than a friendly kiss, but not a kiss that would lead him to believe she was offering more than just a warm kiss right now.

"Good night, Jerry. Sleep well." She winked and smiled at him, just enough to let him know there was interest but not so much as to make him feel uncomfortable.

She closed the door.

Jerry sat for five minutes thinking not about what she'd said, although it did mean a lot that she came to tell him, rather thinking about the feel of her warm kiss on his lips and the feeling of her hand on his cheek.

It was a good feeling.

He put the book on the floor beside him and turned the light off.

For the first time in longer than he could remember, he fell asleep with a smile on his lips.

~ ~ ~

Jerry, as always, was up before the rest of the shelter the following morning. He dressed and started a pot of coffee. He saw Monica sleeping on the floor beside Tony and both looked like they were at peace.

He stepped out the front door to get a feel for the weather. One of the things he missed most was the Weather Channel and the local weather meteorologist. Even though he'd been a farmer all his life, he didn't have the knack for determining the forecast by watching animals, feeling the wind and noting the temperature variations.

It had become his habit that after church on Sunday, after chores and when Randy had gone off to hang with his friends, Jerry would turn on the Weather Channel and plan out what chores he would get done in the coming week.

Those days were gone and since the fall, he'd been winging it day by day and getting a feel for weather changes. He could easily judge the changing of seasons, but the day-to-day barometric changes, high pressure systems and cold fronts were something for that weather lady and her computer models on Channel 13 to figure out and tell him what they meant. She was gone now and Jerry was left to predict the weather as best he could.

Every morning he'd walk outside and try to guess what the upcoming weather would be like. He'd feel the wind on his face, look at the stars or clouds, judge the temperature and do his own modeling in his head. Usually this took a few minutes, after which he'd go pour himself a mug of coffee and go to the barn, milk the cows and feed them before returning to the shelter for breakfast with Randy and the others.

What he saw this morning as he stepped out were the last of the stars being drowned out by the sun, which was still below the horizon, and the clouds themselves. The skies reminded him of the days before hurricanes Katrina, Dennis and Ivan, most recently, came to roar through Alabama and the four that ripped through in the late 90s. They'd all done damage to his farm, but the weather forecasters had warned everyone and Jerry had prepared.

This morning, as he looked at the sky, the long strips of high-level clouds coming in from the Gulf of Mexico could be seen on the southern horizon. There was a light breeze and it was a warm morning for early September.

He knew what they meant without having to be a meteorologist.

He heard someone come out behind him but didn't turn. He couldn't take his eyes off the clouds. His coffee mug was offered to him as he felt a soft hand and arm lay across his shoulder. Kellie's head leaned on his shoulder as she, too, looked up at the clouds.

"Thanks," he said, still looking skyward and not at his beat up mug, the one given to him by a Chambers Seed representative a few years back. He took a sip as the two stood in silence watching the sky.

"It sure is beautiful this morning," Kellie said in a low voice, in awe of reflection of the yet-to-rise sun off the underside of the wisps of clouds that reached out from the horizon. She felt Jerry nod. A light breeze met them in the face, warm and moist and gentle. It was a consistent breeze, not the up and down from a passing weather system, but the constant southwest to northeast breeze.

Jerry, who'd lived in Alabama all his life, had seen mornings like this before.

"There's a hurricane over the Gulf," Jerry said, breaking the silence. "Probably coming this way if the wind is any tell."

"Dear lord. Can you tell how long before it gets here?"

"I'd guess at least a day or maybe two, but Mike knows how to read that barometer thing, so we'll ask him when he gets up. But it does look like we're going to get wet real soon." He took another sip of coffee.

"I'll get some breakfast started for everyone. I'm sure you've got a lot to get done and you'll need some help from your team." He looked and saw she said it with a smile, a beautiful smile. Impulsively he kissed her on the forehead.

"Let's 'git 'r' done,'" Jerry said, mimicing comedian Larry the Cable Guy. They turned to walk back inside, Kellie holding on gently to his left arm with both hands. "I never liked that guy."

"Me either," she said.

Entering the foyer, Monica and Randy were both awake and in the kitchen. Tony was being helped from the bathroom by Mike. Eddie was probably still sleeping. He seemed to always sleep in. "How you feeling this morning, Tony?" Kellie asked.

"Better than yesterday morning," the young man said. "Foot hurts like a muth-....My foot hurts quite a bit, but Monica says that's good. Head still hurts some and my ribs hurt.

But I ain't gonna be complainin'."

"It's good to see you up."

"Thanks, ma'am," he said as Mike helped him back onto the couch.

"Randy, go get Eddie out of bed. We have a lot to do today and we ought to get started. It looks like there might be some weather moving in."

"Gotchya, dad," his son said, placing his bowl of cereal on the table and taking the spiral staircase two stairs at the time. He opened the door to their room and hollered. "Get up! Dad needs us." Eddie said something which no one downstairs could hear, but everyone guessed it was not polite. "Good God, Eddie," Randy responded. "Did you kiss your father with that mouth....oh wait...too soon?"

A pillow flew out of the room and Randy caught it with one hand and tossed it back before closing the door. Coming back the steps, Randy told his dad Eddie would be down in a minute. The smile on his face told the story on how Eddie had reacted to his Randy's comment.

"Good. I'm going down to take care of the cows. I'll be back in about an hour. Kellie will tell you what we saw this morning outside and why we need to get going. Make those lists of what we need and we'll talk about it when I get back." He walked over to the carafe and refilled his mug. Black coffee was the lifeblood of a farmer and Jerry hoped they found some more soon. He was down to his last two cans.

"I'll give you a hand in the barn," Mike offered. "I never had the chance to work on a farm before and you and I can talk a little more about what you said last night."

"Sure, Mike. You want to grab some breakfast first?"

"I'll have a cup of your coffee and that's all the breakfast I need," he said patting his still ample stomach. Kellie handed the large black man a covered mug she got from the cupboard. Mike poured his own cup and snapped on the cover. "I'm ready."

The two men left the others to finish eating breakfast. Jerry knew by the time he and Mike were back, everyone will have made lists of what they thought they needed.

Walking down the path, Mike told Jerry the real reason he had offered to help in the barn this morning. "Jerry, you don't need a financial advisor and you surely don't need any banking advice. I was a Marine almost 50 years ago and am probably out of practice playing war.

"I don't want you to think I'm a survivalist or some Rambo-type. I'm just an old man who didn't die when the rest of the world did. I feel like I'm living on borrowed time."

Jerry thought about what the banking exec was saying. The personality of Mike was solemn and non-confrontational. He was genial, with stories that entertained the group on some evenings. He was well-read, well-traveled, highly-educated and Jerry had just assumed he'd accept the needs of the group and be Jerry's biggest helper.

"I'm sorry, Mike. I thought with your experience, you'd be good at it. I never thought that maybe you might not want to be in charge of things."

"No, no, no, Jerry. You misunderstand," Mike corrected him. "I'll do whatever you want me to do. I just want to make sure you understand I'm not a fighter, even though I was a Marine. I just wanted to make sure you are clear that I'll back you up, but I'll also give you my honest opinions and advice. I won't bullshit you and if I think you're wrong, I'll tell you."

"Really, Mike, that's all I can ask. To be honest, I don't know what I'm doing most of the time either," Jerry said, grabbing a handful of weeds that had grown up along the path. In most years he'd have mowed them down with the brush hog, but now he wanted the farm to look as abandoned as possible so let the grasses grow. He hadn't mowed the lawns of the farm either since the fall came.

"You'd be surprised, Jerry. I've known hundreds of executives and junior executive in dozens of banks who thought they were good leaders, and they weren't fit to be in charge of a doll house. You're a natural and you don't even know it and that's why these people trust you."

"Well, I don't trust me and that's why I need you to help. You're smarter than me by a country mile. I remember my daddy saying the reason he did so well running the farm was because he listened to smart people 50 percent of the time while he worked hard 90 percent of the time."

"There you go again. Your self-deprecating attitude, making sure you let the person you're talking to know you don't think you know it all. For some people, it looks forced and artificial, but you are real and it shows."

They reached the barn and stepped through to the smell of the cows that were already moving into the holding pen. "This is the other reason I came to help you. I've worked in offices almost all my adult life and I don't think I've gotten my hands dirty in the last 50. I've never been on a working farm before and since my former occupation is no longer in need, I think it's about time I learned a new trade.

"Farmer Mike it is," Jerry said in an effort to keep the conversation moving to something besides the discussion of his personality. "First thing we need to do is disinfect the lines," he began as he kicked off his shoes and put on his barn boots. He pointed to Randy's barn boots and Mike slipped them on. Surprisingly, they fit well enough for Mike to work.

For the next hour Jerry showed Mike how to set up milking machines for the 22 cows, which ones needed to have their milk thrown away because of bacteria, which ones needed an injection of anti-biotics and other special instructions. Mike learned how to operate the machinery, how to feed the cows and the two calves and why everything needed to be done in the order Jerry did it.

As Jerry wrapped up feeding the two calves, Mike found a blank sheet of paper and a pen that looked like it had been around for a while, but still worked. He began writing down the supplies he could see the shelter was going to need in the next day or so, then added another column for supplies they'd need long term.

Mike stepped out of the barn to look again at the clouds and to feel the wind on his face.

Remembering what his grandfather had told him, Mike felt he could smell the change and taste the salt in the air. "Moisture is being picked up from the warm gulf waters and brought inland," Mike thought to himself.

Jerry joined him a few minutes later and the two walked back to the shelter. Mike asked a few questions about the soybeans in the fields and what they could be used for now that Jerry wouldn't be harvesting the beans to sell. Jerry shook his head. "I'll harvest them and store 'em and cover them. Since we can't sell them, we'll find some way to use them. The corn we'll use for the cattle and maybe ourselves if we can, and there are some apple trees that will give us some fruit we can store for the winter. I think there's a pear tree or two as well.

"Between those and what we have in the garden, I think we'll have enough to get us through the winter in good shape." They also went over Jerry's plan for the day and Mike made a suggestion that had not occurred to Jerry because he was so use to using his own resources for so long.

The two men entered the shelter and everyone was sitting around the dining room table, except Tony, who was reading on the couch. He looked uncomfortable there with his leg in the sling still, but he had been propped up so he could read with the book on his lap. Jerry could still see the bruises on his shoulder and ribs, his left eye was turning from blue to greenish yellow so he knew it would heal, even if the eye was still bloodshot.

Kellie gathered up the lists, including the one Mike had worked on. Like an executive assistant, she put all the lists together and removed the repeats and gave Jerry just one list after he finished his shower.

Mike looked at the barometer/thermometer and wrote down its settings. Jerry scanned through the single list and then told everyone what he thought they should do.

"I think I should take Mike, Randy, Eddie and Monica up to Trussville where I used to get lumber for the farm. We're going to take the Ford with the trailer and while Mike and I are loading it with everything we can that we might need, you three are going to take Mike's Escalade and the small trailer and see if you can find a pharmacy first and anything else on this list. I know there's a lot on the list, so you guys have to choose a good place. We're going to give you an hour on your own while we load up the truck and gooseneck.

"I want to go to Trussville because I know they have a big fuel tank there and we should be able to fuel up the reserve tank in the truck." Jerry had put a galvanized reserve tank in the truck with a hand pump that would hold 100 gallons of diesel fuel that he used to fuel his tractors in the field.

"You follow us to the lumberyard. We'll talk about what else is on the list on our way because I want to get going soon. I think we'll grab the five gas cans in the barn and strap them to the gooseneck and if we can find some gas, we'll get as much of that as we can, too.

"We don't know how much damage this weather is going to bring, but I think we should ready."

Mike pointed to the barometer. "The pressure has dropped since I looked at it this morning. It's getting pretty low. I'm guessing we'll start getting rain in 12 to 24 hours and a lot of it. We can expect pretty high winds, as we all know, and maybe tornadoes, for the next two or three days."

"Anyone got anything to add?' Jerry asked.

"Can I buy a kite, daddy?" Eddie asked. Jerry gave him a sharp look, ready to put down his levity because of the seriousness of the situation, but decided after what the young man had been through yesterday, if the kid in him still wanted to come out once in a while, that couldn't be all bad. Jerry was aware Eddie knew this was serious business and would be serious when he needed to be.

"Eddie, you get the guns ready with Mike and Monica while Randy and I go hook up the trailers and get the tie-down straps and gas cans loaded.

"Kellie, you think you can keep Tony out of trouble while were gone?" She smiled. "I'm sure I can find some things to keep him occupied and that garden still needs weeding if he gets out of hand. Maybe I'll give him the CB mike so you guys can call in to tell me you're all okay."

"Good idea, but the signal might not reach. I guess we'll find out."

With everyone given a job, Jerry and Randy went to the garage where the truck and SUV were kept. The garage was originally built to house his truck and Andrea's Durango, but she took that when she left years ago, leaving nothing but an oil stain on the garage floor. Mike's SUV was now parked over the oil stain.

Since they were only going to Trussville, Jerry drained the spare tank on the truck and Randy put the fuel in the storage tank over the hill by filling two yellow fuel cans and strapping them on the quad, pouring them in the big tank and coming back for more. If they found diesel, they'd wanted to get as much as they could. The front tank he drained by half. Even with a full load on the trailer on the Ford, it was still plenty of fuel for as far as they were going.

Randy hooked the Escalade up to the 12-foot long trailer they used for the quads. The SUV had a hitch, but the electrical hook up was different. He stood looking at it for a few minutes, wondering how he was going to make the lights on the trailer work.

It was Jerry who had the answer. "Who's going to pull you over? You don't need to worry about lights on the trailer."

Randy tapped his forehead. "Duh!"

Jerry hitched the 22-foot gooseneck trailer to the truck while Randy threw the two-inch straps into the bed of the truck and more into the back of the SUV. One of the tires was low, so Jerry inflated it and the two parked the trucks in the driveway and called on the CB for the other three to tell them they were ready to hit the road.

Tony answered that the three had already left and should be there in a few minutes and then wished them all luck. Jerry could tell the guy still had trouble talking with the missing teeth, but at least he was trying.

That was when the three came around the side of the building with the weapons they'd be taking with them. Mike climbed in the truck with Jerry, and the three younger people climbed in the SUV. Randy drove with Eddie riding shotgun.

Jerry started the truck and pulled out of the drive when Mike pointed at the clouds from the south. Jerry nodded. "Yup, it's coming."

Half an hour later they pulled into the lumber yard. They'd encountered no one on the back roads they'd taken, but saw houses and businesses that had been burned, farm animals that had broken free and were now wandering the fields and streets. There had been a lot of destruction by human hands. Both Eddie and Mike kept sweeping the area through binoculars and Monica watched behind the two vehicles just to make sure no one snuck up on them.

The lumber yard, not a large one, had taken some damage, but it looked more like just a lack of people to maintain the building. The two vehicles parked where there were pallets of lumber. The building itself had two of its oversized garage doors still open.

Everyone got out and had a gun ready.

Jerry and Eddie went around one side of the building while Mike and Jerry took the other side. They met in back and the four worked their way through the building. Jerry and Mike had agreed that without food in the building, the chance of vigilantes or not-deads was minimal and their supposition turned out to be true. Mike found two bodies that had obviously been dead for several weeks, but nothing to endanger the foraging party.

All four met back at the trucks.

"Randy," Jerry said to his son. "Mike and I will be safe here I think. You, Eddie and Monica go find as much on the list as you can."

"We're on it, dad," he said enthusiastically and he and the other two headed to the Escalade. Jerry thought he was a little too enthusiastic and wanted to remind him about the danger. "Don't take any chances, son. Remember, zombies like the dark and vigilantes like the food stores. Try to stay away from those. In fact, do stay away from those. Try to find a small pharmacy with big front windows or something like that."

Stopping at the opened door of the big SUV, Jerry looked back at his dad. "You got it, dad. Small pharmacy first, no zombies, no vigilantes."

"One hour son. If you're not back in one hour and 10 minutes, we're coming to look for you. Go only as far as Gadsden Street," he said after checking his GPS, "or within two blocks of it, no more than a mile either way on County Road 10 so we can find you quickly if you don't show up.

"Yes, dad, one mile east or west, two blocks north or south," he said and started the SUV. Jerry watched them drive out of the parking lot. Mike knew what the father was thinking. "They'll be okay, Jerry. They're good, smart kids. Let's get to work so we're ready in an hour to go find them just in case. I take it you can drive a forklift?"

Broken from his thoughts, Jerry looked around. The first forklift he found was out of propane and refused to start. He then climbed onto a larger Hyster 110. It was gas powered and after a few cranks, the machine came to life.

Mike walked around with a gun in his hand while Jerry loaded a pallet of 12" 2-by-4s, some 5/8ths-inch underlayment and a stack of treated four-by-fours. When nothing and no one showed up to threaten the two men, Mike went to find nails and screws, drills and hammers. He grabbed up some extension cords and rolled a small Honda generator, a 20-gallon air compressor and a couple of cordless tools with extra batteries out to the truck. Jerry would decide what they really needed versus what they just wanted and what would fit in the truck and trailer.

Jerry looked like he was enjoying himself on the forklift. He'd loaded up two more pallets of treated wood. Mike guessed 2-by-12s or 2 by-10s and some OSB. The trailer looked like it was getting loaded with as much as it was going to take. It looked to be enough wood to build an entire house. Mike did his part by loading five-pound boxes of deck screws, 16d nails and truss braces. He also grabbed up some pneumatic nailers and nails for them as well. If they were going to do a lot of building, these would make the work go faster. He also found a pallet of tar which Jerry loaded for him, then finished loading the trailer with two pallets of shingles and another of 15-pound felt for weather proofing.

The two men strapped down the load securely and Jerry looked at his watch. There was 15 minutes left before the kids would come back, so he moved the truck over to the fuel tanks. Between the spare and reserve tank on the truck and gas cans they'd brought, all of them got topped off with diesel or gas. The company must have just filled up their tanks before the fall because they sounded full when Jerry tapped on them.

Checking his watch again, it had been an hour and one minute since the kids had left. He hoped they hadn't got into trouble. He walked around the trailer again to make sure everything was strapped securely when he heard a vehicle coming down the highway. It was in a hurry by the sound of it.

Jerry and Mike grabbed for their weapons and took up positions beside their trailer. They would defend it because they surely wouldn't out run anyone with the heavily laden truck and trailer and there was no time to unhitch the gooseneck.

He heard the vehicle decelerate. It was the kids. They were in a hurry.

~ ~ ~

Randy, Eddie and Monica had left the lumber yard in high spirits. Randy's dad had given them explicit instructions, but enough freedom to make their own decisions. He felt like he'd been given some real authority as an adult and he was going to take it.

They quickly found a pharmacy on the main street of town. Randy thought it was too easy. If they walked in to the pharmacy, got what was on the list, they could be back in the truck and back to the lumber yard 10 minutes after they'd left. Randy's dad gave him an hour. He was going to use all of it and told the other two as much.

He passed the pharmacy and the strip mall it was in. He wanted to see what else was in town before they had to go back. They drove on until they were nearly out of town and Randy was beginning to think this was a waste of time because there were cars and trucks and semis on the main street and they had to maneuver around them.

He was about to turn back when they saw another strip mall and they pulled in. The windows in the front had been knocked of every building and the Winn-Dixie had partially burned.

They were about to leave when Eddie pointed to an electronics store at the end of the mall. Monica guarded the SUV while the young men looked through the front. "Holy mother of God! Jackpot!" Eddie hollered back to Monica. They carefully climbed through the front window and Randy came out first with an arm load of video games. Eddie followed with two game systems and six laptops. They went back in and brought out four flat panel TVs and one more time for the movie display rack that had all the latest releases on it and as many as Randy could quickly grab from the value bin. In all they got about 200 movies and 50 games. They also grabbed several boxes of electronics that were sitting near the doors to the back room, but didn't go near the back room.

Monica asked why they grabbed so many video games. "In case we get bored," Eddie said, like it was obvious. Randy looked at his watch. They had 40 minutes.

There looked to be nothing more at this end of town so they headed back to the CVS pharmacy when Randy glanced down a side street and saw a small gun shop. It was barred up and looked like it hadn't done much business even when it was open, but it was a gun shop and they needed more ammunition. He stopped in the middle of the street and backed up to get a better look. "This might be something," he said, looking through Eddie's binoculars, and hung a left off the main drag. He parked the SUV in the parking lot and the three got out.

Randy and Eddie pulled out their guns and walked around the building while Monica, armed with a .22 caliber rifle guarded the vehicle. They came back and told her the place was locked up tight. They contemplated how to break in, Eddie suggesting shooting the front door locks, but Randy had an easier solution. He tied one of the 2-inch tie-down straps to the front window bars on the building and hooked the other end to the front of the SUV. When he backed the Escalade up most of the front wall came off.

Eddie smiled at his friend. "Cool," he said with a big smile.

All three went inside, sure it was empty. The former owner was dead and rotting in the business's office and Monica almost lost her breakfast when she saw the body. She closed the door quickly and told the boys to not go into that room.

The boys agreed not to.

They looked at the guns in the shop. Most were shot guns

and Eddie grabbed a couple of the bigger ones while Monica was filling bags with shot gun shells. Randy was looking at handguns, including a Desert Eagle he pulled out of a display case he'd opened with a hatchet to the glass. "Damn, Randy! I almost shit myself," Eddie hollered at him after the sound of shattering glass stopped. "Next time warn us before you do that kind of shit."

Randy just smiled at him. He now had a Desert Eagle, something he knew his dad had wanted for a long time. He put it in a holster and then the holster over his shoulder. After that he went for the rifles. He found a pair of what looked like good ones that had names like the guns in his video games. He also found an entire shelf of walkietalkies which boasted 30-mile range and encryption. He grabbed up a dozen packages of them and the display of Duracell rechargeable batteries.

On the counter was a rack of survival magazines. He figured they would be welcome reading by a lot of people at the shelter.

He was grabbing these and any survival gear he could find, while Eddie grabbed as many shot guns and rifles he could get at, ignoring the black powder guns of course, and loaded them onto the trailer. They were getting quite a haul from this little shop.

Just as they were about to leave, Randy saw something behind the counter. It was a ham radio, one of the expensive kinds, with a lot of dials and switches and an amplifier of some sort. He had Eddie go out and look for the antenna while he grabbed the radio equipment and unplugged it from the wall. He had to unscrew the coaxial, but he figured they could find more and dad probably had some at the farm.

He had it packed in the SUV with the guns when Eddie finally got the antenna off the roof and handed down to Monica. Randy looked at his watch and they still had more than a 20 minutes but he decided not to risk looking for more stuff here.

"Let's get back to the pharmacy and then go show dad what we found," he told them. "He's going to love this gun. We'll probably come back for more."

"I got me a Bushmaster 308," Eddie said, "and a 4 by 20

power scope. I'll be able to shoot flies off the nuts of a cow from 500 yards."

Monica rolled her eyes. Randy laughed with his friend. It was good to see his humor coming back. "Cows don't have nuts you idiot. Cows have udders. Bulls have nuts."

"Okay, then I'll shoot the nuts off a fly. Either way, something's losing its nuts to this gun."

Randy shook his head and started the SUV. "Whatever, you dumbass. Just don't shoot one of dad's cows or he'll shoot you."

~ ~ ~

They pulled into the parking lot and stopped in front of the CVS pharmacy. The front glass had been shot out but didn't look ransacked. Randy decided to drive around back of the building. The back door was ajar but there didn't look to be anyone around.

He pulled back around front and the three looked at the front of the building. "Well?" Randy asked them. "You think it's safe to go in?"

Monica answered first. "We do need stuff from in there and without the front windows it'll be bright enough inside to see and keep the zombies away."

"You can probably already smell the candy, huh?" asked Eddie jokingly.

"No, actually, I need tampons, douche bag. Now, do you feel good about your comment?" and she cuffed him in the back of the head gently. "Kellie does too and if we don't get some other products we use real fast, you men are going to really regret having women around."

"Enough!" Randy said. "T-M-I." He put the SUV in park, but didn't shut it off. "Let's get it and hit it."

All three armed themselves, Randy with the Desert Eagle and eight of the .50 caliber magnum rounds that came with it, Eddie with a Colt 9mm and Monica with a Smith and Wesson .38. They went through the front door and allowed Monica to lead the way because she knew what she was looking for. She started in the women's aisle and loaded the guys up one at a time and sent them to the truck with instructions to hurry back for more.

After the second arm load, Eddie gave her a cart and told her to fill it herself. Randy did the same thing. She was careful to only put what she thought the women would need and not fill the carts with frivolous crap.

Randy and Eddie went around picking up soft drinks, boxes of cereal, laundry detergent, tooth paste, tooth brushes, mouthwash, razors, shaving cream, soap, shampoo, and as much coffee as they could put in carts. Each one of the three loaded two carts and pushed them to the trailer. Randy looked at his watch and noticed they had just five minutes left. He asked Monica as he was tying down the last cart if she'd gotten the drugs for Tony.

"I think I got them all, but it wouldn't hurt to check to see what the pharmacist had behind the counter if we have time." Randy nodded. "But hurry."

She and Eddie went back inside to the pharmacist's counter and started throwing pill bottles filled with drugs into a basket, as long as they had a label. Eddie had his back to her when she screamed, and screamed loud. An arm had reached through a slot in the wall and had grabbed her wrist. Then another snaked out lightning quick, then a third and a fourth.

Eddie whipped around and reached first for Monica to pull her away. "Shit, shit, shit," he hollered. "Pull dammit pull!" "I am! I am!" she retorted in a shriek, but was unable break free, instead, she was being pulled toward the slot. The strength of the hands through the slot in the wall was beyond all the strength the two young adults had. The hands through the wall were tearing her skin and she felt like her skin was ripping off the bone or her shoulder would come apart.

Eddie pulled the Colt out of his belt with one hand, afraid to let go of Monica, and began shooting through the wall next to the slot. Three of the four hands grabbing his friend released her. He heard deep, throaty grunts from behind the wall and continued to shoot until his gun was empty.

At the sound of the gunshots, Randy came running. He heard the screams and more gun shots as he ran through the store and he was going to help his two struggling friends.

There was panic in his body language and in his face, but he wasn't going to lose the two best friends he'd ever had.

The two were still struggling with the last hand holding onto Monica's wrist. Randy pulled the Desert Eagle and held it with both hands and shot the same place Eddie had. Six loud shots deafened the three, but finally, with the sixth shot through the wall, the hand let go and the young people fell backward.

They started running when Randy turned back and grabbed the two baskets of drugs Monica had filled. He wasn't going to leave without getting some of the priority products for which this trip was planned and that his dad had instructed him to get first. He grabbed the baskets and got a glimpse of the zombies through the holes and slot. They had misshapen heads with oversized black eyes. Their mouths were distended and the two he saw had what looked to be dried blood on their face. They were looking right at him and one had a new bullet wound in the face and the other had a new hole in its neck and one in the shoulder, but the holes didn't slow them down or make them look any less dangerous.

Holding the baskets in one hand and the Desert Eagle in the other, he shot at them again. The gun almost flew from his hand and he shot the floor eight feet in front of where he thought he was aiming. "Shit. I'll leave this part out when I tell this story to dad," he said to himself and ran from the store.

Some of the drugs fell out, but he didn't stop to pick them up. Whatever he had was going to have to be enough. When he got to the truck, Eddie and Monica had already gotten into the back seat and he threw the drugs into the passenger seat, barely taking time to close his door. He dropped the shifter in drive and stepped hard on the gas.

They raced all the way back to the lumber yard, laughing and crying and repeating their fears and heroics to each other. They were loud because the gunshots in the close quarters had temporarily deafened them.

Randy brought the SUV to a sliding halt and all three jumped out. Monica was holding her wrist that was badly injured, but not broken and yammering about almost dying. Eddie was going on about shooting two zombies and Randy was just pleased as hell to see his dad.

It took 20 minutes for the three to explain the drama they'd gone through in the past five minutes. Jerry let them release and asked Randy if he'd like Mike to drive the SUV back to the farm and Randy declined. He'd finish the job he'd been asked to do.

Jerry let the kids calm down for a few more minutes while he looked over the merchandise they'd picked up. It looked like they'd picked up a lot of stuff they would need. "Okay, let's load up and head back home," Jerry directed. "And let's have a little less drama on the way?"

Pulling out of the parking lot, Jerry and Mike discussed what the young people had done and Jerry didn't let the shaking he was feeling inside show on the outside. He kept his speed down to 25 miles per hour. It was a pleasant drive and Jerry could see in his side mirrors that Randy was smiling and talking with his two friends, so while they might have had some reality scared into them, they were none the worse for wear.

Mike was recalling some story from his youth in which he had to run from someone. Jerry was not paying real attention, just enjoying the pleasant drive home and thinking about his son. He was checking side mirrors again making sure the boy was still following and talking with Tony on the CB. "Yeah, we're all okay," he was saying while passing a drive that was hidden by decorative shrubbery. A small car pulled out of the drive and into his front bumper.

Who was more surprised would be talked about for months. Jerry hit the binders several heartbeats later than he might regularly. The driver of the little car was equally surprised and also hit the brakes. It was too late for both, but the car took the heaviest damage and the big Ford, easily pushed it out of the way as Jerry brought it to a stop.

Randy, Eddie and Monica were out of their vehicle first. They each had their guns drawn. Jerry was next because the hit was on Mike's side of the truck and the hood of the car was next to his door. The driver of the car was turned, looking at something in the back seat. Jerry heard crying, the kind kids make when they are scared but not hurt, and the bark of a very big and very mad dog.

He let his gun drop, knowing his three young people in the Escalade would have their guns ready after the terror they'd been through in the last hour. The driver turned around. There was no fear on her face. In fact, to Jerry, it looked like she was ready to get out of the car to kick his ass until she saw the three young people with guns pointed at her in her rear-view mirror. She put her hands up.

The very big dog barked at him from the passenger seat of her car. It looked to be a Bull Mastiff, like the dog he had when he was growing up. He pointed to the dog and made a hook with his finger indicating he wanted her to hook the dog up before he tried to help her out of the car.

She fumbled around and found the dog's leash and hooked his collar.

Jerry went around to the passenger door, still afraid to open it because the dog was 2/3rds the size of its owner and with his strength could easily break free. He'd hate to have to kill the dog, especially in front of his kids and the kids who were in the car.

He made the motion for her to slowly roll down the window, but just a little bit.

She did and he heard the woman tell "Boomer" to shut the hell up.

"You okay, ma'am?" he asked, slowly allowing the dog to sniff at the back of his hand.

She held onto the big dog while he leaned over to Jerry's hand. "I think so. I've got two kids in back, don't kill us, please!"

"We're not going to hurt you, ma'am" he assured her as gently as he could. But let's get everyone out of your car and get it away from the truck. He then stood up. "Quit aiming those damn things and get over here," he said to his kids. "We got children in the car."

All three holstered their guns as they quickly ran up to

help. "No more drama, huh, dad?" Randy asked. Before Jerry could respond, added "I know, shut up, boy."

It took them all a little while to get everyone calmed down and make sure no one was injured. Jerry found out the woman, Tia, was the wife of an Army major stationed at Ft. McClellan over by Gadsden. He'd died along with everyone else on the Army base and she was driving back to Reno where she hoped to find her family.

She'd stayed on the base for three weeks after everyone else had died, not knowing why she and her 12-year-old son, John and eight-year-old daughter, Hannah, had survived. She'd decided yesterday that they would drive to Reno and had made it this far last night when she pulled off the interstate and found a church for them to sleep in.

They hadn't seen any vigilantes nor heard about the not-deads, but Tia was a religious woman and felt the Baptist Church was a safe place for her and her kids. They had just packed up and were going to look for a gas station or another car when she pulled out and hit Jerry's truck. "I just didn't think there's be anyone around," she told them.

Randy was talking with John who was not crying, Eddie was playing with the big dog and a tree branch while Monica was sitting on the side of the road with the little girl named Hannah.

Jerry explained what they knew about the world, the vigilantes and the not-dead, and the chances of Tia and her kids making it to Reno. Tia didn't break down like he thought she might. She just ran her fingers through her hair and looked around. "Well, there's a storm coming, so if you'll help me, we'll find another car and then be on our way to find some shelter."

"We won't stop you ma'am, but we have a place not far from here where you and your kids and dog are welcome to stay." Suspicious, Tia almost declined until she heard Kellie call on the radio. "I hope you picked up some more clothes while you were out," Tia heard the woman say. "I'm tired of wearing flannel."

Mike picked up the microphone and filled her in on the accident. Tia heard Kellie's response. "Well bring the poor dear and her kids here and stop screwing around. There's a lot of work to be done and little time."

"Who's she?" asked Tia.

"Someone like you we picked up about three weeks ago. A teacher," Jerry explained. "And a garden weeder."

Tia smiled for the first time.

Jerry, Mike and Tia looked over the car. "You won't be driving this anymore," Mike said.

"I think I'll take you up on your offer, Jerry," Tia said, looking at her kids as they talked with Monica and Randy.

Tia and Hannah were packed into the back of the truck while John wanted to ride with Randy in the Escalade with his new friends and Boomer. They got all the clothes out of the car and some food Tia had brought along, including two 50-pound bags of dog food for Boomer. Tia lifted one by herself and Jerry grunted just a little when he grabbed the other.

Packed up, they left Tia's car where it had died and headed back to the shelter.

Driving through Moody, everyone kept a look out and Randy was surprised when his dad pulled over in a big parking lot of a strip mall that looked mostly ransacked. Jerry got out of the truck and motioned for Monica to get out of the Escalade.

"I almost forgot to get clothes for you girls," he said to her. "Do you think you can find what you need over there in that store there?" he said pointing to a clothing retail outlet that had the front windows shattered and doors off.

Monica smiled and just asked for covering fire while she shopped.

Jerry, Mike and Tia all armed themselves while the two adolescents stayed in the vehicles. They stood guard while Monica loaded Eddie and Randy up with clothes for the women and made them carry the clothing to the rear hatch of the SUV. Someone heard Randy say "get this bra off my head" at least once and Eddie ask "Seriously, you wear that size?" followed by a head slap.

It took all of 10 minutes to load up everything Monica

could find that she thought those living in the shelter might need and the troop got back on the road.

They arrived at the shelter with the three new people just in time for Kellie to serve them leftover stew for lunch. They all recounted their experiences to Kellie and she listened to every word, smiling at the right places, showing concern and consternation when appropriate. She was the perfect hostess and made sure Tia and her two children felt comfortable.

After the lunch, Jerry suggested jobs to everyone. Mike, Kellie, Tia and her two kids would unload the Escalade while he, Randy and Eddie would unload the truck and trailers and start boarding up the garage and barns in preparation for the heavy weather that was coming.

The winds picked up through the afternoon. Everyone worked hard and as night began to fall jobs that had to be completed outside were finished with flashlights.

The first rains began falling around midnight.

Everyone found a place to sit in the overcrowded living room or in the dining room area. It was more crowded now and Jerry reviewed everything that had gone on during the day. He talked about their mistakes, his included, how they could avoid them in the future and what the storm damage would probably be like on the farm. Mike made some additions and handed out complements to Eddie, Randy and Monica for their quick thinking that day.

Everyone could hear the storm winds picking up outside. Jerry reminded them the shelter, built into a hill, was safe and everyone believed him. But that didn't stop them from thinking about the barns and garage and fields and anyone else who hadn't found a shelter as secure as theirs.

When Mike said he was going to bed, Kellie told everyone of the new sleeping arrangements. Tia and her two kids would be sleeping in the room she and Monica had been in. Monica had volunteered to stay in the living room with Tony. Now that he had a splint on his ankle and drugs for the pain, she wanted to stay with him to make sure she'd medicated him right and had already gotten an inflatable bed and put it on the floor.

Mike, who snored rather loudly, had volunteered to sleep in the cellar. "Now you volunteer to sleep in the cellar, old man? Why didn't you think of that three weeks ago?" Eddie asked and tossed a pillow at the elderly black man. Mike caught it and smiled. He then shrugged and replied mildly, "You didn't either, and you're smarter than me."

"We've done all we can," Jerry said, breaking up the emerging pillow fight before it could start. "Why don't we all get some sleep if we can? I know I'm beat." Everyone seemed to agree, but no one moved right away. They all listened to the winds outside, muffled from the amount of earth that protected them, but loud enough to let them know nature was still alive.

It was Tia who moved first, gathering up her kids and Boomer was let outside to do his business. Jerry patted the dog as the animal walked by and Boomer wagged his tail, hitting everyone within reach.

In response, Molly, on Kellie's lap, lifted her head, and then put it back down. To her, Boomer was just another one of Kellie's friends.

The boys and Mike went next, the two younger up the stairs and the one elder to the cellar. Jerry made sure the front doors were locked tight when Boomer returned to the shelter. He went to his room while Kellie checked to make sure Monica and Tony were comfortable, everything in the kitchen was turned off, and the three new guests had blankets and pillow and everything else they needed for the night.

Jerry would have liked a shower before bed, but he had put in 18 long hours and was as tired as he'd ever been. He stripped to his boxers and crawled into bed, barely noticing a pile of clothes Monica had picked up at the fashion store were now on his floor in a corner.

He'd just closed his eyes and was nearly asleep when his door creaked open. Molly came in followed quietly by Kellie. "Shhh," she whispered to the dog as she used a pen light to navigate around the room. Not coming fully awake, Jerry realized Kellie had never said where she'd be sleeping, now that Tia and her two kids had taken over the girls' room.

Now he knew.

Kellie slipped off her flannel shirt and bra, and took off the new pair of jeans Monica had found for her and crawled into bed, the one Jeff had been sleeping in. They had been arranged to make room for the clothes they'd picked up and also so both people in the room could use the same lamp with which to read.

The heads of both beds touched at the corner, with Jerry's going down the length of the back wall and the other along the wall on which the door was hung.

All the space in the room was used.

Kellie turned her penlight off after Molly had gotten herself comfortable and the room went totally dark except the red glow from the digital clock on the shelf by the door. Jerry felt Kellie's hand stroke his head and he reached for it. "Good night, Jerry," she whispered. Still holding her hand, he fell asleep before he could wish her the same.

~ ~ ~

Morning came with rolling thunder that shook all of them. It was still very dark in his room when the rumble woke him. The digital clock on the wall was out and the light between the beds refused to turn on. He heard Kellie getting out of bed too and was happy with the total darkness for the moment.

Jerry reached for his pants and pulled them on. He had a penlight on the keychain he carried and turned it on to locate his shirt and work boots. Kellie was sitting on her bed hurriedly trying to locate her clothes too and Jerry noticed, but just briefly, because something loud was happening downstairs.

He could hear crashes and voices that sounded like Monica and Tony. He heard the wind outside their shelter and by the sounds of it the storm was hitting them hard. Using the light from Jerry's penlight, Kellie was able to find her pants and a tee shirt in the pile of clothes. Jerry tried not to look like he was looking, focusing instead on pulling on his boots the rest of the way on, but he had to admit to himself, she was an attractive woman.

"You going to be okay?" he asked as he was leaving the room, making sure to not direct his light at her eyes. "Sure, go," she said, waving him out. "I'll be there in a second."

He rushed out of the room, making sure to close the door to keep Molly from following him. He passed Tia's room just as she opened the door to look out. He heard her kids asking questions and told them things were okay and that he was going to check on what the noises were.

Looking down the spiral stairway with his light, he saw Tony on the couch looking to where Monica was by the front doors. He saw the doors must have been blown open and she was trying to find a way to keep them closed in the feeble light put out by Tony's small flashlight.

Jerry grabbed the big flashlight he kept on top of the bookshelf and turned it on. A bright blue light filled the foyer as 32 LED bulbs lit up. He rushed to the doors and leaned against them with Kellie to keep them closed. Kellie took the flashlight from his hand and stepped back to give the two a better view of what they were doing. The doors were closed again, but the locks were broken. The door stayed closed for the moment and Jerry and Monica stood back.

They could hear the ferocity of the winds outside and the rain pelting the doors.

"Wow," Monica said, still standing by the doors in her underwear. "That wind is strong, Mr. Saunders." Kellie brought Monica, who didn't realize she was still standing in her underwear in the reflected light of the flashlight, a blanket to cover herself. Mike opened the door from the cellar and shined his light on the group.

"Everything okay?" he asked.

"The doors blew in. Broke the locks top and bottom. Must be something hit 'em hard because the wind shouldn't be able to do that," Jerry said. He heard Tia and her kids at the top of the stairs, but Randy and Eddie hadn't even stirred yet.

Kellie was shining the light on the doors, looking at where they had been damaged when they flew open again. Hard horizontal and stinging rain and wind came through the door and she dropped the flashlight to cover her face as she and Jerry rushed to close them again. Monica and Mike also helped push against the doors to keep them shut.

"Randy! Get down here!" Jerry hollered as water cascaded over the four and wind battered against the double doors. Randy and Eddie were both on the stairway in seconds, both in their underwear but they didn't care. They saw what was happening and rushed down to help Jerry and the others. Eddie grabbed two chairs and wedged them against the door handles while Randy put his not inconsiderable weight into keeping the doors shut.

The wind still howled but the amount of water coming through the doors was significantly lessened. Jerry's luck or foresight, he didn't remember which, had been to make the entryway to the shelter slope away from the inside of the shelter. The water that came through the cracks in the door frame didn't flow into the room, but it was easily three inches deep by the door.

One by one everyone moved away from the doors. Randy was the last to move and he did so gingerly, making sure they were going to stay shut. Everyone watched for two full minutes before anyone moved too far from the door. They were all soaked, but no one wanted the doors to come open again.

Mike broke the silence. "Power's out too, I see."

Jerry accepted the flashlight from Kellie and walked over to a grey box on the wall. He lifted the latch and opened the front cover. "Yup," he said. "It looks like we blew the main breakers.

"When I built this place and put in the electricity, I only knew half of what I was doing, but if the water wheel down at the river or the wind turbines got to giving the batteries too much juice, the main breaker would shut down.

"I never thought it would work, but it did just like I hoped it would."

He switched the breaker back on and every light that someone had tried to turn on in the darkness came on.

"Sweet," Eddie said, removing a lot of the tension from the room. There was a lot of water on the floor and Mike and Jerry started mopping it up, being more fully clothed than anyone else. The others were deciding it might be a good idea to get into some dry clothes. Tia and her kids, who had remained out of the way, came down to the foyer to help. They joined everyone and it was little Hannah who said something that only the innocence of youth can get away with. In a stage whisper, so her mom could hear her over the noise coming from outside she said, "Mommy, that lady's shirt is sticking to her boobs."

Everyone looked and saw that Kellie's tee shirt had in fact gotten wet and everyone could easily see the gifts with which God had given her. Tia shushed the little girl and smiled apologetically at Kellie. Kellie took it in stride and gratefully accepted the kitchen towel Jerry was handing to her. He was seeing the same things as Hannah had seen when the lights came back on and had the chivalry to avoid staring. Eddie and Randy, he noticed, did not. They raced back up the steps as they were still in their underwear and needed to hide.

"Uh, yeah," Jerry said to no one. "Let's get out of these wet clothes. Anyone know what time it is?"

"It's Oh-Six-Fifty-Two, sir," John said looking at his watch. Jerry could tell he was an Army child.

"I guess we're all awake for the morning," he said, using a towel to dry his head and face. "If the doors stay shut we'll have to just find ways to keep ourselves occupied while the storm moves through."

"With the power back on," Randy said, emerging from his room wearing jeans and a tee shirt, "We've got games in our room the kids can play." John and Hannah looked at their mom and she nodded they could. Randy asked for a few minutes before the kids were allowed in so Eddie could finish putting clothes on.

Monica said she would grab a movie for herself, Mike and Tony to watch and Tia said if no one minded, she'd only had an hour of sleep and she really could use some more. No one minded.

Mike declined the offer, saying he was going to finish the book he was reading in the cellar.

Monica was heard, as she picked up a pair of men's underwear from a pile under the spiral stairway, say to Eddie as he emerged from his room to gather up John and Hannah

"Seriously, you wear that size?" Jerry chose to ignore them and started looking at the power levels of the batteries which stored the power from the wind mills and water wheel generators. He heard Kellie go up the stairs to change as well.

His shirt was soaked, pants were wet and shoes made squishing noises. There was no way he was going to mess with the electricity in the shelter with this much water on him. He checked the door again and used his towel to tie the two handles together, just in case the chairs slipped. They were as secure as he could make them for now so he went to change into some dry clothes.

Forgetting that he had a new roommate he walked in on Kellie changing into dry clothes. He slapped his hand across his eyes and backed out as fast as he could, apologizing repeatedly for intruding. He stood in the narrow hall until she came back out, embarrassed about what had just happened. She opened the door a minute later, fully dressed and pulled Jerry into the room. "I'm sorry," she said. "I didn't even think to lock the door. I thought you were going to work on the electrical stuff. But thank you for being a gentleman," and she kissed him that kiss he had enjoyed so much two nights ago. "I'll put coffee on," she said as she left the room.

Jerry locked the door after she left. He didn't want anyone walking in on him.

The storm raged.

Chapter Five

Jerry spent the day shoring up the front doors and checking the electrical systems in the house with Mike. Tia slept until noon and came down to have lunch with everyone. Her kids, who played games with Randy and Eddie for an hour before going back to sleep with their mom, came out of the room around 10 in the morning, wiping sleep from their eyes asking for breakfast.

Tony watched two of the movies found the previous day and played with the CB radio while Kellie and Monica organized and sorted through some of the bounty that had been brought in.

Randy and Eddie had entertained John and Hannah and kept them from being underfoot and their minds off the storm until they were tired. Every so often the people downstairs could hear the laughter and giggles coming through the open door to the boys' room until the little ones had retired back to their mom's room for more sleep.

About 9 o'clock that morning, the winds died down to almost calm for about an hour. The eye of the storm was passing nearly overhead of them. The winds returned in a hurry with the same ferocity for another six hours. It had been a big hurricane and Jerry knew there would be damage to his farm. The storm continued through the morning and didn't noticeably begin slacking off until late afternoon.

It was 7 p.m. when Jerry finally believed it was finally safe enough for him and Randy to go check on the cattle. The winds had died down considerably and they could hear rain falling, but not as hard as it had been. They donned raingear Jerry had kept in the basement. He slid one of the walkie-talkies inside his rain coat after testing it with the one Randy had and the one Mike was using. Everyone had their own walkie-talkie now and it gave a feeling of safety. Randy put his in his front pocket so he could get at it easily under his rain gear.

Jerry undogged the front door and he and Randy saw what had broken the door early this morning. It was still raining steadily, more of a dousing rain than the sideways wind-driven rain of earlier. Randy closed the door behind him and his dad.

There was a 20-inch limb, at least 35-feet long outside the front door, across the parapet. Jerry didn't have any trees that big within 200 feet of the shelter, so whatever wind had brought it this far, had to have been a real doosey.

"Damn, dad. Look at the size of this. We're going to have to get a chain saw to move it," Randy said as they climbed over it.

"Yeah, it's too big to move now. We need to take care of the cattle first, if there are any left. Let's go."

As the two men trudged down to the barn, the rain kept them from seeing too far. The hurricane winds had died down to less than 30 miles per hour, Jerry guessed, but there were still gusts that reached over 60 mile per hour.

As they neared the barn, Jerry could see the farm house had taken a lot of damage. Most of the roof was missing and three of the walls had caved in. There were dozens of large trees in the yard that were up rooted and two of the smaller outbuildings he used to store his lawn tractor and some of his equipment was gone. The lawn tractor had been blown into the tree line, along with a lot of other debris.

The cattle barn and garage had some major roof damage, but some of the steel and framework held. The damage was over the pens in the barn and not the equipment so it wasn't a priority. The cows could stand to be wet, but he noticed eight of his herd was missing. The milking parlor no longer had a roof, but the equipment, lag bolted into the floor of six-inch reinforced concrete seem mostly intact except for a few of the plastic lines.

The garage had taken a bad beating as well. Most of the siding had been ripped off, and the roof was gone. The big

Ford and the Escalade had been pushed around and dented and some glass knocked out, but they were still there. The big Massey-Ferguson tractor was still sitting where he'd parked it, but it had a tree limb every bit as big as the one behind the shelter sitting across its hood.

Both trailers were upended and now leaning against one of the supports in the back of the garage. There was nothing he could do about it now, but when the rain stopped, probably tomorrow, he and the rest of the people at the shelter had a lot of work to get done.

Jerry counted himself lucky both buildings had been built into the hill and protected by the trees. The other out buildings were gone and the old concrete silos which Jerry had stopped using years ago had collapsed.

It took almost two hours for Jerry and Randy to get the cows milked and taken care of for the night. They let the milk go down the drain in the holding room because they still had six full gallons in the refrigerator at the shelter and he didn't want to start the refrigeration on the milk storage tank.

Randy cleaned the stalls and pushed the manure out the back of the holding area with the skid steer Jerry had left parked inside the barn. There was a small lake where the manure pit used to be. He guessed they'd received about 20 inches of rain so far which meant the soybeans and corn and probably everything growing on farm would be ruined.

Randy couldn't do anything about it now but he hoped this hurricane hadn't destroyed their ability to keep the shelter as a safe haven. He heard his crotch say something so he reached in for the walkie-talkie he'd put in his front pants' pocket.

"How's it going?" asked Eddie. "Need any help?"

"We're just about finished here, Eddie. We should be up shortly."

"Okay. Kellie wanted me to tell you guys supper'll be ready in about 20 minutes."

"Thanks," Randy said, then put the walkie-talkie back into his pocket and parked the skid steer.

He met up with his dad who was also finished. The rain had lessened in the two hours they'd been in the barn and there were peeks of sun coming through the cloud cover, very near the horizon. They were both awestruck by the cloud formations curling across the sky.

Before they went in for the night, Jerry wanted to check the water wheel and generator by the stream. As he suspected, the river had flooded well over its banks and the wheel was long gone, but the generator and its housing were still bolted to the concrete platform he'd constructed and poured. It was salvageable.

The wind turbines were gone from the back hill. He could see they'd been snapped off the poles on which they'd been bolted. If they were lucky they'd be able to find and repair them, but he wasn't going looking tonight.

The antenna tower for the CB radio was also knocked down, probably taken out by the tree that was now pinning it to the ground.

While they were on top of the hill next to the antenna, the two men looked around their farm. There were gullies in the fields still flowing violently, but less now that the rain had slowed. There were trees and limbs and debris everywhere, including, from what they could now see from this vantage point, more damage to the roof of the garage where Jerry stored the wood they'd gotten yesterday.

From the pattern of fallen trees that protected the front of their property and kept dust from the dirt road from the farm house, Jerry guessed winds had easily topped 190 or 200 miles per hour.

Those same trees had outlasted at least seven other hurricanes, but now a lot of them were broken or uprooted.

"Let's get inside son. We'll have a lot of work for us the next few weeks."

Once inside and with their gear hung up to dry, the two told of the mess they'd seen outside. The shelter, most of the cattle, the trucks and tractors were safe, but first thing in the morning they'd have to fix either the water wheel, which probably wouldn't be practical until the water levels went down, or one of the wind turbines. The charge in the batteries in the basement would probably last another 24-36 hours Jerry guessed from the charge monitor on the wall.

"We survived better than I thought we would," Jerry said positively. "But we're going to be pretty busy getting the farm back in shape.

"The important thing is we made it," Kellie said. "I'm willing to bet not everyone who survived the fall of the world survived the hurricane." There was a long silence at the table for a while as that fact sunk in.

It was Tia who broke the silence. "Do you think it's safe for Boomer to go outside? He's been a good dog today, but I think he might be exploding real soon."

"Sure, just open the door and let him run," Jerry suggested. "He probably won't run off and I doubt he'll hurt himself out there. He might try to get around the cows, but they can take care of themselves."

"Oh I doubt he'll go far," Tia said as she got up to let the big dog out. "We used to let him run around the housing complex and he never caused trouble with anyone and won't go far, but I'd be careful where you step outside tomorrow. Some of his piles are epic."

Boomer ran outdoors into the dark that had fallen. The rain had slowed some more and there was a cool breeze out. Jerry asked Tia to leave the door open to allow the cool air to circulate throughout the shelter, replacing the air that had gotten a little stale. Molly, Kellie's dog, for the first time that Jerry could recall, ran outside with the big Bull Mastiff. Her tiny little hid legs were churning to catch the big dog and everyone laughed.

Kellie didn't chase after the little dog she loved so much. "They've been playing all day. It's good to see even she has a new friend." They could all hear the dogs playing now that they were free of the confines of the shelter. It wasn't so bad for the little four-pound mutt, but the 80-pound dog needed room to run.

Quiet fell over the shelter as the rain lessened to a gentle thrum. It'd been one bit of excitement after another over the past week. The group of Jerry, Mike, Jeff, Randy, Eddie, Tony and Terrill, Kellie and Monica had been torn asunder. Jeff was now three days dead and the time for mourning had passed. Jerry hoped Terrill, who sacrificed himself for his friend Tony, was finally at peace as well. Jerry would forever remember what the young veteran had done and swore he would somehow erect a permanent marker for the man.

Tony, who'd been captured by vigilantes and used as bait, would probably spend the winter rehabilitating from his broken ankle and the severe beating he'd received. There was no dentist available, so he'd have to live with the missing teeth.

They had also taken in Tia and two adolescent children who would have to grow up in a new world and with new ways.

Jerry had always been a bit of a loner, used to being out of doors, working the land, making his way in life as best he could. He'd been uncomfortable around large crowds, he wasn't highly-educated or trained to be a leader of people, but neither was he an ignorant "good-ole-boy." Jerry had graduated high school, but because his dad had died and left him with the farm, his continued education was mostly night classes at the community college when he could arrange it.

All things considered, before the fall of civilization, Jerry felt himself to be in a safe life, happy enough, but still with hopes and dreams. He'd raised a couple of kids who did okay in school and never got into trouble so deep the cops had to get involved.

Here sitting at the dinner table with nine people looking to him for leadership, he sometimes felt almost overwhelmed because decisions he was making affected others. It was worse when those decisions, like the one yesterday morning to send his son and his two friends off by themselves to look for supplies, might send people he cared about into danger.

The dogs came running back into the shelter, giving everyone something other than their own thoughts, for those who were lost in them, or those who were just finishing up dishes and talking about the weather, to see some pure joy.

Boomer had an expressive face and a big tongue he wasn't afraid to use. When he came running in, his huge paws were covered in red Alabama mud and he tracked it to every place in the shelter he could splash it. He ran first to Tia and John who were in the kitchen, after slip sliding around the dining table, then to Jerry for a quick pat from him and finally over to where Tony sat on the couch. Tired from his run he laid down on Monica's bedding and looked at everyone like he was surprised they were all yelling at him to stop running around.

What increased the simple joy was Molly, who had followed Boomer in and was also covered in mud. The little dog's black and red tongue was hanging out and dripping when she came through the door and found her favorite spot in the world: Kellie's lap, on to which she immediate jumped, muddy feet and belly and all.

Jerry and Mike both got a chuckle from the mud now on Kellie's new clothes as she struggled to hold Molly above her lap. Tia, John and Hannah immediately dove for Boomer to get him off Monica's sleeping area. Tia was pledging to clean up the mess and apologizing while John and Hannah man handled the big dog over to a mat by the door someone had found.

Everyone was, for the first time, Jerry reflected, concerned with something other than the hell they were living. He saw they were actually living life in what was now their normalcy.

The evening was an enjoyable night of frivolity and playing with dogs, shared memories of previously owned pets, and John teaching Mike the right way to play a video game while Tia taught Monica how to braid hair using Hannah as the subject.

It was the release of tension the group needed so Jerry kept his serious discussion, in which he had planned on talking about the clean up and what they might have to do now that his crops were most likely destroyed, on hold for the next morning.

Jerry, Randy and Mike were up before first light to get the cattle milked, cleaned and fed. Boomer joined them. Jerry was pleased to have the other two to lend a hand and get this chore taken care of first. As the three walked to the barn just as the sun was rising they could see better the damage the storm had wrought.

While work Mike asked how much they should actually clean up the area if they wanted to remain hidden from casual view of anyone. Jerry hadn't thought of this. He'd planned on sawing up the fallen trees to use as fire wood for the winter and hauling all the branches into a large burn pile. He'd always taken pride in his lawn and having dead branches lying around went against his nature.

Mike proposed leaving as much damage as possible where it was. This would give anyone, should there be anyone left in the area, the belief the place was abandoned.

Jerry felt differently. He felt they needed to maintain the property to give the people living here a semblance of the life they had before the fall. If the people living here thought they were always hiding or had to live like they were afraid of being discovered, they would be living in fear and that was something Jerry didn't want.

Both men gave it serious thought and debated each side of the issue casually while they watched Boomer run around the barn yard picking up different sticks to be thrown. It was Randy who found the compromise with which they could both live. Randy suggested cleaning up the areas that couldn't be seen from the road. They could fix the damage in the barn and garage, but only clean up the debris on the back side of the hill where the doors to the shelter were.

Instead of building a pile of branches for a bonfire, throw them all on the old farm house and burn it to the ground. That would lessen the chance of someone thinking there was something worth salvaging from the place.

Randy also suggested it would probably be a good idea to allow the cows to free range now. He knew they'd come back at milking time because cows were creatures of habit and it would be less of the drain on the dry feed they had in stock.

He looked at his dad and told him they were going to have to change the way things had been done, to ways that now would make more sense. "Eddie and I have been doing a lot of talking about this," Randy said to his dad, while he, his dad and Mike headed back to the shelter. "We think we've come up with some good ideas on how we can make our lives easier and still be able to keep this place going."

"You and Eddie?" Jerry asked incredulously. "That boy has trouble pouring piss out of a boot with the instructions on the heel. His idea of work is ten minutes of doing dishes. Don't get me wrong, I love the boy, but his biggest challenge before the fall was if he was going to be a stand-up comedian, a domestic terrorist or play video games for a living."

The other two laughed with Jerry at his description of Eddie. It was wholly accurate.

"Seriously, dad. We don't just play video games all night, well, sometimes we do, but we also talk a lot about what our future is going to be like."

Mike, who had stayed out of discussions between Jerry and his son did add his thoughts but in a way to make sure Jerry didn't think he was intruding. "Things do change. They did before the fall and they will continue. A year ago, I was making $850,000 a year and had a boat on the coast. Things changed. Sixty years ago, I couldn't ride in the front of a bus. Things changed. One hundred years ago, my granddad couldn't own property. Two hundred years ago, my ancestors couldn't be free.

"Everything changes, Jerry. Your son might have a point."

"But not all changes are good, Mike," Jerry said without much enthusiasm for his side of the discussion. "We'll look at some changes, but let's not go overboard. Let's start small and see where it gets us. Right now we're doing okay. I don't want our changes to make us less okay."

Jerry and Mike both seemed to accept that position.

Boomer came up to the three men walking back to the shelter. This time he had the biggest limb he'd brought to them yet. It was easily six feet long and four inches in diameter. "Why don't we find a way to harness his energy for the electrical system?" Randy jokingly asked. "He ain't too right in the head."

"Speaking of that," Jerry said as they walked into the shelter. "Let's start on that first, right after breakfast."

~ ~ ~

For the next week, there was an unspoken rule that the shelter and farm needed to be the first priority. Everyone knew it was uncomfortable and crowded and everyone had to make the effort to not lash out when angry, although harsh words did get spoken and brows were furrowed more times than could be counted.

Jerry and Randy, with John as their gopher, worked to repair one of the two wind turbines. It had taken three full days to get it working properly and they had to use parts from the second one they found that was beyond repair. Electrical usage in the shelter was brought down to a minimum and even then the gas generator had to be started to keep the batteries charged for the work in the barn.

Mike, Eddie, Tia and Hannah did a lot of the farm work. Tia had a farming background in upstate New York and knew how to drive tractors and other heavy equipment. Mike and Eddie bowed to her expertise and Jerry just had to give her only very general instructions on which fields needed harvesting and which ones weren't worth the effort anymore.

With the cows free ranging, there was no need to feed them every morning and night. Eddie got permission to take down the fences and allow the cows to go wherever they felt the need. The second day only two hadn't returned for morning milking but surprisingly, by the end of the week, the herd went from 12 cows up to 23. Jerry figured the hurricane had torn down fences all over the state and the cattle joining his herd just wanted to be with other cows.

Kellie spent most of her time improving the inside of the shelter to make it as comfortable for everyone as possible. She continued making a list of stuff they needed, now more blankets and inflatable beds, storage containers and dry goods. She also spent time in the garden and was able to save some of the peas, tomatoes, carrots, potatoes and sweet corn.

Monica began organizing the loot she, Randy and Eddie had gotten. The survival magazines were stacked on the dining table for everyone to read regularly and look through for tips or tricks to help the shelter survive.

With everyone else fully employed, Tony felt like he wasn't doing his fair share and insisted the CB antenna be re-erected and the shortwave radio antenna get attached to the very top of the lattice tower. When Jerry balked, it was Mike who came to Tony's defense. "How would you feel not being able to contribute, Jerry?"

"We still have things which need repaired or replaced that are far more important than the antenna," Jerry pointed out. "If I could, I would, but we need to get power re-established and repairs done to the barn and garage before some other storm comes up and slaps the shit out of us."

"Tell you what, you tell me what to do to get that antenna up, and I'll have Tony help me," Mike suggested. "I'm not much help farming, and Tony isn't doing anything but sitting there moping. If we can do it, we'll get it done. If not, you're not out of any time."

Jerry let the foolish old man have his way, but he was right.

Tia had Mike doing very light work that really didn't have to be done right away, but that she'd made up so he'd feel useful. Jerry wouldn't be losing any great amount of time by having Mike help Tony. Tony's better mood immediately affected everyone and Jerry even let Randy loose for a couple hours late in the afternoon to use the chain saw to remove the tree that had downed the antenna tower.

The next morning Tony, despite being in pain and using crutches, helped Mike on the top of the hill. They rolled logs out of the way, to be picked up later by Tia, Eddie and Hannah with the tractor, and for the next two days, Mike and Tony worked to get the antenna tower's lattice work straightened and braced. Tia, it seemed, also had a talent for stick welding and she did the brace-work for the two men.

Just before dark on the second day of work on the tower, they raised the antenna tower on its foundation and bolted it in place. The guide wires were tightened and coaxial cables zip tied to the frame and buried deep enough to avoid anyone tripping over them. Tony had spent the day snaking the coaxial for the CB and shortwave transmitter through the shelter and hooking them to the radio.

Tony wanted to try the equipment that evening, but Jerry put him off for another 24 hours while the batteries fully recharged. The one wind turbine was spinning slowly in the gentle Alabama wind, but it was charging the batteries. The balance was off on the one propeller Jerry had made and he and John sanded smooth. Jerry set the rpm rate of the propeller to six to keep the 15-foot tower from shaking itself apart until he could balance the whole thing.

Jerry promised that once the batteries were fully charged, Tony could turn on the equipment and give it all a try. He also let everyone know that he and Randy would be re-building the water wheel for the next two days at least. Jerry and John found the paddle wheel about a mile downstream, lodged on some trees when Randy was helping erect the tower.

Mike clapped Tony gently on the shoulder and told him they'd worked too fast, but tomorrow they could work on building a shelving unit for the equipment so it wasn't setting on the floor and taking up space on the couch.

The following morning at breakfast, Tia mentioned that while she appreciated the use of the room, she wanted her own shelter. Jerry said he too had been thinking about enlarging the place but wasn't sure they had the room to do it now that just about every square inch of the shelter had something stored in it.

"Why do we have to build underground? I want something to live in that has windows. I really miss windows."

Jerry scratched his chin and thought about it. "Well, I have thought about it, but we really don't have the kind of experience to build a house that you could live in."

"What about those houses on wheels?" asked Hannah, who was playing with Molly on the floor.

"What about that, Jerry?" Kellie asked. "If we could find some modular homes still on their wheels, do you think we could drive one or two of them here for houses?"

Jerry had never considered it, so now he did. "No. I don't see how. There's no way to get one down the roads from the highway. We'd have to clear a path and that could take days or weeks," he said shaking his head. "And I can drive tractors and forklifts, but I don't know anything about driving a semi. I think I'd probably wreck it. I don't think its practical Hannah. Sorry."

"Mommy can drive a semi!" She said brightly.

Everyone setting at the table looked over at Tia. She smiled and admitted, "Yeah, I did it for a year before I met my husband. But Jerry's right, a modular home wouldn't work. If we cleared enough room to get it in, it'd be like carving a path for anyone wanting to find the farm.

"But what about an RV? We could pull it on the back of your truck easily enough and we would be comfortable in one of them if we could find one." Jerry arched his eyebrows to consider it, so Tia went on. "Actually, that'd work better. I could use the tractor to clear out a spot near the trees down that way," she said, pointing the same way as the garden. "I'm sure we could get it plumbed and electrified without too much trouble. If we found one with electric stove and refrigerator, we'd have more room for everyone."

"That's a good idea, Tia, Hannah," Mike said. "What do you think, Jerry?"

"Hey, dad," Randy chipped in, "if she gets one, can me and Eddie get one for ourselves? I'd like living in a camper with windows."

"If they get one, I want onc!" Monica said petulantly.

"I wouldn't mind not sleeping in a cellar anymore myself," added Mike.

Jerry could see he was out numbered, but he wasn't ready to start a RV park on his back 40.

"First off, I don't know where to start looking for RV," Jerry said, lifting one finger, "second, even if I did, the hurricane probably destroyed everything around." Another finger came up, "thirdly, there is still a lot of debris and repairs to do here, and fourthly," another finger, "we'd probably have to clean the road to get it in here. That's a lot of work to expend right now when we still haven't finished what we need done now."

With every finger he raised, the faces of everyone in the room dropped from big grins to straight lips and a few frowns.

It had been a difficult week for everyone, working from nearly sun up to sun set and all were starting to feel a little frayed at the edges.

To finish off he raised his thumb, Eddie and Randy looked like they were ready go up to their room and Monica went back to looking through the magazine she had. "And fifthly, if we do it, we'll go after one and bring it back here and see if it will work before we start bringing in a convoy of RVs here." The smiles and good cheer in the room was back instantly.

"But first we need to finish fixing the barn and garage, and get the water wheel generator fixed for power. And then we'll go over a list of other things we need before we go, just like the last time." It wasn't much of a consolation, but it gave everyone something to work toward.

Hannah clapped her hands, making Molly bark. When Molly barked Boomer barked and ran for the door. Everyone laughed at the big dog as he cocked his head and looked back at Molly, as if asking her to open the door for him. Hannah got up from the floor and let both dogs outside. Both started barking at nothing and having a good time playing.

"Let's plan on five days from tomorrow. That'll give us time to finish the repair work on the farm, Kellie and Monica time to finish inventorying what we have here, and the rest of us time to make a wish list."

"730 George Roy Parkway, Calera, Alabama, 35040," Monica said. Everyone looked at her, wondering what she was talking about. She smiled. "Ad in this magazine says they have a huge selection of RVs, and it's just 45 miles from here."

Eddie chipped in his two cents. "Road trip!"

Chapter Six

Five days of hard work had the shelter back in shape. The water wheel had been repaired and the batteries were now charging well even with the moderate use from the equipment in the shelter and barn. The battery storage system and power grid Jerry used had been set up by his friend Nick from the church. Nick had scavenged the batteries from his marine business and hooked them up in the cellar for Jerry for a minimal price.

Jerry had purchased most of the equipment off the internet like the lights and kitchen accessories. The stove and refrigerator he picked up at auction. He installed them himself as they arrived via the big brown truck. The refrigerator had arrived on the last day before UPS would never deliver again.

While checking the batteries in the basement, Jerry found three of the 24 packs in the power set had failed to recharge. He made a note to get replacements and extras. The internet wouldn't help him anymore and he'd like to keep this set up working as long as possible.

Tony had been thrilled to get the shortwave radio turned on finally. Everyone sat around him expectantly when the unit came on. He ran through the dial on several bands but heard nothing. The excitement slowly faded over the next hour as no voices from the airwaves came through the speakers. There was an automated signal in the 900 megahertz range but when Tony tried the microphone, Monica noticed it wasn't working. It took and hour with small screw drivers for Tony to find out it never would.

A new microphone was added to the list of wants for the shelter.

Tia suggested some more equipment for cooking outdoors.

All of Jerry's equipment had spread to the countryside with the winds. She was big on cooking on the grill and added charcoal to her list. John was hoping for a quad his size and Hannah wanted M&Ms.

Kellie and Monica wrote down a few things to make their lives easier, but nothing of real importance for the run Jerry and Mike were planning. Randy and Eddie were the same with the exception of the addition of a video surveillance system to augment the early warning system Eddie had suggested earlier.

~ ~ ~

The morning finally came for the trip. Kellie walked with Jerry to the garage. Randy and Eddie had gone down early to make sure the truck and SUV were prepared. Something they'd also done the previous night. Jerry mentally added to his list a mobile CB unit for the Escalade.

"We're going to spend as much time as we can on the highway," he told her. "I know we'll be going by a lot of towns and possibly drawing attention to ourselves, but I want to get there and get back here as soon as we can.

"We know where we're going and we should be able to get there in less than two hours if we take the interstate, even if there is a lot of debris."

You and the kids, Mike, Monica and Tony should be fine here. We haven't seen anyone else since before the hurricane and Mike thinks the vigilantes who were out there," he couldn't bring himself to talk about Jeff yet, "were probably killed in the hurricane or at least are too busy trying to find a way to survive to come after the shelter."

"We'll take care of the shelter. You take care too," she said, taking his rugged hand in her hand that was quickly becoming as calloused as his. The intimacy was as close as they'd gotten. He was in no hurry to push her, and she set the pace. Both seem okay with it.

Boomer took that moment to come running up, followed by John and Hannah who were enjoying the early morning air and the lack of morning chores usually handed out by their mom. They knew where she was going, but she'd glossed over the danger that they could run into.

Boomer licked at Jerry's hand, the one Kellie was holding and they both released and wiped off the slobber. He then went for Molly who was walking beside Kellie and knocked the little dog over with his big nose. She got back up and started chasing him, barking happily, leaving Jerry and Kellie and the two kids in good humor.

Mike was in the barn with Tony and Monica, having volunteered to do the chores early so the four going on the trip could sleep in. Tony took every chance he could to get out of the shelter and help where he could, even though it wasn't much because he was still healing and the crutches were an inconvenience.

They met Jerry and the others as Randy drove the SUV out of the garage and Eddie brought out the big Ford. The guns were already loaded in the vehicles and there wasn't much reason for a long good-bye, but for some reason, it was becoming one.

Breaking the standing around, Jerry asked everyone to load up. Kellie closed his door as he climbed behind the wheel of the Ford and put his seat belt on. Tia was riding shotgun for him. Eddie was driving the Escalade with Randy in the passenger seat.

He turned to say good bye to Kellie again when her face came in the window to kiss him. She then withdrew as he put the truck in "D" and headed down the drive. Tia spoke, once the truck moving. "She seems to like you." Jerry thought so too and waved out the window at her and the others. She waved at him with her beautiful smile which he saw in his side mirror.

When they were out of the drive, he focused on road in front of him. There had been a lot of damage from the storm and there was no more department of transportation to clean up the messes.

The two-vehicle convoy was slow. Debris had the road blocked in several places, but not so much as they couldn't get to the interstate. Twice they had to find alternate routes because trees were too large to drive over, the road had been washed away, or in places there was no way to drive around the debris. Jerry had expected to take two hours to get to the RV sales location, but after 30 minutes, they'd only made it as far as the interstate. He called Kellie on the CB and let her know they were running slower than expected. He also told her they hadn't seen where anyone else had been on the roads and that brought a sigh of relief from everyone who heard.

Driving on the interstate was easier. The storm had moved what cars had been on the four-lane to one side, or off the road completely. There were overhead signs that had been blown down, but driving over them or around them was easy for the two big trucks.

They stopped and checked a half dozen semis that had been thrown around, checking the trailers for goods they might need, but it was more effort than what it was worth. All the food was bad and smelled that way. Tia said opening refers would be a bad idea to keep doing. The goods in the other five were damaged beyond use. They decided to stop wasting daylight as they were already nearly two hours into the trip and they had just reached the first Birmingham exit.

The damage was both worse than they thought and much worse than they could have imagined. Birmingham's skyline was not the one they all knew. Gone was the mix of southern antiquity and modern skyscrapers. The hurricane and fires had ravaged the city. It'd been a week since the hurricane, but still they saw fires smoldering and belching black smoke.

The two vehicles merged from the 20 to the 459 bypass. The bridges had either collapsed or were so littered with smashed vehicles they were impassable. Jerry, however, was able to lead them off road and onto the bypass without much trouble. From the bypass they could see more of the city and it didn't look any better from this side. Jerry was sure this city wasn't the only one that had suffered. He knew there were hundreds of other places that had taken the same or worse type damage. He recalled his dad talking about the damage done to Gadsden back in the late 1970s by Hurricane Frederick.

They passed several places they might want to stop on the return trip if time allowed, but Jerry felt it would be best to find the RV dealership first. Randy tried to convince him to let them stop while he and Tia continued on, but he rejected that idea as well. They were already well behind the schedule he had wanted to follow and were now out of CB range with the shelter. He wanted them all to stay together.

The transition from 259 to 65 south was no easier than the previous interchange. It took the two trucks 20 minutes to get on 65 south and the first three bridges after the interchange were also down. They used the on and off ramps to get around the fallen bridges.

Tia pointed to a ramp exit sign that had been blown over and stuck in the concrete of a bridge abutment, but was still readable. The next exit was the one for which they were searching. It took another 45 minutes before they finally found the RV dealership Monica saw mentioned in the advertisement.

The place was destroyed. There were campers and RVs strewn about and buildings that had been torn apart. Jerry was not feeling good about finding a camper for Tia and her kids.

The four of them walked around the park, looking for anything that could be salvaged. Jerry suggested using the truck to set some of the campers back onto their wheels to see if they could be salvaged and they all kicked the idea around.

It was Eddie, who'd gone off on his own to relieve himself who came back with an idea.

"Why not use what's in that building?" he said pointing to a building at the far end of the mess that was partially damaged and barricaded by fallen trees, but not totally so. He'd seen something through the large overhead door that had been knocked off its track, but not off the building.

The four walked up to the building and, using flashlights, they saw something that made Tia smile like she hadn't in a very long time. Inside the partially destroyed building were a Winnebago motor home and another vehicle. The building had been protected from the harsh weather by another building with a steel frame, what had been the repair shop by the looks of it, and a show room. All three RVs in the showroom were wrecked beyond use, but the luxury Winnebago in the building Eddie noticed looked to be in very good shape.

Everyone had been thinking of an RV that would be pulled by Jerry's truck's fifth wheel, no one had thought about getting a rolling house on wheels. Tia took one side of the vehicle, Jerry the other while the boys walked around the outside of the building, looking for a way to get the big motor home out.

Tia opened the door of the home and looked inside. It was clean. There was no damage inside and there was no smell of rotting food or dead animals. It was like the home had been readied for someone, then stored here in the building. She sat in the driver's seat and Jerry came to the window. "It looks good from out here. There's no major damage that I can see. Tires are all inflated. If we can get it out and it runs, I don't see why this wouldn't be better than a camper."

"I have to know, Jerry. The keys are in it. I'm going to start it!" Tia said excitedly. Jerry couldn't see why she shouldn't so nodded to her. She was going to do it anyhow, whether he said yes or no.

She turned the key and the dash lit up. She waited for the diesel's glow plugs to heat. It started after two turns of the starter. All the gauges came up and the Winnebago idled like it was brand new. The fuel gauges read full. Tia couldn't quit smiling.

Randy and Eddie came running at the sound of the truck. They decided the expedient way of getting the 13-foot tall, 42-foot-long motor home out of the garage was to pull the overhead door off with the Ford, which took about 10 minutes to accomplish. Jerry offered to drive the Winnebago, but Tia wouldn't let him. She told him she'd driven semis before and behind the wheel of the behemoth she felt right at home.

With the large overhead door off, Tia to pulled the vehicle into the light. It was better than she'd hoped, bigger than they needed and Jerry was just a little envious.

Eddie was not. He found something else in the garage. Part of the roof had fallen on it, but it wasn't badly damaged. "Randy, you gotta see this!" he hollered.

Randy went to find out what Eddie was so excited about as Tia and Jerry looked around inside the Winnebago.

Eddie was grinning like someone who had just found the

key to the backdoor of the cathouse. "Lookie what I found!" he said and pointed.

It was a three-axel Emergency Response S.W.A.T. truck.

Eddie was almost frothing like a rabid dog. There were no stickers on the truck and it was still flat black from the heavy-duty tires to the periscope air vent on the roof, with no external accessories, except three antennas. It had a heavy-gauge grill guard on the front and gun ports, which were more likely ports for releasing tear gas.

"This thing better freaking run because I'm driving this bad boy home," Eddie said as they ran for the driver's door. Eddie climbed in and rummaged for the keys. They were in the console on a plastic key ring from this RV dealership.

Inside, it was unfurnished except for a driver and passenger seat. There were no radios or weapons which Eddie had hoped to find, but he wasn't upset.

Eddie started the truck. He grinned in the same way Tia had done when her new vehicle had started. Randy climbed in the passenger seat and was looking at the dash video screens when Eddie said "Hang on." Randy looked up, startled, and Eddie dropped the shifter into gear and stomped on accelerator. He drove through the garage door, laughing all the way. The roof collapsed behind them as they pulled out.

Jerry and Tia had to come see what Eddie had done. There was no reason they needed a SWAT vehicle at the shelter, but Eddie made all sorts of deals, like making sure he got the fuel for it, taking care of it, finding a place to park it so it would be out of the way and rationalizing that it was a vehicle they might need someday. He also found a 75-gallon fuel tank that had been in the garage that was still near full. He and Randy strapped it to the back deck of the SWAT truck.

After giving in to the young man, Jerry told them of a couple of stops he wanted to check out on the way back to the shelter. There was now more than enough room to carry stuff in one of the four vehicles.

The clock was still running. They'd been gone now for nearly six hours and out of contact for four.

Headed back the way they'd come, the four-truck convoy

was able to move fast, now that they knew what to expect. Jerry pulled off the interstate twice to check out areas that hadn't seemed to suffer as much damage as others.

They refueled all the trucks from a wrecked tanker truck they found at a Pilot Truck Stop. They all used diesel except the Escalade so it was a simple matter to pull into a Pilot truck stop. Jerry pulled out the manual pump and they pulled fuel right from trailer which was on its side, but not broken open. There was a brief discussion about trying to right the entire rig, find another semi, but their time constraints put that idea to bed for another time.

The doors to the store were open in front and back and there were a trio of torn up bodies near the doors. Zombies were here, but they wouldn't be out in the bright sunlight and no one wanted to go inside anyhow.

The next stop was a strip mall at the 459 / 20 interchange area. The four vehicles circled the mall and all the doors were closed. Glass had been shattered in the fronts, roofs had been ripped off, but the place didn't appear to have been ransacked.

From the outside, they could see how much damage the wind and rain from the hurricane had done to the insides of the stores. None of them had any real hope of finding something they could use, but since they had some time while the other vehicles were fueled, they did look around.

Jerry was able to get several microphones from a Radio Shack, some more AA and AAA batteries, a couple of antennae for Tony and a toy remote control truck for John.

Tia found some goods for her mobile home. She located a nice grill still in the water-soaked box, picked up all the charcoal that hadn't been too ruined by the weather that were stacked outside of the K-Mart, and two gumball machines that were still filled with M&Ms. She also loaded more clothes for her and her children.

Eddie and Randy found a book store. Most of the contents were ruined, but along one back wall there hundreds of still-dry books, shelves full, which they loaded into the SWAT truck. Mike loved reading and the two boys had become quite fond of the elderly black man. He never got mad at them, only offered advice and never talked down to them.

They loaded back into their respective vehicles and headed east on 20. Jerry tried reaching the shelter on the CB, but got no response. He was sure they must be outside because it was a beautiful day. He'd instructed Kellie to have someone monitor the radio so the convoy could check in every hour. He'd try again in another 20 minutes when they were another 10 miles closer.

Ten miles later Jerry heard why Kellie hadn't answered his call.

~ ~ ~

Kellie waved to Jerry, Tia and the boys as they pulled out of the driveway. She watched the dust on the road for more than a mile and she felt alone. It was Mike who came up, not quietly, but not in a way where she felt like he was intruding on her private thoughts.

"They'll be fine," the kindly man said to her. "Why don't we get these two kids breakfast. Tony and Monica are running some more cable to the windmill tower so he can move the short wave antenna. That'll keep those two busy for hours.

"I think John could use a little distraction to keep him from thinking about his mom so I'm going to teach him to use some of Jerry's wood working tools. I'm sure you and Hannah could find something to keep her busy." Kellie understood Mike was also finding a way for her to engage her time with young Hannah so she wasn't worrying about Jerry.

Following breakfast and with the dishes cleaned and dried, Hannah said she wanted to build a doll house for her dolls the same way Jerry had done for her, her mom and brother.

Mike had already left with John for the garage.

Kellie found a couple of hand shovels and the two ladies started digging in the rim of the parapet. Molly tried to help with the digging too, but she got tired and laid on the rim with her head on her paws. Boomer ran around the field for a while then lay down in front of the shelter door.

Everyone was working on non-critical jobs, enjoying the light duty while the others were away. Kellie kept the doors open to the shelter so she could hear the CB. Jerry checked in while they were in range and had told her they would be going further than the CB could reach, but to not worry. He'd let her know they were running behind schedule, but assured her they'd be back before dark.

Kellie thought she'd heard something from the radio so left Hannah to dig while she checked. She called several times but didn't get a response.

She'd just returned to where she and the little girl were digging when she heard a gun shot report. She actually heard the echo from the hills that ringed behind the shelter. She wondered if it was Monica or Tony who was shooting.

It sounded like a heavier caliber gun than the .22 Monica used. She then heard a truck coming up the drive. Something didn't feel right to her. If it had been Jerry, he would have radioed her and the gunshot she heard before the sound of the truck bothered her.

Hannah heard the truck too and looked up to Kellie. "Is that mommy?"

"I don't know, sweetheart. Let's get you inside and in the cellar and I'll go find out. If it is, you can surprise her when she comes in." She smiled a smile she didn't feel and took the little girl's hand and led her inside. Molly followed with Boomer. She sent all three to the cellar and told Hannah to lock the door. She had given the little girl a walkie-talkie, but told her not to use it or to unlock the door until Kellie told her to.

She then picked up the Remington 20 gauge, which was loaded with six rounds of buck shot. Jerry had showed her how to use it and she'd fired it half a dozen times, but only at a target.

She picked up her walkie-talkie, changed to the channel Tony and Monica were using and placed it on her belt. She was afraid, but she had to know what was going on. She looked out the door and saw no one. She didn't want to use the walkie-talkie in case it would alert someone to her presence. She waited and listened.

~ ~ ~

Monica saw it happen.

Tony was between the hills, but she was on top of the taller one where the windmill was and where they were going to put the short wave antenna. She saw Mike talking with someone. She hadn't seen from where the man approached her friend, and she was too far away to hear what was being said.

She saw Kellie and Hannah playing in the dirt outside the front door of the shelter and at the sound of the gun shot, Kellie had calmly taken the little girl and dogs inside and shut the shelter doors.

Mike must have walked out from the barn where he and John had been working.

It was an ugly scene.

~ ~ ~

Mike had heard someone calling in the driveway. It was a voice he didn't recognize. He and John had been sanding on one of the new propellers Jerry would be using for a second wind mill. Mike told John to go hide while he checked on who the person was in the driveway. John nodded and ran to the back of the barn and lay down inside one of the old tractor tires. He held his walkie-talkie in his hand and tried not to be afraid.

When John was well hidden, Mike opened the door of the barn and saw a large black man wearing a dirty red shirt, a brown jacket and pants. Mike had a pistol holstered under the leather jacket he had put on before leaving the barn. He didn't want the stranger seeing the gun and start shooting before talking.

Mike walked slowly toward the man. He was shorter and darker than Mike, and had 100 pounds on him, but he didn't look threatening. "Morning, mister. Can I help you with something?" Mike asked pleasantly, stopping 10 feet from the stranger.

"You got any food, mister? We need food and water," the man said. He had a gravely voice, deep and harsh like he'd been a smoker for 50 years.

Mike looked around. "I don't see anyone else. Who else did you bring with you?"

"I didn't bring anyone, mister. You got any food and water.

I ain't had anything good to eat in days and am real hungry," the man said, looking nervous now that Mike had noticed his mistake in mentioning "we" instead of "I."

"What 'chyou got in that barn there? Cows? I like steak."

"Mister, we don't want any trouble. If you're hungry, we will share our food with you," Mike said, trying to placate this man who was looking more nervous as the conversation continued. He hoped the offer of food would settle him down some. Mike had face a bank robber early in his career in banking and the robber had settle down after Mike had given him four thousand dollars in cash.

The robber had left the bank without killing anyone and was caught a week later, but no one had died.

"You said 'we' too, mister," the newcomer said. "Who else you got here? You got women? How many are here?"

Mike raised both his hands to show the man he had nothing to fear. "Mister, my name is Mike and there are a number of men who live here. We don't want any problems. If you want food, we can give you some and send you on your way."

The man's feral smile was filled with rotten teeth. "Your menfolk are gone. We saw 'em leave. I bet yer the only one left here 'cept the women."

Mike's hands were in the air and he wasn't prepared for the swiftness the man in front of him moved. It was just registering with Mike that the man was reaching inside his jacket when he realized he'd made a mistake. Fifty years separated him from his Marine training and years of sedentary living slowed his reactions. He'd just started reaching for his gun when the man's gun came up, aimed right at him.

The sound was loud, but Mike was dead before the echo faded.

It was surreal for Monica. Mike and the other man were talking for a moment and Monica supposed Mike was just trying to find out if the man was a drifter who had just showed up or something more devious.

It was the latter.

As Monica watched, the man reached into his jacket and pulled out a gun and shot Mike in the head. The old black gentleman who had been kind and helpful to everyone in the shelter, who had never said an unkind word, dropped.

Monica was shocked into inaction. Tony also heard the shot. He had to say her name three times before she responded. She ran down the hill when she saw the truck come up the driveway. She hoped she hadn't been seen. She met up with Tony halfway down the hill and she told him what she'd seen. Tony, who had been unrolling coaxial, sat down in the knee-high grass with Monica.

"We have to get back to the shelter," Monica told him.

"No, you have to. I'll never be able to get back there without someone seeing me, but you can sneak back and call Jerry for help," Tony told her. They'd become close friends, closer than Tony'd been with anyone, but there hadn't been a physical relationship. Only Tony knew that Monica had a crush on Eddie, and in one of their late-night talks, he admitted he had a bit of a crush on Randy, a secret she swore she'd take to her grave.

Monica nodded at Tony's suggestion. "What're you gonna do?"

He lifted his head above the grass. "I'm going to crawl all the way down there, then up on top of the hill where the hatch is. I'll be able to see everything from there. If I can get Jerry on the radio, I will, but also, I want to make sure John stays wherever he is hiding.

"Sounds like a plan, man. Be careful." She kissed her friend on the forehead and started off through the grass, trying to follow the path Tony and she had already made on the trek out to the windmill.

Tony, tossing his crutch aside pulled out his 9mm and began crawling the hundreds of yards he'd have to navigate to get to the base of the tree line so he could go up the hill under the cover of the trees.

Monica moved quickly. She was a large young woman, but the panic she felt gave her the extra energy to move through the field. She had her .22 rifle with her; she carried it with her all the time now after the death of Jeff and of learning of the callousness of the vigilantes.

There were about 100 yards of cleared field between Monica and the shelter. She was hesitant about crossing the area, not knowing who might be watching. Instead she laid down at the edge of the field and waited until she saw Tony finally reach the edge of the tree line.

Monica had been caring for Tony and he was healing well. She hoped he didn't hurt himself scrambling the way he was. She was using what she'd learned from three years of working for Dr. LaFavre at the clinic.

~ ~ ~

Her parents had doted on her growing up. She hadn't liked sports and wasn't good at music, except listening to it, but she did enjoy eating. She'd never been lithe and slender, but she did have an athletic build prior to junior high school. That was when her parents moved from the country to the city for her dad's job.

She was at a new school with no friends she began spending more time enjoying the friendship of comfort food. By the time she was in high school, she was topping 200 pounds.

Her grades were excellent, but her friends were few. She was able to test out of classes and started nursing school during her senior year. That was the same year her parents divorced and after 18 months of nursing school, she had to drop out and get a job.

Dr. LaFavre needed a receptionist at his small clinic and Monica was able to earn enough to live on her own in a small apartment not far from the clinic. After three years she felt like a part of a team at the clinic. Mrs. LaFavre worked part time while her husband and his partner Dr. Belewa saw patients. The clinic catered to lower income patients, some with questionable injuries or illnesses, but Dr. LaFavre was an honest man in treating patients and if they were fakers or malingerers, LaFavre wouldn't allow them to use him as their doctor of reference.

Dr. Belewa wasn't as honest. Belewa had his own receptionist, but she and Monica shared duties with billing and scheduling, but only Belewa's assistant would take care of certain patients. Monica asked why one time and was told to mind her own business by Dr. Belewa.

When LaFavre took a week off to work with Doctors Without Borders, Monica was left with little actual work to keep her busy. She was sitting at the reception desk when a patient came in. Dr. Belewa was very busy this week and he and his receptionist were in one of the back examination rooms. She knew the man was one of Belewa's patients and she took his name and put him down as a walk-in.

When the man demanded to see the doctor right away, Monica firmly told him to have a seat and said she would page the doctor. She paged Belewa and told him he had a walk in and the doctor told her he would be with his current patient for another 15 minutes.

Monica passed on the message to the walk-in customer at which time the man pulled out a two-way radio and said "Move in."

Seven police officers rushed through the door with a warrant.

Belewa and his assistant were both handcuffed and led out, along with the "patient" they were seeing at the time. Monica was threatened with arrest if she tried to leave so she sat back down and started crying.

The officers took the computers and the files and searched every room in the building, taking garbage bags full of drugs and paperwork. When they were finished taking evidence out, a female detective lieutenant questioned her for nearly six hours before telling her she could go home, but they warner her to not leave town.

Six months later, Belewa and his assistant were serving time for fraud and drug trafficking.

Dr. LaFavre had his license suspended for failing to report the illegal activities of his partner which he should have known about. LaFavre blamed Monica and any career Monica had believed she had in the medical field died when the news was printed in the newspaper and heard it on the local radio and telivision stations.

The only thing good that had come out of those years was that she had been able to use what she'd learned to help Tony, and now Tony was helping her.

~ ~ ~

She saw Tony work his way slowly up the hill through the trees and take up a position near the base of the CB tower. Monica now wished she'd given him her rifle. The 9mm didn't have a lot of range.

She heard him whisper on her walkie-talkie.

"There's five of them. Two women and three men. There seems to be an argument going on," he told her. "They're looking around now."

"Okay, I'm going inside with Kellie. Did you reach John?"

"Yeah, he's on channel three. He heard what they did to Mike and he's hiding in the tractor tires in the back of the barn. I told him to stay there until one of us tells him to move."

Kellie, knowing the vigilantes couldn't see her started for the doors to the shelter. She called Kellie on channel five to tell her she was coming. She wasn't even half-way across the clearing when Tony told her the three of the five were coming up the path while two others were starting to go toward the garage.

Monica turned and ran back to where she had been hiding in the tall grass.

When she was down and hidden, she called Kellie and told her to lock the door and don't let anyone in. She saw Tony work his way toward the hatch and Monica cautioned him to stay low.

The three who went up to the shelter's entrance did so with a confident swagger. Like they knew they were in charge of the situation. Monica watched as the one started banging on the door hollering at Kellie inside.

Monica lifted her .22 to her shoulder and looked through the scope, putting the crosshairs on the one beating on the door.

She pulled the trigger.

Nothing happened. She rolled over and looked at the rifle to make sure she had loaded it and had a round in the chamber. She cursed herself for forgetting to flip the safety off. She rolled back over and pulled the weapon up to her shoulder just in time to see the door explode.

~ ~ ~

Kellie had blockaded the door with the table and the braces Jerry had made to keep the door closed during the hurricane. She didn't know if it would work, but it was all she had. She heard Tony tell Monica that three were coming up the path and they were all armed. Tony had told her to hide Hannah because of what the man had done to Mike. Kellie couldn't believe the kind old man had been shot down in cold blood, but this was a world so different than the one she'd lived in all her life.

Now there were three people coming to her door. She hoped it wasn't with heavy weapons and she feared for the life of Hannah and John if something were to happen to the adults.

She tried the CB several more times but there was no answer from Jerry.

If she hadn't been so scared she might have cried. She pulled Tony's couch out from the wall and used it for cover. If they did have heavy weapons, she wondered if the couch's stuffing would save her.

She heard the man at the door. He was hollering at her to open up. He told her no one would be hurt, that they were just looking for a safe haven and some food. She didn't believe him. She heard Tony on her walkie-talkie tell Monica to shoot to kill.

Tony told his young friend that from his vantage point, he could see the man with a bandolier and he was pulling out one of the hand grenades, but from 250 feet, he would never be able to get a good shot off.

Monica clicked the mic twice, acknowledging his transmission, but she had a small .22 caliber rifle. It had no real knock-down power and from 200 yards, Monica would have to be very lucky to get all three, and then only if they were stupid enough to stand there and be shot. There were two others who might come after her.

~ ~ ~

Kellie heard the man holler again to open up or he would open the door his way. She wasn't sure how he knew someone was in the shelter, but she was sure he'd not think twice about blowing the door off.

It was Tony who said "He's got a grenade!" over the walkie-talkie.

Kellie didn't stop to think anymore. She flipped off the safety of the 20 gauge and from seven feet away shot through the door, pumping four shots through the wood.

~ ~ ~

What Monica saw was the door erupting outward and knocking all three people in front of the door to the ground. One of them stayed down, but the woman, who had been more off to one side, started crawling away, obviously injured.

Monica saw the one who had the grenades had been slightly protected from the blasts from Kellie's shotgun. He was gravely wounded, but he was still grabbing for a grenade, probably hoping to throw it through the new hole in the doors.

Monica looked through her scope and pulled the crosshairs down, just like Eddie had showed her. Three shots later, the man wasn't reaching for a grenade anymore. He had new holes in his shoulder, his neck and his head.

~ ~ ~

From Tony's vantage point, he saw the three knocked back and fall to the ground, one man lay still, one man writhing in pain. The woman had been hit peripherally and was crawling toward the truck that was in the drive. He watched as three more shots stopped the writhing man who was reaching for a grenade.

Tony turned in time to see two other people come running out of the garage, the fat black man who had shot Mike and a heavy-set woman. John apparently hadn't been found and Tony was glad.

Too far away to hit anything with his pistol, he none-theless fired off five rounds, aiming high and hoping one of the rounds would hit something near enough to the two intruders to give them a fear of what they couldn't see.

Tony wanted their attention trying to find him, not trying to save their comrades.

The man and woman lifted their rifles and shot in his direction, but he'd ducked down before they could locate where he was hiding. They jumped in the truck and tore out of the driveway, leaving their three comrades to their own luck.

Two minutes later Tony, Monica and Kellie had the woman securely tied up and gagged. She was slightly injured but no one cared. They left her lying on the ground.

Kellie let Hannah, Boomer and Molly out of the cellar. She instructed Hannah to listen for Jerry on the CB and if he called, to call Kellie on the walkie-talkie before answering.

Hannah, who looked so frightened, said she would do it.

Boomer was the first reach Mike's body. The big dog whimpered and licked at Mike's face. Monica told them the old man had died before he hit the ground with the way the back of his head was missing. All three cried while they wrapped his body in a tarp Monica found in the garage. Then the three went to get both kids. They were scared and clung to Monica and Kellie, tears falling freely.

Chapter Seven

It was Kellie who heard Jerry calling on the CB. They were 10 miles away and were asking where everyone was. He sounded very happy with how the day had gone.

Jerry and Eddie both had CBs operating and heard the whole story. Jerry was pissed and slammed his hand on the dash of the Ford. Eddie was pissed too because he'd been good friends with the old banker and he knew Mike had probably given his life to save the kids and the others at the shelter. Eddie's dad had never been around and while Eddie didn't think of Mike as a father, he did feel like the gentleman would have been a right fine grandfather to him.

"They left here about 10 minutes ago in a small black truck. There are two of them, a heavy black man and a heavy white woman. He's wearing brown clothes and she is wearing yellow and red. Watch out for them," Kellie warned, relaying to Jerry what Tony had seen.

Eddie had taken the lead in the convoy. His stout truck was both more powerful and had a better front grill guard than the Ford which would be an asset on the two lane roads. They had exited the highway and were less than a mile from where they would get off Highway 10 and take the back roads to the shelter when Eddie saw the truck.

The truck was on the side of the road with a man refueling it from a red gas can. Eddie had just come around the curve when the man saw them and dropped the fuel can. He forwent putting the gas cap back on and rushed to get into the truck. The woman in the front scat lowered her rifle out the window and aimed it at Eddie's oncoming truck.

Eddie didn't even duck when her rifle bucked and a star appeared in his windshield. The woman's aim was good, Eddie had to admit. If the windshield hadn't been bulletproof, Eddie might have been hit in the face.

Instead of being dead, he put his right foot to the floor.

The man had gotten the truck started, but Eddie continued to accelerate. He heard Jerry telling him to not do it over the radio, but Eddie was positive these were the people who killed Mike in cold blood. He wasn't giving them a chance.

The little black truck just started moving backward when the 9,000-pound SWAT truck hit it at 73 miles per hour in the right front quarter panel. The big truck's steering wheel pulled at Eddie's hands, but he had been expecting this and held on tight.

Eddie felt satisfaction seeing the airbags deploy in a blink and the man, who had not been belted in, nor had his door completely closed, punted like a spinning rag doll out of the truck and onto the car he'd so recently siphoned gas. The amount of blood coming from the broken body was enough to let Eddie know he was gone.

The woman who had shot at Eddie was saved from instant death by the airbag and seat belt, but the crushing weight of four and a half tons of SWAT truck pushed the dashboard into her chest and ample belly microseconds later. The heater core and accompanying venting crushed her shins as the little truck began spinning out of the way of the big truck.

It was the grill guard that ended her thoughts forever as it pushed the quarter panel and windshield support member through her neck and face.

The woman's life ended there on the road seconds after her partner.

Eddie slowed but didn't stop. In his rearview mirror he saw the damage his truck had done. The little black truck had just started catching fire. He almost smiled before he realized he had just killed two more people. He was pissed that he'd not given it more thought, but also glad he hadn't given it more thought.

Those two were responsible for Mike being dead. That he'd been able to kill them made him feel like vengence had been served.

Mike was one of the good people who had lived through the hell that had happened to the world. The world needed good men like Mike. Those people had taken him.

"That was for Mike," he said to Jerry on the CB. "They're now rotting in hell." He then turned it off.

The convoy followed him back to the shelter.

No one stopped to check on the two people from the truck.

Randy and Tia who had been bringing up the rear were filled in by walkie-talkie courtesy of Jerry.

The positive mood everyone in the convoy had carried back with them was now gone and a solemn drive home was something none of them had expected.

Everyone but the wounded woman who remained tied up and gagged and laying on the ground were graveside when Jerry and Eddie lowered Mike's body into the hole they'd dug a few feet off the path they took from the garage to the shelter entrance. Kellie fashioned a cross and stuck it at the head of the grave.

Monica refused to tend to the woman's injury until Jerry asked her for the third time. She did leave the gag in the woman's mouth because no one wanted to hear what the woman had to say or her cries when Monica tended to her. She pulled the shot gun pellets out without pain killer and slapped bandages on the wounds. That was all she was going to do.

Monica did it because she respected Jerry's authority sake, not because she wanted the woman to live.

~ ~ ~

Tia moved her motor home to the back side of the hill, down from the shelter entrance and hidden from the road. She and the kids moved into the home that evening, not because she wanted to be away from the others, but because everyone needed the space and Tia wanted to talk with her kids about their feelings in private. It would be hardest on John over the next few days. She needed time to be a parent to her children.

Eddie parked his truck beside the Winnebago and took a few of the extra weapons and cases of ammunition in the shelter and filled the truck. From now on, anyone who threatened the shelter would feel the full wrath of an armed SWAT truck.

The men who had died from Kellie's blast through the door, and Monica's well-placed shots were burned with the farm house and the brush that had been cleaned from behind the shelter. No one said any words for them. Eddie's non-verbal comment spoke volumes. He pissed on the fire and walked away.

No one was sure what to do with the woman they captured. To make sure they could sleep in relative safety, Jerry, Randy and Eddie decided to secure her in the barn that night. She was put in the barn's office where there was nothing she could damage, but she'd be out of the weather and safe, without being in their way.

Making sure she was secure, Jerry finally took off her gag. She started crying and begging for mercy, but she had been one of those who caused the death of Mike, someone they all loved.

Jerry told her to shut the hell up and that if another word left her mouth, he'd put the gag back in. There was a fierceness in his voice he was glad Kellie couldn't hear.

Jerry put a lock on the outside of the door in case she did get free of the ropes with which Randy and Eddie had tied her, but he was pretty sure in the morning she would be sitting in her own filth, just where they were leaving her now.

They'd deal with her in the morning. The group from the shelter was in mourning and they had no want to deal with the woman.

That night, as everyone went to bed, they reached for comfort. Kellie, who had always gone to bed after Jerry, slipped herself under his covers before he was fully asleep and let him hold her close as she cried. Monica and Tony moved into the spare room that Tia and her kids had vacated. They slept in separate beds, but she held her friend's hand and they talked about what they'd seen and could have done differently. There was nothing.

Eddie and Randy played video games until the early hours of the following morning, losing themselves in the fantasy world of electronic games.

Despite the sadness of the day, Tia and her kids were happier now that they had their own home and tonight they would sleep in one big bed, even though the Winnebago came with two queen-sized and a single bed.

~ ~ ~

The following morning when Jerry, Eddie and Randy checked on the woman they'd captured, she told them her name was Cheryl. She claimed she was a victim of circumstance. She said the men had captured her and threatened her and that she was just following them because they made her. Jerry and Eddie didn't care to hear it and if she could have walked, they would have sent her away.

As it was, she had been hit with buck shot in the leg and arm and couldn't walk very well as yet.

Neither Kellie nor Monica would have anything to do with the woman and Tony said it would be better just to kill her. Randy had the softest heart and was given the job of caring for her until she was well enough to be sent away. Everyone might hate her, but Tony wanted to kill her where she sat.

Cheryl, as Randy was told, was a 27-year-old former legal clerk. She'd been captured by the vigilantes less than a week after the fall of civilization. She said they beat her, raped her, threatened to kill and tortured her. She had no other way to survive.

Randy listened and didn't make any comments. He dressed her wounds, there was two pellets he found that had to remove from her leg, and then left her alone to clean the rest of herself. She had to do it from a bucket of warm water he provided. He found clothes for her so she could change into something cleaner than the blood soaked and dirty, stinking clothes she had on. He gave her privacy, but only in the old barn office.

She would ask him questions but he refused to talk to her.

It was Eddie who came up with the idea of a way to keep her controlled during the day when Randy asked for something other than the ropes he had to untie three or four times a day. They used Boomer's collar and put a combination lock on it to keep Cheryl from taking it off. The collar was attached to chain Randy bolted to one of the walls in the barn's office after it had been cleaned out. They left her a place to sit, a table to eat from and a bucket to piss and shit in. Randy brought food to her in the morning when the cows were milked and again in the evening. He brought her water when he remembered to and that was the way she began her first week of captivity.

No one wanted the woman on the property, but no one really knew what to do with her. It was out of sight, out of mind for a week for everyone but Randy. Some evenings, during the last meal of the day, they would discuss what they should do. Tony's opinion stayed the same. Other ideas were floated, but nothing they felt they could do with the morals they had.

The seventh day after Mike's murder, and no one called it anything but a murder, Jerry and Randy were going to make a quick 15-mile trip Birmingham-ward down the interstate to see if they could find some batteries for Jerry's power grid and few other necessities.

Also, it was a time for father and son to talk away from everyone else.

They had gone three miles on I-20 when they saw a convoy of three vehicles coming at them on the same side of the road. They hadn't expected to see anyone and were actually within shooting distance when Jerry slammed on the brakes.

Both men had their guns out while Jerry called back to the shelter. Eddie, Kellie and Monica could be there in 10 minutes or less with a lot more weaponry. He wouldn't lead a convoy of three vehicles back to the shelter and he hoped the show of force would be enough to turn them back.

The convoy in front of them stopped. The front truck had a camper on the back and the back two were a mini van and full-sized Chevy pulling what looked like a pop-up camper.

People got out of the trucks. They were all armed, but did not look threatening.

The man who appeared to be in charge reached back into his truck and pulled out the microphone for his CB and held it up. He then made a show of holding it to his mouth. Jerry reached in to his truck and turned the CB up louder. He started scanning the channels until he heard the man's voice.

"We have women and children and we're sick. We've been running for days. We beg you for help. My name is Josh and my daughter is sick. Please I beg of you, help us," he pleaded over the radio. Jerry wasn't much of a poker player, but he could tell sincerity when he heard it. When the man finished talking Jerry asked him to put his weapon down. Josh put his weapon on the ground and reached back into his truck and pulled out a little girl who looked like she was dead.

Jerry's heart might have been hardened by the vigilantes who had killed his friend Mike, but it hadn't become that hard. He told Randy to cover him and he put his Desert Eagle back in its holster. He reached under the driver's seat for the first aid kit he always carried and approached the man who was carrying the girl toward him.

Josh kneeled and laid his daughter gently down on the pavement, a few feet in front of Jerry and looked up with pleading eyes. "Please, she's been sick for days. We don't know what to do," he cried.

Honestly, Jerry didn't either, but he checked to make sure she was alive and breathing. The four others from the three-truck convoy stood where they'd unloaded their vehicles. They showed no threat. There were two older people in the van and two men in the truck pulling the camper who showed themselves.

Jerry heard Eddie's SWAT truck in the distance and told Josh to not be afraid. He reached into his pocket and pulled out his walkie-talkie.

"Come in, Eddie," he said to the two-way.

"Yeah, boss, this is us."

"Get Monica up here between the trucks and hurry," he told them, while looking at Josh. "She's the closest thing we have to a medic, and she's really good," he said to the man kneeling beside his daughter.

The SWAT truck careened around Jerry's truck and Jerry was glad to see Josh's eyes get huge. The big black behemoth did look intimidating. Eddie slammed on the brakes 30 feet from the two in the middle of the highway and Monica came running with her "doctor's bag" before the truck was fully stopped.

Kellie followed her quickly with her shotgun and Eddie popped out a moment later with his high-powered rifle aimed at the convoy. By then Monica was kneeling beside the little girl. Josh related the symptoms his little girl, Marissa, had shown and Monica surmised some type of poisoning. She picked up the little girl and told Josh to come with her.

Inside Eddie's truck, Monica started an I.V. drip and told Eddie he'd better drive smoother than a baby's ass back to the shelter, where she had some medicine she hoped would take care of the very sick little girl.

Eddie looked to Jerry and Jerry felt himself nod.

Jerry's compassion for others had not been lost and Kellie's hand on his arm told him he'd made the right decision. She stayed with Jerry as he walked up the highway to talk with the others in the convoy. He found out two others of the eight were showing signs of being sick. He asked if they were willing to follow them back to a safe haven.

There was a great sigh of relief and agreement and everyone but Kellie put their guns away. Josh had trusted Jerry with his little girl, they would trust Jerry too.

It was a five-vehicle convoy back to the shelter. Randy drove Josh's truck and Kellie rode with Jerry.

The week ended with tally of one loss, the beloved Mike, and 10 more people living on Jerry's once peaceful farm and one living in the custody of their "jail."

"This is the Smith Compound calling anyone on this frequency, please come in," the shortwave transmitter finally spoke after weeks of Tony's tender mercies. "This is the Smith Compound calling anyone on this frequency, please come in, anyone. Someone tell us we're not alone, over."

The broadcast had come during the evening meal. Tia had fired up the grill and had cooked steaks for everyone. One of the cows had been put down earlier that week and Josh, who used to be a butcher, was able to cut the animal up in short order. The garden had produced enough potatoes, sweet corn and tomatoes to make a good meal for everyone. The potatoes had done especially good this year which was fine with Jerry.

He enjoyed a good baked potato on the grill.

Everyone on the farm was eating together tonight, something Jerry proposed they did every few days.

The lone exception at tonight's meal was Cheryl, who hadn't given anyone any problems and looked contrite and scared all the time. She was shackled with a pair of ankle cuffs, provided by the former corrections officer Juan deJesus and his wife had in their minivan, during the day and the collar which had a chain bolted to the wall at night.

She was allowed to go wherever she wanted, as long as it was no where near any person other than Randy. She was also forbidden anywhere past the barn and garage, and no where near where the campers were parked, or in any building except her room in the barn. She ate what Randy brought to her and slept in the barn office on a cot he'd built for her. Jerry hadn't told her what the penalty might be if she broke a rule, and honestly he didn't know, but she hadn't broke one yet. She did nothing but walk around and stumble once in a while when her ankle cuffs snagged on something.

~ ~ ~

Hannah heard the radio first and yelled to Tony who was still on crutches. Tony and Monica raced to the living room and listened for the call again.

"This is the Smith Compound calling anyone on this frequency, please come in, anyone. Someone please answer," the call came again. It was almost covered by static as the radio had been set for automatic scanning, but Tony worked the dial to clear up the signal. He then looked up at Jerry.

Jerry who'd followed Tony in to the shelter nodded to the young man. "Go ahead, this is your gear."

Tony picked up the powered microphone. He'd practiced this first conversation many times in his head and now he was going to do it. He lowered his voice an octave before answering, "This is God. What can I do you for?"

There was silence on the radio and Jerry looked down at Tony. His grin was barely suppressed. "Really? After all your work, you're going to pretend to be God?"

Tony shrugged. "You spend all your time on this couch and

see how crazy you become."

"Hello? Hello? Is someone there?" asked the person on the shortwave asked again tentatively.

This time Tony answered the call with a little more decorum. "This is the Saunders Station calling the Smith Compound. Please come in. I repeat, this is the Saunders Station calling the Smith Compound. Please come in, over"

"Oh my God! Are you for real? I mean are you really real?"

"Yes, we are real. My name is Tony and I am part of the Saunders Station. Who am I talking to?"

"This is Keith Bennett and we're the Smith Compound in Kentucky! Oh my God. I can't believe I finally got someone. Pendleton said I should quit wasting my time! I can't wait to tell him there are more people out there. We thought everyone was gone except for the flesh-eaters. How many of there are you? Where are you at? Are you close to us? Are there a lot of you? Do you have food? We have some food, but not a lot. Oh my God, I can't believe this worked!"

Tony was finally able to get a word in and asked Keith to slow down and take it easy.

Jerry and Tony had already spoken about what information they would and wouldn't share on the short wave.

"My name is Tony Marks and I'm a member of the Saunders clan of survivors. There are a couple dozen of us and we're in Alabama. We have food and water, but little extra. Where is your compound located, over."

"Pendleton said I can't tell you for fear of you guys coming to take our stuff," the young man said. Tony figured him to be around his age. "We've had a lot of that around here. We were attacked by brigands who killed three of our guys, but we're getting better at defending ourselves, over."

"We have the same issues you have. We call them zombies and vigilantes, over."

"Zombies? I'll tell Smith that's what you call them. He'll like that. He hates them because they killed his friend. Pendleton Smith is in charge here and he keeps us alive. The brigands are worse though. They killed two of our scouting parties and attacked us here, but we held them off. I'm not supposed to tell you, but it probably won't hurt, we're on Fort Knox military base. We can defend ourselves good, over."

"We've had a similar problem but we're pretty well hidden. Did you suffer a hurricane three weeks ago, over."

"We had a lot of rain a few weeks back, and probably tornadoes, but no hurricane. We didn't get too much damage here on the base, but the towns around us are wasted. There's fire in one of them, over."

"Before I forget, Keith. Write this down. Every night at 2100 hours I will monitor this frequency for you. Let's keep in touch and maybe we can help each other, over."

"That's a great idea Tony. Every night I will try to be here. It might not be every night because we have to be on guard duty too, over!"

"Sounds like your signal is fading, Keith. It is great to hear you and now we know that more people are out there. Let's keep in touch and see if we can reach others. I'll let you know if I get anyone, over."

"Will do, Tony. It was great hearing from you. Keith out."

Tony turned the radio back to scanning and looked back at Jerry. He had a big smile on his face. "We're not alone, Jerry. There are other places like here. Isn't that great?"

Jerry smiled at the young man. "We've never been alone," he said. "But now we know there are more people who aren't alone too." Jerry left Monica and Tony to the radio and went back to finish his supper. He finally had an idea what he could do with Cheryl.

~ ~ ~

Randy had taken Cheryl's meal to her and Tia and Kellie were sitting talking with Juan and his wife. Juan had worked as a corrections officer for 30 years before retiring. His wife had been a teacher of Spanish in the local school district and later an administrator. There was something special about those two and both Kellie and Tia enjoyed talking with them.

Josh was shutting down the grill and preserving the leftovers. His daughter, along with the others who had suffered from food poisoning, which had been complicated by their living conditions, were doing much better now that they were re-hydrating and getting some decent and safe food.

The others in the group had set up tents or were sleeping in the campers. Tia and Jerry both had spoken to each other earlier when the new people arrived. They agreed that new people coming would have to provide their own shelter. Both agreed they couldn't disrupt their homes every time someone new came along.

Jerry was touched by the deJesus couple's story, however. They had been sleeping in their minivan for the past two weeks, hadn't showered and had just met up with the other two vehicles in the convoy in Mississippi the previous day. They were both underfed and, in an open moment of honesty, Juan told him they'd wanted to see to Gulf Coast one more time before they died, which was what they had planned on doing.

Jerry pulled Mr. deJesus aside and suggested he and his wife sleep in the cellar of the shelter until a motor home could be found for them. He also offered them showers and safety. There was something warm about the gentle old man and his kindly wife. Maybe it was that the Mexican immigrant somehow reminded him of Mike.

There were another four men, Danny, Sade, Rusty and Nick, and one woman, Katie, from the convoy, and three younger children without parents who had been rescued along the way; the oldest was a 16-year-old boy, Jamal, who was currently playing video games with Randy and Eddie, and twin girls, Tara and Sara who were John's age.

The twins were playing with a rubber ball someone had found along with John and Hannah. Tia, like Jerry, had taken in the twin girls who had been riding in Josh's camper. The girls were no problem for Tia as there was more than enough room in her motor home. "But that's it," Tia said with a smile. "No more kids for me."

Kellie saw that Jerry was deep in thought. "Let's go for a walk, Jerry," she said to him and took him by the hand. Jerry wasn't in a mood to walk, but he couldn't say no to her. They walked past the campers, stopping to make sure those sitting around outside had gotten enough to eat. People were getting ready to call it a night. When they saw Jerry and Kellie, they were effuse in their gratefulness for allowing them a safe haven.

Jerry and Kellie smiled and walked on. Kellie was doing every thing she could to get Jerry away from everyone. When they were far enough away, so no one else could hear she asked him what was on his mind.

They walked for a little longer before Jerry was able to put his thoughts into words.

"Cheryl is a drag on us. She brings everyone down just being here. We can't continue to ignore the problem. We're going to have to do something with her one way or another."

They walked further along the trail. The sun had set, but it was still light enough to see. "You have an idea how we can do this without killing her?"

"I think I do. What if we moved her? What if we gave her enough food and water to last a few days, then drove her somewhere blindfolded. We could drive for a few hours then find a place and drop her off near another camp, tell her which direction to go, and let her fend for herself," Jerry said even as he was putting together the plan in his head. "I can't see killing her, even though she probably was part of the reason Mike was murdered. It's just not in me to do it."

"Jerry," Kellie said, leaning her head against his shoulder and holding his hand while they walked. "I don't know what to do either, really. I see the way she is around Randy. She smiles at him and looks down and acts like she is subservient, bites her lip, and will do anything he tells her to do, but I think it is just that, an act.

"I haven't talked to her, but maybe we should, before we make any decision. I might be wrong about her, but I have had a lot of experience with abuse and she isn't acting like an abused woman." Jerry had never asked Kellie about her husband. Reminiscing about past lives was a very sensitive subject. No one could go back and change what happened before the fall, and most people had secrets they felt were better left forgotten. Kellie talking about being abused shed a little more light on why she acted the way she did with him.

"Maybe you're right," he allowed. "Tomorrow, let's you and me talk with her. If we are convinced she was just a victim, we'll make arrangements to let her go on her way. There's no way I want her here, even if she was coerced by those men. No matter what, she was walking freely and she could have run from them, but she didn't.

"But if she was more than just a victim, then she was part of Mike's murder and I'll drive her ass to the middle of Texas and drop her off myself," he said through gritted teeth.

"Sounds like you have a good plan," Kellie said after thinking about it for a few paces. "You know, it's funny, in a sad kind of way. Under the old judicial system, she might be able to convince a psychiatrist and a judge and a jury that she is innocent when everyone else knows she was guilty and she could walk away free to do it again.

"Tomorrow, we'll be the psychiatrists, judges and jury and decide her fate. What uses to take months and years, we'll do in a day. I wonder if we're improving on the old system or making it worse."

Jerry thought about it. "Right now, I don't know if she is guilty or not, I guess. I've been told I'm not a deep thinker. All I know is, I need to do what is right and the only laws I really know are the ones that were written on a tablet of stone. Everything else people added afterward."

"You're a religious man," Kellie said as a statement, but with enough inflection to make it sound like a question.

"No," he said after some thought. "I believe in God and I believe we were all put here for some reason. I don't know what that reason is and probably won't be told." There was a long pause while the two walked and watched the stars grow brighter. "I try to live my life so when I die and have to face The One who made all of this, I don't have to apologize."

"I hope you're right. I don't know what to believe, but I do believe in you," she admitted. "I was so afraid after the fall of the world...when everyone I knew died and I continued to live. I didn't know why and no matter what questions I asked, no matter how much I prayed, I got no answer. When you found me and Molly, you found a walking dead woman.

"I was glad you found me and maybe that was the answer I was looking for. I don't know. But I don't feel like dying anymore. I thank God for you being there, being here, for me."

Jerry had never thought of himself as a theologian. He went to church regularly and believed in God. When the minister spoke of the bible, Jerry was never really sure how much of it was true and how much made up by man. He was grateful God had spared both him and his son, and still prayed for the wellbeing of his daughter.

The final sermon given by his minister, on the weekend before the all churches were closed, when the end looked like it was coming for everyone and the church's pews were nearly empty, he spoke of the end of times being upon the land. Jerry hadn't understood most of what the minister was trying to say, but the death of nearly everyone on earth was surely the end of normal times. If Armageddon had happened, it didn't happen the way the bible said it would.

"Tomorrow, we'll talk with Cheryl and we'll decide," he said as they turned and headed back to the shelter. They heard a violin being played by someone. "I didn't know anyone had a violin let alone played one."

"But it sure is nice," she agreed.

Kellie agreed. There was peace about and it felt good. That night she slept in the same bed with Jerry and did not cry, just allowed herself to be held close and comforted.

~ ~ ~

Morning broke in silence. Jerry awoke and rolled out of bed. Kellie'd laid out clean clothes for him as she had begun to do every morning now. Usually she'd sleep in for another hour, but usually she slept in her own bed. This morning, however, she was in his bed. She sat up and swung her feet off the other side of the bed and started putting on her clean clothes.

"You're up early," he said, surprised she was getting up. "Planning on milking cows with me and Randy this morning?"

"I thought that might be something I'd like to learn someday, but this morning, I thought it might be a good idea to have a talk with Cheryl early. I think if we do it this morning, before everyone else gets up, we'll probably not be interrupted."

Pulling on a clean flannel shirt, Jerry considered what she suggested and agreed. Once everyone on the compound was awake, there'd be very little time for a private talk. Jerry recalled the time before the fall of the world that he and Randy might go most of the morning without speaking, not because they were mad at each other, it was just their way. Now it seemed everyone wanted to talk with Jerry and the time he used to have for himself could be measured in minutes rather than hours.

Jerry and Kellie met Randy outside the shelter. Jerry's son looked tired. He'd probably been up late with Eddie and Jamal.

"Morning, dad, Kellie," Randy said as they all began walking down the path to the barn. The weeds were taller than Jerry'd ever let them grow and once they crossed the crest of the hill between the entrance to the shelter and the outbuildings that included the barn and garage, it was like looking at two different properties. The "front" of the farm was overgrown, debris was scattered about and was looking mostly abandoned, to the casual observer, while the back side, where everyone spent their off time was kept cleared and clean.

"Morning, Randy," Kellie said to him, putting her hand on his shoulder as they walked to the barn. Randy had come to like Kellie a lot. She never forced herself on him, but he knew she was fond of his dad. Randy knew his dad had been alone for a long time and when Kellie moved into his dad's room in the shelter he and Eddie made many sexual remarks behind their closed door.

But in all honesty to himself, Randy didn't give his dad's relationship with Kellie much thought. Kellie never tried to mother Randy, but would listen to him and give him sound advice without judging his opinions, something a lot of older adults were unable to do. She seemed to be a nice lady who his dad liked and that was good enough for Randy.

"We need to have a talk with Cheryl this morning," his dad told him. "We want you to be there. You and her have been talking a lot."

"Yeah, she's an okay lady," Randy told him. "I think she just got mixed up in a bad crowd and they took advantage of her."

Jerry nodded as they entered the barn and began the morning milking. Randy cleaned the barn floor and took care of the calves. Kellie watched Jerry work and learned some of the simpler tasks. She'd never worked on a farm before and found it fascinating. She'd taught children about farms, but the one field trip she'd been on with them, was more of a tourist trap than a working farm.

When the jobs were finished, Jerry took a drink from the same hose he used to wash his hands and boots. Kellie washed as well, but didn't drink.

"Let's get it done," Jerry told them.

~ ~ ~

Randy had knocked on Cheryl's door and opened it when he heard her respond, barely above a whisper. He always tried to be respectful to the woman.

Cheryl was sitting on her bed where Randy usually found her in the morning when he brought her breakfast. She was dressed in a simple tee shirt which showed her midriff at the top of the pair of shorts which seemed a size too small for her.

The collar with which she'd been fitted was creating a callous around her neck and chained to the wall by her bed. She wore a pair of worn tennis shoes Randy had found that fit her better than the combat boots that she'd been wearing when she had been captured.

She was still wearing the bandages on the wounds received when Kellie shot through the door of the shelter, critically wounding the two men who were with her. One bandage covered half her upper neck where door splinters had hit her, another on her upper right arm and the worst injury was bandaged on the inside of her inner right thigh and went under the pant leg of the very short pair of shorts.

Cheryl was a waif of a woman. She had dark brown eyes which matched her hair. Her complexion was that of her classic Spanish ancestry. She had smooth, blemish-free skin with pouting lips and long, dark eyelashes. Sitting on her bed like she was, she looked harmless and beaten. She had her hands folded on her lap as if she were waiting to have someone tell her what to do. She acted like she'd given up living.

She smiled when Randy walked in, perfect white teeth and the appearance of joy at seeing him. When Jerry and Kellie followed him through the door, her smile looked less genuine. "What...what's this about Ran?" she asked the young man, using her nickname for her jailer. "What's going to happen to me?"

"My dad wants to ask you a few questions, that's all. So he can decide what to do with you."

"I...I'm scared," she almost whispered. "I don't want to be killed. I...I don't want to be afraid anymore." Tears welled up in her eyes and Randy started for her to give her comfort, but Jerry put a hand on his shoulder to stop him.

"Just tell me why you came here, from the beginning," Jerry said. "And then tell me why those men killed my friend Mike in cold blood."

Cheryl looked down at her hands. Jerry pulled one of the two chairs in the room away from beside the bed and offered it to Kellie. He took the other one and they both faced Cheryl, waiting for her story.

Randy, not wanting to get too close to Cheryl right now and provoke his dad's ire, sat on the floor near the door.

After a moment of sniffling, Cheryl began her story.

~ ~ ~

"Before everyone started dying, I was the athletic trainer at North Florida Community College. My biggest concern every day was if I had enough tape for the kids who needed their ankles taped up. It was an easy job I took so I could be close to my boyfriend, Dale, who owned a body shop. We were planning on getting married and having kids. Dale was a good man, a hard working guy who had six brothers, all younger than him, who he helped support with his mom. Their dad had died and Dale started the business to keep the family together. That was important to him and he made it important to me."

Randy cringed a little as Cheryl talked about Dale, but

didn't let his dad see it. Randy wasn't so naïve that he believed he'd ever have a chance with a woman like Cheryl before the fall of the world, but now that the situation had changed, there was hope in his heart.

"Dale was all about family. We talked about starting our own and he'd even talked to my dad before asking to marry me. He was so traditional. When he died, part of me died with him. He died the same day as four of his brothers and both his mom and dad. His other two brothers had died the day before," Cheryl continued. "They were the entire world I had left down here. My parents, two older brothers and two younger sisters all live…lived, in Indiana. They died too. My mother called me the day dad died to tell me not to come home because there was no one going to be left in my family.

"I wanted to die too," Cheryl said, sparking the memory in Jerry that this was the same thing Kellie had told him weeks ago. "I was driving back to Indiana so I could die at home when I was caught by those men you killed. I tried to get away but they wrecked my car and took me as their prisoner. They said they needed to repopulate the world and needed all the women they could find because they didn't have any.

"They were cruel and sometimes wouldn't feed me. They beat me and raped me. They were terrible and killed any man they came across. For weeks they kept me tied up. When I refused to eat, they would hit me. One of the guys you killed use to put a gun to my head and tell me what he'd do to my dead body. He'd pull the trigger on an empty chamber just to scare me. Sometimes I was so scared I peed myself.

"He said if I didn't get pregnant soon, he would use me as bait for the zombies and I couldn't think of anything worse than being eaten alive by them. I gave up and did what they wanted. I was dead anyhow. I ate when they told me, got naked when they told me, did the work they told me and never said anything. I didn't care anymore.

"We were attacked one time and I just stood out in the open hoping someone would shoot me, but I watched those men shoot and kill three people. The man in charge hit me for not hiding from the attackers.

"Then I was taken with them to get food and they made me go inside the buildings first, in case the zombies were there. I did but was so afraid but more afraid to stay alive. I was lucky to survive when we were in a food store and it appeared to be empty. The men came in and were getting canned food when the zombies attacked from the back. Two men were killed and I wasn't touched.

Kellie tired of hearing about the trials Cheryl had gone through. She wanted the woman to get to the point. Everyone had gone through hell and it sounded to her like Cheryl was attempting to garner pity.

"How did you find out about us?" Kellie asked.

"You had a gunfight with another group of vigilantes. They'd captured two people and were using them as bait for a store that was still in good shape. The men were tied outside and when night fell, the zombies would come out and eat their flesh. That's when the vigilantes would kill all the zombies with a grenade.

"They weren't expecting a rescue party to come after those two men. You killed four of their group and the old black man who killed your friend and the woman were the only two left of them when you were done. They figured out where you were hiding and told the men who captured me. They wanted revenge on you."

"But why would they bring you?" Kellie asked. "That doesn't seem like something a vigilante group would do.

"I don't know why they brought me," Cheryl said. "I guess they thought they would take over here and they'd want me here so they could make babies for them. Maybe they thought you had a good place that they could live in. I just don't know and just did what they told me to do.

"The day we came here, they saw two vehicles leave so they waited for a long time. When they saw that there were just a few people left, they parked down the road and walked up to where the man was in the garage. I didn't hear what was being said, but I saw the man shoot your friend in the head.

"They then waited for the other guys to come up. When no one else came out of the barn, the two you killed told me to follow them around back to see if there was anyone else. That's when they saw the door and were going to blow it open when they were shot. I was lucky I was off to the side and was lucky…or maybe unlucky…not to be killed.

"Monica found me and tied me up. Everything else you know," she finished, her head down and sniffles coming from the woman.

"I'm sorry you had to go through that," Jerry said noncommittally. "We'll talk about what you've told us and let you know. Until then…."

Jerry was interrupted by Jamal from outside the barn

Chapter Eight

Jerry! Jerry! Come quick! Tony's reached someone else on the radio and you're going to wanna hear this! Jerry! Come quick!" Jerry and Kellie left quickly, leaving Randy with Cheryl. They'd talk about the story she gave later. Right now, it sounded like something significant had happened.

Jamal was a tall teenager. His accent was all southern Cajun and his dark skin gave a brilliant contrast to his big smile. He was a very active youth who wanted nothing more than to play in the NBA when he was older, but those dreams had died with the rest of the world.

Jerry was about to go back to bring Randy along when the teenager grabbed all of his attention. "Come quick. Tony reached someone named Commander something. He sounded Russian. Come quick."

The three ran most of the way back to the shelter. Tony was on the couch listening with his headset on. When Jerry and Kellie arrived he took them off and told them the news.

"The International Space Station is still inhabited!" Tony told him excitedly, putting the microphone back on the shelf. "They just went out of range, but there are four astronauts up there and they want to come home."

Eddie and Monica were in the living room as well. The deJesus' were just now coming out of the cellar. There was an air of excitement in the room and Jerry waited a moment for everyone to get in the room and was ready to hear what Tony had to say.

"I heard you guys go to the barn this morning and I couldn't get back to sleep. Monica snores pretty loudly." That comment earned him a soft swat in the head from the young woman. "I was scanning the bands and I heard a voice, but didn't recognize the language. I answered him and he responded in English.

"He's the commander of the International Space Station. He and three others are still up there but will be running out of food and air in a few months. They don't want to die in space. They want to come home, but not to a dead world. They've been calling for weeks trying to find someone alive."

Jerry considered this for a moment and asked what the ISS crew wanted from them.

Tony filled him in. "The commander, I can't remember his name, who is Russian, said they have a re-entry module but it will only fit three.

It usually lands in the desert, but can land anywhere if it needs to. Shallow water is better than hard ground if there is a boat available to pick them up.

"He said two men and one woman would be sent back and then he'd push the ISS into its highest possible orbit, open the hatches to the emptiness of space, preserving the station for as long as it stays in orbit and 'give himself to the universe.'"

"But the three coming back will die from the virus, won't they?" Kellie asked.

"I asked him that and he said the scientists on board thinks the virus is dead by now, but either way, they would rather die here on earth than in the vacuum of space. "I think we have to help them if we can," Tony said, looking directly at Jerry. "Two of them are Americans, the other is Canadian."

"We'll do what we can, but I don't know anything we can do that can help them," Jerry told him. "I'm just a farmer and no one here is a rocket scientist."

"I don't know either," said Tony. "But they'll be back in range in about an hour and a half. I'll ask them then. If we can help them, I say we should."

Jerry nodded. Everyone in the room was somber after hearing what was being asked. Three people would rather risk coming to earth to die than spend another six or eight months living in space. One man would stay in orbit for as long as it took, then die alone on one of man's greatest achievements.

The hell everyone lived in wasn't being fair at all.

Jerry looked around the room at all the faces. He thought about asking everyone here to keep this a secret, but he didn't want to. Everyone should know what was going over their heads.

In another 90 minutes they'd know more, but until then, there were two other important issues which needed attention.

One issue concerned everyone, the space station, the other concerned just Jerry, Kellie, Randy, Monica and Tony alone and that was what to do with Cheryl.

While everyone moved singly and in pairs to the kitchen to get breakfast, Jerry waited for everyone to get something to eat before laying out plans.

Tia knocked on the open door and let herself and four kids, two of her own and the twin girls, in. "I hear there's some excitement going on." She was followed in by the others who lived outside the shelter.

Randy followed a minute later, coming to get breakfast for him and Cheryl, who did not come in. Jerry assumed she was still in the barn.

When everyone was settled, Jerry stopped Randy from taking Cheryl her breakfast for a few minutes and cleared his throat. "We're going through our store of food pretty quick. The garden food isn't going to get us through the winter. I think we have enough people now to start raiding some of the stores in town for canned food and anything else that we can find.

"I think we need to arm everyone who can shoot a gun and go into Odenville or Trussville and get whatever we can. Any volunteers?" he asked, knowing the closest city to them, Moody, had been effectively wiped off the face of the earth.

Everyone in the room except Monica and Kellie volunteered. The clan they'd formed was ready to do something more than exist and if it was going to, everyone was going to have to pitch in.

"I don't want you thinking this is going to be easy," Jerry told them. "Some of you haven't encountered the vigilantes or the zombies out there. One is vicious and the other are killers. The vigilantes will shoot to wound and then use you to draw out zombies. The zombies hide in the dark, but when they come out, they're almost unstoppable. They're super strong and eat flesh while you're still alive. It can't be a good way to die."

"Monica here was lucky that Randy and Eddie had big guns when they grabbed at her, but even then, the zombies were hit four or five times and still didn't die right away." The looks on everyone's faces were less excited than before.

It was Nick, one of the five men who came in the most recent convoy who spoke up. "I don't care if they're vigilantes or zombies. I'll kill every one of them. My family is all dead. My kids, my wife, my dad and my friends….all of them are dead. But this place is better than being alone so I'll defend it," he said with complete conviction.

There were agreements around the room.

Jerry looked at Monica, who had not raised her hand. He wondered if she were afraid to go foraging. "Sorry boss," she said, mimicking Eddie. "Me and Tony are going to set you up a security system so we know if anyone tries to sneak up on us. He's got some good ideas we were going to show you this morning, but since you brought this up, I figured you'd want to know what we're up to."

She started to bring out a note pad her and Tony had been using. Jerry held up a hand. "Let's decide how we want to do the run to Odenville first. I don't want to send everyone.

"Eddie, you'll go for sure since you know the area." Eddie smiled. "Take your truck with two others as protection.

"Danny, why don't you drive my truck with a trailer and someone for protection? That makes five going, three always holding guns. You should be able to clear a building, but don't take any chances. If you get a chance to get more diesel fuel, great, but don't risk yourselves. We have one full reserve and the other is mostly full." Rusty, Josh and Sade were also chosen to go foraging.

"It'd be best to leave in the morning so you can scout around the location for vigilantes. Look for tracks around any place you go in to. Be real careful of the hurricane damage because you might go into a building and have it collapse on top of you if you touch anything.

"We also need seeds if you can find any. We'll start growing as much as the gardens will let us and the weather allows."

Katie, the other woman besides Mrs. deJesus that was part of the most recent convoy, was a middle-aged woman whose face showed the loss of her world. She raised her hand. She talked little, but always helped where she could. "I ran a Christmas tree nursery with my family in Arkansas. I can help."

Jerry, seeing an opportunity to engage the woman in something other than her thoughts, nodded to her. "Thanks Katie. You're now our head gardener. Make sure the people going on the foraging trip know what seeds we can use best.

"Bullshit. I'm going too," the woman said, surprising everyone with her intensity. Jerry would not stop her from going after that declaration.

There was some more housekeeping details Jerry went over with everyone and then the group broke up into smaller groups outside the shelter. Jerry and Kellie finally got around to having their first meal of the day. He hadn't realized how much time had gone by until Tony began calling for the International Space Station again.

Jerry had work to do on the farm, but he couldn't bring himself to go outside yet. He had to learn more about what the ISS wanted with them.

Tony spoke with headphones on to better hear the station. Jerry, Kellie, Monica and the others listened as he spoke with the man in the stars. After a few moments, he pulled one of the headphones off. "Commander Rustov, I think his name is, said he is sure the emergency escape ship can land in the Gulf of Mexico. He said they are very accurate with landing the ship and if we can have a boat ready off Gulf Shores, Alabama tomorrow evening, they will try for there.

"The commander said they can land an hour before dark, in the orbit they are in, and land close enough to us to make it feasible."

Jerry knew where Gulf Shores was and told Tony to tell the Russian space station commander that they could be there and they would find a big enough boat to rescue his crew. He made sure Tony wrote down the details for everything, from the time of day they should expect the rescue ship to come down, how far out from shore to be, to how to open the ship up when it landed. Jerry told Tony that he needed to be the expert on everything and make sure the people going on the rescue knew as much as they could and have all the tools they needed.

Juan, who had been silent through most of the morning, spoke up. “I’m really not going to be much good doing any heavy work around the farm, but me and my wife know a lot about boating and navigation. Maybe we can help?”

Jerry smiled at the elderly Mexican. “Sir, you will do just fine. You’re now in charge of the rescue. But just so you know, I want to go with you.”

Juan smiled back. “I thought you might. But anyone going better not get easily seasick. I’m sure we’ll be going out past the breakers and it’ll be rough. And that hurricane hit pretty hard. It isn’t going to be easy finding a boat, so we better get started. There are a lot of unknowns and two days isn’t a lot of time. I say we should leave very early in the morning tomorrow.”

“Okay, very early tomorrow morning, we’ll leave. You find out how many need to go to make this happen and we’ll let everyone else know.”The meeting broke up and everyone began their personal chores before really starting on the day’s work.

~ ~ ~

Monica answered the CB when the call came in. Eddie and his crew were leaving the drive now for Odenville and foraging and were making the radio check. She would be their contact while on the road. Jerry heard the tone of Eddie’s voice and knew while he didn’t want anyone getting hurt, the five men and one woman wouldn’t mind a fire fight with zombies and there was no way in hell a vigilante group would get the drop on them.

He turned to speak with Tony who was working on some RJ45 connectors for a computer network he was building, “Is there any way we can keep in touch with you and the space station all the way to the coast?"

"I don't know. Let me and Monica work on it while we're sitting here," he said and started pulling out electronic manuals.

That left Randy with whom Jerry needed to talk. He'd give his son, who'd left with Cheryls breakfast, until lunch time to digest what Cheryl had said this morning. He was sure he knew what Kellie'd say, but decided he better ask her in case he was wrong. He looked at her and she saw his eyes dart for the door. She nodded and they both got up to go for a walk and to talk privately.

Once they got outside, they saw Tia and her four kids in the garden, pulling weeds and harvesting the ripe vegetables. Tia, who seemed able to drive anything with wheels had fixed the garden tractor and pulled it around back with the small, two-wheeled trailer for the kids. The other new arrivals were working with her, knowing the garden would be providing them with food over the winter to come. Jerry and Kellie made toward the antenna on the far hill, in an effort to disguise that they were talking about something as serious as banishment. Once they were out of earshot of everyone, Jerry finally asked the question he thought he knew the answer to.

He believed Kellie would side with Cheryl as a former victim herself and Jerry would have both her and Randy on one side and himself undecided. Kellie surprised him one more time.

"I don't believe her. I think she is a lying piece of shit," she said vehemently, "and I think she is trying to play you and Randy. If you're asking me, send her away as soon as possible before she hurts someone, because she will. I can't put my finger on it, but there is something wrong with her story and I don't believe her, not for one minute."

Jerry stopped in the middle of the field. Kellie walked a few feet more. The woman who had become Jerry's closest confidant and friend over the last three months because of her compassion and thoughtfulness and willingness to give everyone a fair chance, just told him she wanted the woman in the barn sent away. Jerry didn't know how much truth there was to Cheryl's story of how she had been captured and raped and possibly tortured, but even if it was only half true and Cheryl had been exaggerating and embellishing in hopes of not being sent away, he could probably forgive her for that. It was a ferocity he hadn't seen in her before.

Kellie turned around and looked at Jerry.

"I'm sorry, Jerry. I just don't believe her," Kellie said with grim intensity.

Jerry looked at her. He knew Randy had spent a lot of time over the past 10 days with Cheryl and he hadn't once said anything about Cheryl trying to get away. If her story hadn't jived with what she's told his son, he was sure Randy would have said something. He wasn't experienced with abused women and didn't know how they acted or should act. Maybe Kellie was right about Cheryl and their prisoner was just making something up to save herself.

He didn't know which side to come down on.

"Maybe it was that she said everything exactly right to evoke the greatest sympathy response from you and Randy. Maybe it's because of the way she dresses. I know Randy took her a lot of clothes, but she chose what to wear. Maybe it's because when she was captured by Monica, she was wearing Army boots and now she wears tennis shoes," Kellie explained, not giving him proof, just justifying her feelings about something being wrong. Jerry knew Kellie had a degree in something and as a teacher, she had a lot of psychology, so he didn't dismiss what Kellie was saying, but it was still just circumstantial.

Maybe what would be best for everyone would be to put her some place where she wouldn't be a danger to anyone, like an island.

A light seemed to go off in Jerry's head. "I have an idea that might allow all of us to sleep at night."

Randy knocked on Cheryl's door. When she didn't respond he knocked again. The door opened a crack. He looked through the crack in the door and Cheryl was lying on her bed.

"If you've come to send me away, just shoot me now while I'm not looking," she said, a tremble in her voice and not looking to see who was at the door. “I’m not going to go anywhere by myself. I won’t let you do that to me again. Just kill me and put me out of my misery.” Her body was curled into a fetal position, turned away from the door so only her back was to him.

Randy entered the room and sat Cheryl’s breakfast on the chair his dad had so recently sat in.

Randy could only see her trembling and heard what sounded like sobs. Her long dark hair had been brushed and left to hang, like she did every morning and how he liked seeing it. She must have done it before her conversation with his dad and Kellie.

The tee shirt she had slid up on her torso and showed off her slender form. She had light olive colored skin and from where he was standing, he saw she was not wearing a bra. With her knees folded up and her arms holding them tightly, Randy could see the shorts she was wearing hugging tightly to the curve of her hips. He could see the uppermost tan lines on the back of her legs from where she had bikini tan lines on her incredibly long, well-tanned legs.

For a 22-year-old man, here was a drowning woman and he wanted to save her. She was drowning in sorrow and he was a life preserver.

“No one is going to hurt you,” he said with authority. “Not while I’m in charge.”

“But you’re not in charge,” she said, no longer sobbing. “That woman, Kellie is, and I can tell she doesn’t like me.” She planted the first wedge between Randy and his father. Now she planted another. “She’s very pretty and I can tell your dad loves her and will do anything she says.” She let her voice crack a little for effect.

Randy didn’t realize he was being played by an expert. “No, I am in charge of you. My dad trusts me and I believe you’re a victim. I’m going to tell him you can be trusted. He’ll listen to me over Kellie. All you have to do is make sure you don’t do anything that will cause him not to trust you.”

Cheryl rolled over to look at the young man. Her face was wet with tears. Her movement uncovered her left breast to

Randy, who, try as he might to not look, saw the well-formed breast. She pulled her tee shirt down swung her legs to the floor. "You'll keep me from being sent away?" she asked in a whispering voice.

"Yes," he said, feeling his body react to how close she was moving to him. "Don't you worry about it. I'll convince dad you're not a threat to us."

Cheryl stood up and hugged Randy like he had saved her life. "I won't do anything to make him not trust me, Ran," she whispered in his ear. He felt her hard body against his, her arms under his and pushing on his back to her body, pulling him close. Her face was buried in his neck and he could feel her eyelashes fluttering. He wondered if his statement about protecting her caused her to cry again. If she was falling for him, he was fine with that so he hugged her back, pulling her as close to him as he could.

Cheryl felt his body respond and released from him when his hand reached the small of her back. She knew Randy was hooked and she was going to keep him on the hook for as long as it took to secure her freedom.

"I hope you're right, Ran. I was so scared and you're saving me. I won't forget it," she said. He was getting ready to reach for her again so she innocently deflected his advance by going for her breakfast that he'd brought for her. She pretended not to see his reach. "I'm really hungry now. Thank you for bringing me something to eat."

Randy knew the moment for intimacy had passed, but he looked forward to more intimate time in the future. "You know what would be nice, Ran?" she asked as she sat down on the bed. She crossed her long legs and leaned over just enough to tease Randy, but not allow him to see anything without moving.

"A deserted island with no one but me and you and a shit load of ice cream?" he said, trying to sound witty.

She gave an obligatory smile and giggle. "Not what I was thinking, but along those same lines. I haven't had anything good to drink in months. I sure would like some beer. I used to get so drunk with my boyfriend, I'm surprised I didn't get pregnant already."

And with that sentence, she dropped the allusion that when she got intoxicated, she would put out. Randy knew he was going to get some of dad's beer and Cheryl and he were going to party. Randy didn't have a chance against her. She had him controlled and he didn't even know it.

Chapter Nine

Eddie drove to Odenville with the same enthusiasm he had been doing everything lately, with gusto. He was driving his SWAT truck and he was hoping he got a chance to use some of the firepower he and a couple of the other guys riding with him, one of them a machinist, had done to improve the truck's lethality.

Morbid curiosity drew him to the food store where he'd first shot at another human target. It was the same store where Spec. 4 Terrill Ellison Jackson gave his life for his friends, so that they might live. Time and circumstance prevented them from returning for Terrill's body, but Jerry had found two pieces of slate on which to engrave the names of Lt. Michael "Mike" Jamison and Spec. 4 Terrill Jackson. He placed them side-by-side on the hill where they'd laid old Mike to rest. Eddie thought it a fitting yet simple memorial to the two men who died after surviving what had killed more of the world.

It had been over a month since that morning he, Jerry and Terrill had gone looking for their missing friends. He put it out of his mind now.

Eddie was more interested in seeing what effects of the storm had east of the shelter. There were chain link fences, signs and all matter of debris on the highway, houses ripped from their foundation, cars smashed and littering fields and entire forests of trees blown down. There were dead carcasses from wildlife, both domestic and wild that had been preyed upon by vultures or other animals.

Most promising, however, was there were no telltale signs that anything had been cleaned up or moved. He slowed as he drove up to the crossing where he and Jerry had crossed the road beside the store itself. The billboard under which they'd hid was gone except for the three telephone-sized poles that had held it up.

The store was damaged extensively. Half the roof appeared to be sagging; the glass in front was all gone. Terrill's body and all evidence that he'd been there was washed and blown away by the massive hurricane, which was what Eddie had hoped. The building from which vigilantes had shot at Jerry and Terrill was gone completely as well.

While Eddie was sure no one would still be there, a part of him hoped that they were so the fight they'd had before could be resumed – this time however he had six people with guns and his SWAT truck, not just himself with a bolt-action rifle.

The lamp posts in the parking lot had all been snapped off like matchsticks and the area looked so different than the last time he'd been here. He figured this must be what a city hit by a bomb would look like.

Followed by the Ford and its trailer, Eddie directed the truck to park in front of what was left of the food store and illuminate the inside with both the two-million-candlepower spotlights that had been installed.

Danny, who was driving the Ford, followed his instructions and after a careful search called it clear. Eddie drove along the back of the store. The doors were closed in back so there was no way to tell if there were not-deads inside waiting to ambush them. The SWAT truck had two thermal imaging guns and he asked Josh, a butcher by trade, and Rusty, a former tattoo artist, to pull them out of their cupboard in the back of the truck.

Eddie had talked to everyone on the foraging crew before they left the shelter about the encounter he'd had with the not-deads. "The zombie will kill you," he told them. "They are not real zombies, they've just mutated somehow. They're stronger than a freaking gorilla and twice as mean. I shot one three times and it was still coming after us. The only reason we're not dead is because of a brick wall and a big-ass amount of luck."

"A bullet from this will put it down," Rusty had said confidently, patting the Smith & Wesson 500 he had holstered on his hip.

"Don't bet your life on it, and don't bet my life on it, man," he said to the tattooed man. "We shot one five or six times at close range with a Desert Eagle and a 30-06, and it still wanted to eat our brains out. It had half its arm missing, a hole you could see through in its chest and part of its neck gone and it didn't stop that damn thing."

"So how do we kill them? Blow them to smithereens? I didn't bring any TNT with me and wouldn't that kinda blow up the whole freaking place? Seems like the hard way to go shopping to me."

"A good head shot that takes off the brain stem will work. They don't seem to bleed much, but if you can shoot their legs or arms off, do it. Don't waste ammo on the gut or chest because that doesn't seem to stop them very fast. They'll be eating your face and your eyes will be falling out the hole you just shot in its stomach. You'll be dead and it will eat your brains before it dies. It won't care that you killed it and you'll be dead.

"Also, don't think these things are like zombies in a movie. They move faster than hell and they will bite the shit out of you first chance they get. Shoot 'em a lot and shoot 'em again and don't stop shooting until the son from the pits of hell is flopping on the ground like a fresh caught catfish.

"They look like a human on triple doses of steroids, but don't think their moaning is going to give them away. They come out of nowhere and their huge black eyes see really good in the dark. A bright light will blind them, but they don't give a shit, they'll still come after you and snack on your pancreas.

"They gather in groups of two or three, maybe more, in dark places. I don't know how they survive or why they want to eat us who haven't been turned into zombies. There're plenty of slow moving cows and dogs still around they could snack on. If there were any scientists left we could ask them, but we don't so it's a mystery, but I know I don't want to become a McHuman for those creepy bastards. I'd rather blow their head off and watch them flop on the ground like a drunken college cheerleader."

Eddie wasn't sure of all the "facts" he'd given them and he might have exaggerated some, but he wanted these people to know how dangerous and scary the zombies were.

Eddie parked the SWAT truck and Josh and Rusty climbed out of the truch. Eddie followed the two out and directed them to either side of one of the doors.

"Okay, turn 'em on. When I open the door, you," he pointed to Josh, "go left and you," to Rusty, "go right." Both men, AR-15s with 30 round clips in their right hands and thermal imagers in their left, nodded to Eddie. For just a moment, he wondered what the men, both well over 10 years his senior, thought about the 22-year-old giving them orders. The moment passed when he opened the door.

The thermal imagers showed heat signatures in the distant corners of the building, but they weren't clearly defined. Eddie motioned the men back out of the building and slammed the steel door.

Pulling out his walkie-talkie he called Katie and her crew to the back of the store. When they arrived he laid out his plan. "We need the food in there and they don't. Let's go in in threes. One with the spotlight, two with guns. We shoot anything that moves and we shoot it until it doesn't move no more."

"Josh, you and Rusty take the lights. You guys know where you saw the images on the thermal. Katie and I will go for the right side, Danny and Sade, you go for the left side. If they start getting to close, say within 10 feet, start screaming your ass off and we'll all back out. Sound like a plan?"

Although he was asking, it was still the plan they were going with. Josh and Rusty got the hand held spot lights out of the truck. The others made sure they had the safety off on their guns, a round in the chamber and their side arm ready. "Don't hesitate," he told them, "because they won't."

When everyone was ready, Eddie took the handle of the door in his hand. The spotlights which were held over the head of everyone were on and creating shadows of Katie's and Sade's head on the door frame. They'd go in first, followed extremely close by Eddie and Danny and then the spot lights.

Eddie pulled the door open quickly and two zombies were right there waiting for them. Sade was caught by surprise, but Katie started pulling the trigger on her AR-15 like a sewing machine. The zombie was a large, heavily-muscled woman, and Katie had to put six rounds into the damn thing's head before it stopped reaching for her. It went down and Katie put two more rounds into the thing's black, greasy hair. She was then being pulled back out the door by someone.

The spotlights didn't seem to slow the zombies at all. Sade hesitated for a heartbeat and almost died for it. The zombie grabbed his throat and was leaning in for a bite before the Nigerian-born American started shooting. The zombie's abdomen was being turned into Swiss cheese but the beast had him in a choking death grip.

Danny got his AR in play with surprising speed, pushing Eddie and Katie to the side. He had a dozen rounds into the zombie's neck and jaw, splattering the two men with zombie flesh, blood and bone as Katie and Eddie backed out.

Grabbing a knife with a 12-inch blade from his hip, Danny sliced through the sinew and tissue of the zombie's arm as it began to fall, trying to take Sade to the floor in its dying seconds.

Eddie pulled Sade and Danny back out and Rusty slammed the door. They tripped and fell over Rusty.

With the door slammed shut they looked at each other. Both had blood and flesh splattered on them and Sade had dark bruises on his neck.

Sitting on the ground, wiping off the blood and guts Danny looked up at Sade. "What the hell, man? Why'd you hesitate?" Sade looked at Danny. He was still in a little bit of shock. He didn't know what to say for several moments. "I thought it was Bill Murray. You know, from that zombie movie."

Danny's jaw opened and stayed there. Katie rolled her eyes. Eddie knew the reference and started to laugh. "What, you were going to ask him? 'Bill, wanna play golf?'" everyone then started laughing. Maybe they didn't know the movie, but Bill Murray and the golf reference were so out of place in what they had experienced in the last 15 seconds, it had to be funny.

When they had settled down and the ones who had fallen got back to their feet, Sade deadpanned, “I like to golf,” and everyone broke into laughter again. They moved back to the far side of the SWAT truck and cleaned themselves of the gore.

“I think we need another plan,” Eddie admitted. “They knew we were coming and they were waiting. I thought they would be stupid and didn’t give them credit. Next time we do it different.”

“We got any rope?” asked Danny. “I got a plan.” Eddie climbed inside his truck and brought out a length of repelling rope. Danny cut a piece off. He tied one end to the door handle and walked back to the rear of the truck.

“Eddie, you and Katie go lay over there,” he said pointing to the back of the trailer the Ford was pulling. “Take the light Eddie, and don’t forget to reload, Kate. You went through a lot of ammo. Me, Josh and Rusty will go over here,” he said pointing to an opposite oblique from Eddie and Kate. “Sade’s going to pull the door all the way open from back here, 20 feet from the door.”

“Okay, I see what you’re saying. Let’s outsmart those dumb asses,” Eddie said and got into position with Katie. When they were all ready, Eddie gave Sade a signal. Sade pulled the door open.

Katie got the first kill with a three-round grouping the size of a quarter through the neck of a large male zombie. The back of his neck blew out along with what was left of the thing’s spine. It dropped.

Danny and Josh combined to put down the other zombie that had been waiting at the door. There were now four badly mutilated bodies of zombies lying in or near the doorway of the food mart.

“Spot lights!” Danny called. “See anything?”

Neither Eddie nor Rusty could see any more Zombies lurking.

“Let’s try the thermals again,” suggested Danny, who seemed to have a firmer grasp on the situation, so Eddie let him lead. Sade and Rusty grabbed the thermals they'd put behind the SWAT truck. They moved carefully to the sides of the door, staying clear of the fields of fire of Katie and Danny. Eddie and Josh swept the spotlights to the limits they could reach from their positions with one hand and held their pistols in the other.

"I see nothing," Sade called back to the group after sweeping the area with his thermal imager.

"Me either...," Rusty started to say, "wait! Up high!" He grabbed Sade and dragged him to the ground. A large shape came jumping down from the racking. Josh had the first shots and bullet holes appeared in the zombie's chest and legs. As the beast staggered under the onslaught, he came into Katie's sight picture and she finished the thing off with shots to the face and neck. It dropped to the floor, twitching. Katie and Josh hollered "clear!" so Sade rolled into a sitting position and shot four rounds from an M1911 into the zombie's head until it quit twitching.

"Who's golfing with me this weekend?" Eddie asked everyone. "do you think there are any courses still open?" Everyone ignored him, but they did so with smiles.

The crew checked the building again, first with thermals then with the spot lights. There was nothing left in the building but rats, mice and a family of raccoons, but they were easily shooed away.

Once cleared, they started loading cases of canned goods and other non-perishables onto the trailer and then into the SWAT truck.

It wasn't a large store, but it had more than enough salvageable merchandise for the two vehicles. They took turns loading and keeping two others on perimeter making sure no one had been drawn by the sound of gunfire.

When fully loaded with as much as they could safely carry, the day had nearly run its course. Danny finished strapping the load to the trailer when Eddie called the shelter telling them to expect the foraging crew in an hour.

~ ~ ~

Randy spent the day with Monica and Tony setting up

the video surveillance system for the shelter. He climbed the trees and towers while Monica ran the wiring. When Monica, Randy and Eddie had raided the electronic store on their trip to Trussville, they didn't realize all they'd recovered from the store.

When Monica and Kellie were going through the spoils, they found the boys had loaded a complete Q-SEE Advanced Series Surveillance System with eight outdoor cameras and four that had microphones. They'd also unknowingly grabbed seven rolls of wiring for the unit.

Monica threaded the wiring through the shelter while Randy put cameras on both the antennae, aimed both ways down the road, one pointing along the path in front of the shelter, one down the path to the garage and barn. The seventh had the longest run of wire as it was places on a tree over Tia's motor home and the eighth Randy pointed out across the garden.

Randy got help from Cheryl with setting up the four audio cameras. These he placed as far from the shelter as possible and hid them high in the trees. He believed this would give the shelter advanced warning of invaders.

Out of deference to the fact that Monica hated her guts, wanted her dead and would spit on her corpse, when Randy would tell Cheryl that Monica would be in the area, she would find some place else to be.

Randy didn't understand the depths of Monica's hate for Cheryl. He thought it might be jealousy because Cheryl was long, lithe and beautiful, while Monica, while no longer obese, was still larger than average. Monica had become a stout woman rather than fat, her double chins had receded and her once fat face had toned up to where she was looking less like an over-stuffed couch and more like a roller derby blocker.

When Randy knew that Monica would be in the area he'd let Cheryl know and he'd hear her shuffle off, chain clinking like little bells. He didn't talk about his friendship with Cheryl to Monica because he knew how women were and he didn't want to get in the middle of a cat fight. He also didn't want to do anything to mess up his chances with Cheryl.

The talk his dad and Kellie had with Cheryl this morning didn't trouble him. He believed even Kellie would see that Cheryl had been a victim, that she was not in any way responsible for Mike's death or the attack on the shelter. Cheryl was just an abused woman who was being held captive in a barn, without trial, and threatened with being banished, which Randy knew would be a death sentence.

Randy didn't see what Monica had seen the day of the attack. Cheryl had been standing by the door with the two men, not as a beaten woman just following her captors, but as a participant. She'd told Jerry what she'd seen and that's what prompted Jerry to finally speak to Cheryl herself. Monica had told Randy the same thing, but what she saw wasn't what Randy heard. The pretty, sultry voice of Cheryl's sounded a more plausible reason for her being there.

~ ~ ~

Tony worked on the set up in the shelter. He plugged the DVD into a 42" television in the main room so he could see it easily. As Monica ran the wires to each of the cameras, he'd check the adjustment of each one, and then tested the microphone pick up. He was still recovering from his broken ankle, although he was getting around better. Monica figured another three weeks before she dared take off the make-shift cast.

After that, Tony would still need a splint and physical therapy, but he was making progress and that was better than being dead. There were three orbits in every 16 in which the space station was within the line of sight for contact the shelter. Tony made sure he was available to listen and speak to the people there as well as working on the surveillance system. There was not much the people at the shelter could do for the ISS crew who were returning to earth, but Tony wanted to know everything he could to help them.

The Russian commander gave explicit details on the recovery capsule, how to open it, what tools to have on hand and what precautions to take if the three mission specialists returning survived re-entry.

Everything about the recovery was a long shot, but the people coming back accepted the risk. They knew chances were good they would die, but the two Americans and the one Canadian would rather die on earth than in space.

Jerry collected the information from Tony and spent the afternoon arranging the recovery mission with Juan. Tony's answer to real time communication between the shelter and the coast was dead end. The shelter had nine CB radios and it was about 300 miles to the coast. On a good day, which according to the station commander, the weather for landing tomorrow afternoon looked perfect on along the coast, the base station might reach up to 30 miles if tweaked, but the mobile units could only hope to reach five to 10 miles at best and they didn't have enough time or power to set up a system. Tony also thought about getting a radio station working, but he didn't have the talent or knowledge to get the Moody AM station back on the air and even that would be a one-way communication.

Jerry told him to forget worrying about it. The station commander would be able to transmit to the receiver Tony already had. Tony would spend the evening hours putting his short wave receiver and an antenna in the Ford. The station commander would update Jerry and his rescue crew, but Tony doubted the short wave would reach 220 miles into space.

They were just finishing the surveillance set up when Eddie called in that the foraging for food had gone well and they were on their way back.

Tony and Monica began cleaning up the living area. Tia and the others who weren't living in the shelter worked in the garden while the kids played. The fields had been as completed as possible so it was more housekeeping around the farm.

Jerry, Randy and Kellie met at the final camera position. Cheryl wasn't anywhere in sight. On and off during the day Jerry and Kellie had chances to talk about their morning conversation with Cheryl. Jerry had come to a decision which would make no one happy. He remembered during his divorce a judge saying if no one was happy, then it's a fair deal.

"Randy, I want to tell you I know you have been spending a lot of time with Cheryl," he began as they headed back to the barn, being careful not to dismiss his son's feelings or maturity. "I've given it a lot of thought today and I tell you, it hasn't been an easy decision. I don't think we can trust Cheryl. Maybe what she said is true, but I don't think all of it is."

"Dad, she's been through a lot. She's screwed up in the head and she's told me she is. I think we owe it to her to give her a chance, just like we have all those other people we have living here."

Jerry was getting pissed. He wasn't asking for more input on his decision because he'd already had enough of the whole situation. He'd already made up his mind. Cheryl was bringing drama into his life and he hated that. He had to nip this situation quickly or a rift was going to come between him and his son and he wouldn't tolerate that from anyone.

Kellie was smart enough to see Jerry's temper was being pushed. There was tightness in his jaw that she'd seen before. She had the good sense to say nothing, nor to try to comfort either of them. Whichever way she leaned, she'd alienate the other. She had to remain out of this situation. She walked between the two men, not touching either, but near enough to show Jerry she supported him, but also to show Randy she was not afraid of being here with them, that she stood with them, as a family should.

"What I want to do is transport her to some other place, maybe find another encampment for her. While she is here and until we find another location for her, she is to remain in the leg irons," Jerry said with finality.

"Tony has talked to the Smith compound and in time, he may find something closer. But while she is here, she is bad for us. She is a constant reminder of the death of Mike. Somewhere else, maybe they can accept her, but I don't believe all of her story and others here suspect she's lying too. No one will be able to trust her."

"But dad, they don't know her like I do. She's been abused, raped and tortured and now you're sending her away to someone else who might abuse her. She said she feels safe here. She doesn't need to be in those damn leg irons like this is the 16th Century."

"She is safe here, but she's not welcome, son," Jerry said.

"If it was just me and you, that'd be one thing, but now we have kids here and other people who depend on us. We can't take the chance of trusting her. Hell, if some people had their way, we'd drop her in the middle of no where and let her fend for herself. There are others who would do worse." He didn't tell his son Eddie would gladly stand Cheryl against a wall with a blindfold and a cigarette. Monica's thoughts weren't much better toward the woman.

"Will you at least talk to her again before you send her away?" Randy pleaded.

Jerry thought about it and could see no harm. He knew he wouldn't change his mind, but sending her to another encampment might be the best for everyone, and it would let Randy know he was at least willing to listen to his son on important issues with the shelter.

His decision, however, had been made and there'd be no bad feelings against her at a new place unless she wanted to share her story of what happened here.

Jerry said he would talk to her again before making a final decision, but made sure Randy knew his mind was probably made up already. The three started the evening chores with the cow herd which had grown to 45 head. Randy wasn't happy with his dad's decision, but it was better than just dropping her off somewhere in the middle of no where.

It wasn't what he wanted, and that was to tell Cheryl she was free to be part of their clan here. No place else but here would be good for him to build a close relationship with her.

However, his dad had said he would speak with Cheryl again after their return from the coast, so Randy would use that bit of hope when he spun the decision Jerry made to Cheryl. It might be enough to keep her from panicking and retreating into the curled up ball of tears on the bed.

~ ~ ~

The people on the farm were just finishing chores when Eddie and his foraging crew showed up. They had loaded the vehicles with a lot of canned food to the cheers of everyone. The evening was filled with moving the food into the garage and stories of conquest over the zombies.

Kellie and Tia's kids would begin sorting it in the morning.

Eddie, helping Randy and others unload the SWAT truck, showed his best friend the stash he'd found in the back of the store: two full cases of Bud Light. Randy was pleased because now he wouldn't have to steal from his dad's stock of beer. He and Eddie were not drinkers, but Eddie had liberated some beer before the fall of the world from his mom and the two got half-tanked and were giggling and falling down drunk after less than a six pack.

"I bet I can get Monica drunk and there's enough here to make her look good too," Eddie said with a lecherous laugh. "I don't even want to think about it," Randy told him and continued to work. He was busy making other plans for an evening with someone who looked a lot more inviting to him than Monica did.

With both trucks unloaded and re-fueled, everyone moved like a herd to where Tia had set up picnic tables near the garden. Kellie and Mrs. deJesus had prepared the evening meal of southern fried chicken, baked potatoes and okra. Mrs. deJesus had also found the fixings for home made chocolate chip cookies which everyone agreed were the best damn cookies ever to have baked in the history of cookie baking.

As the kids finished and went off to play, the adults relaxed while Jerry and Juan cleared the dishes into the shelter. Everyone settled down to enjoy cool evening and Jerry took this time to lay out his plan for the rescue mission.

"I want to take Eddie, of course, with his SWAT truck for defense. I would like him to have Juan with him, and Monica. I'm going to take Rusty and Tony with me in my truck. Tony will operate the radio and try to keep in touch with the ISS commander and Rusty, I hear, is pretty good with the AR-15."

"We'll be leaving at 4 a.m. tomorrow morning, so Randy will be staying here to take care of the farm and finish some work he started today. It's about a 300 mile drive, so we'll be gone all day and most of the night. We'll probably be back the day after tomorrow, but don't send a rescue team until the day after because I don't foresee any problems and we'll be able to defend ourselves pretty well.

"I also want to make sure every one knows the Russian commander is giving this a 10 percent chance of success. But I think we still have to do our part because it is the right thing to do.

"On another note, Tia wants take three people in the Escalade to Anniston to pick up another motor home. She and I have talked about this today and she recalls a dealership near the military base there. If she can find one, it will go a long way to housing these people we're going after in the morning.

Tia spoke up here to let everyone know she'd already picked her crew for the drive to Anniston. "I'll be taking Sade, Josh and Nick. Nick is going to be my radio man and Josh has some experience driving straight trucks. Sade, I heard today, is a good golfer, so I had to have him along."

The people who heard the story of Sade's golf comments in the middle of a battle with the zombies laughed. The others would be told about it later.

Josh's daughter had fully recovered from the food poisoning as did the others of the three-vehicle convoy so Josh felt safe leaving her on the farm.

"That leaves Kellie, Mrs. deJesus, Danny and Randy here with the kids. I know it isn't an ideal, situation, but we're under some time constraints," Jerry pointed out.

It was Mrs. deJesus, no one it seemed could bring themselves to call the grand motherly woman "Margarita," even her husband, who spoke up. "I was a school teacher for more than 20 years and a principal for another 25, Meester Jerry. I think I can keep this young lady and men and children from tearing up the school while the director is gone."

It wasn't what she said; it was her purposeful lapse into thick Spanish accent that made everyone laugh. Jerry could see why Juan loved her so much. She was easy to like and knew how to keep the tension level down.

"In that case, unless anyone has any questions, I'm turning in early tonight and I'd suggest the rest of us going to the gulf do so too. It's a 300-mile drive tomorrow and I figure it'll take about 10 hours, if the highways south are anything like the highways near Birmingham.

"Once there, we'll have a couple of hours to find a boat and get five miles off the coast." There were a lot more details to the rescue which Tony had written down, but now was not the time to go through it all. Tomorrow, they'd need a lot of things to talk about on the 10-hour drive, so Jerry didn't go into all the details tonight.

"Good night everyone," he said and excused himself. Kellie touched his hand as he left the table. He wanted to get a good shower before going to sleep. It was early for him, the sun having just gone down over the horizon, but he had a knack for forcing himself to sleep when he really needed to.

Eddie and Monica also went into the shelter to sleep. Juan and his wife got up, but the two were going for a walk, hand in hand, before he retired for the evening.

Danny headed back to his truck and camper.

Tia and Sade gathered up Nick and Josh and the four went off to discuss their trip to Anniston. They'd be leaving hours after the rescue crew, and Tia wanted her kids to play themselves to exhaustion tonight.

~ ~ ~

Randy waited until everyone had committed to what they were going to do before getting up from the table. To throw off suspicion, he walked up the path to the antenna on the hill above the shelter. If anyone was watching, it looked like he was going to check on the equipment he'd been working on.

During his dad's meeting, he thought for sure all his plans were going to be ruined. He thought for sure his dad was going to take him along for the rescue. When his dad said he would be staying behind, and that half the people currently staying on the farm would be gone for two or maybe three days, a full-blown plan popped into his head.

He was so excited about the turn of events, he wanted to run to Cheryl and tell her his plan, but instead, he slowly worked his way up the hill, past the antenna and down the other side to enter the barn through the cattle stalls.

As he was passing through the barn he had to slap the rump of a couple of cows to get them away from the door which led to the interior. He didn't bother being quiet because he knew Cheryl would be awake still, probably reading or playing some of the music Randy'd put on an MP3 player for her.

Cheryl did hear him coming, so she quickly arranged a reception for the young man who was infatuated with her, like so many men before had been. It was so much easier now that she didn't have to wear those damned leg cuffs at night. Until last night, if she'd needed a change of clothes, she had to wait until Randy came with her food, unlocked the cuffs and wait outside until she changed, then he'd come back in and put the cuffs back on.

This morning, shortly after he'd brought her breakfast, Randy had put locks on all the doors that led to the outside of the building so she wouldn't have to wear the cuffs unless she was outside the barn. It had been his idea of giving her "more freedom." Things were much easier now for her.

She cracked the door to the interior of the barn just enough to make it look like she'd left it open to allow the air from the small window, too small for her to squeeze through, to create a draft through the room. Her timing was nearly perfect.

The door which led outside was barred and locked as was the door to the parlor, but if she had to use the bathroom, there was one available between the former office she was living in and the parlor. If she really wanted to escape, she could probably break out if she had some tools, which she didn't, but Randy told her everything was covered by the cameras and she believed him. She also promised not to escape and he believed her.

Randy saw the door to her room was cracked opened when he closed the milking parlor door. There was a light on in her room so he was pretty sure she was awake. He walked up to the door to knock before entering and through the opening he could see Cheryl preparing for bed. Her back was to him so she obviously didn't see or hear his coming in. She was in a pair of powder blue panties and was leaning over her bed, picking up a clean tee shirt. The smooth curve of her back showing the ripple of each bone in her spine, and long legs excited Randy. He caught just a glimpse of a breast again as she picked up the shirt and slipped it over her head, pulling her long dark hair through the head hole and flinging it in back of her.

Right then, he should have knocked and entered, attached the collar to her and left. He should have just done that and left her secured for the night, like his dad had told him to do.

Instead, Randy backed away from the door, feeling dirty, like a voyeur. He stepped back very quietly two or three more steps. He thought about some things his dad had taught him. Jerry had tried to instill in his son a moral righteousness. Randy's dad had never forced the boy to attend church with him, but Randy did go about once a month to make his dad happy. The sermons usually bored him because he felt they didn't pertain to him. He was living at home with his dad and the amount of sin Randy had in his life amounted to impure thoughts from the pictures he looked up on the internet and little white lies, more exaggerations than lies, he told to Eddie. Randy didn't give much thought to faith in God, nor if there was a supreme being. He just didn't care to think about it because he just didn't have the desire to think about there being a God watching over him and seeing his every thought.

Right now, he wasn't thinking about God. He was thinking about what his dad had told him about the right to privacy and the sanctity of that right. He wondered how he'd feel if someone was peering at him through a crack in his door.

What he'd just done brought a feeling of guilt washing over him. This wasn't the internet where no one was looking back at him. The pictures he looked at on the internet, he rationalized in an effort to justify himself, were just pictures of women who wanted the attention, who wanted to be looked at. What he'd done – looking through a crack in a door – he'd done to real live woman. What if she'd seen him and screamed? What if she had been embarrassed and told his dad that Randy was spying on her like a common pervert? What if she'd seen him and saw him as the kind of man who preys on frightened women like so many had done before to her? She'd surely reject anything he had to say or any apology he tried to make claiming innocence.

He recalled the farmhouse, which was now a pile of ash,

where he had grown up and less than 200 yards from where he stood right now, there used to be piece of wood that hung in his room. In the wood was carved the sentence "Do what is right, even if no one is looking, because someone is."

Randy knew it wasn't right to peek through a door at a woman, no matter how accidental it had been, no matter what her status was on the farm. There is knowing what is right and doing what is right. The woman trusted him because Randy was a good man who was trying to make her feel safe and welcome here. Sure he had fantasies that she and him would become a couple, that she'd see him for the good man that he was and they'd become like Kellie and his dad, but those were just dreams.

He was also 22 years old and hormones ran through his body like water rushing down a mountain ravine. Randy, still standing quietly, told himself he was wrong for looking through the crack in the door and promised himself he wouldn't do it again. He heard Cheryl sit down on her bed. He couldn't bring himself to move as his morals fought a battle in his head. Minutes later he saw the light turn off.

He'd missed his chance to talk with her tonight by one or two minutes. If he said anything now that her light was off, she'd know he'd been spying on her and maybe all the trust he'd built up with her would be thrown to the wind. He had frightened himself into not moving a muscle.

He stood, staring at her door in the near darkness, wondering if he should say something and every second that passed, he knew he couldn't and wouldn't.

He stepped further away from her door, being careful to make no noise. The door to the milking parlor opened and shut quietly. Randy locked the door as silently as he could, but the deadbolt clicked loudly. Hopefully Cheryl had been asleep or if she had heard it would think it was one of the cows. He worked his way out of the barn and back up the hill the way he'd come, still feeling guilty by what he'd seen.

He forgot to put the collar on her and realized it when he was almost back to the shelter. He kept thinking of her body and how beautiful she was. He knew he could trust her, though, and didn't go back. If he did, she'd know he didn't really trust her and he wanted her to.

Maybe on their "date" she'd remember how much he trusted her.

~ ~ ~

Cheryl's plans went awry because of the morals Randy's dad had instilled in him. She'd heard the young man entering the barn when he had slapped one of the cows. He was really just a boy playing at being a man. She'd had to hurry to get undressed and then had to wait again, standing half-naked by the door until she heard the door to the milking parlor unlock. She then ran back to stand by her bed to make it look like she was just now getting ready for bed.

She timed it perfectly and she knew Randy would see her body through the crack she'd left in the door. She knew he'd watch her and want her. Men were like that. Her body turned men into easily malleable pieces of clay and she would use him just like she'd used others.

She bent over the bed, her back side pointing straight at the door to give Randy the best view of what she could offer, making a real show of straightening the tee shirt before reaching high over her head, stretching her arms fully toward the ceiling before allowing the shirt to fall gently over her body. She made sure not to turn around and accidentally catch him looking at her. This was an act she'd played out before and she knew when it would be the right time to move forward with allowing him just a sip from her cup, and with the lights on was not it.

Cheryl pulled the blanket and sheet down on the bed and made her movements clear so Randy, if he was still looking through the gap in the door, would know she was about to get into bed. If he was smart, he would be sneaking quietly back to the door to the milking parlor to make sure he made enough noise for her to hear him "come in" to her living area. After a moment, she thought maybe he'd back away from the door to give her time to finish "dressing" for bed, so she lay down and picked up a book she wasn't reading.

Still Randy didn't come to the door. She wondered if he

was still watching her. She couldn't look at the door to see because then he'd know she knew he was there. After a few minutes of pretending to read, she decided he was waiting for her to turn out the light, probably hoping to catch her just before she fell asleep, hoping she'd invite him to lay with her for a while, so she "could feel safe" while she fell asleep.

Cheryl was prepared for that too. She turned off the light and waited. Any minute now she would hear Randy pretend to open and close the door to the milking parlor. He'd then knock gently on her door and ask if she was awake. She'd mumble a fake "who is it?" and Randy would say it is him. She'd tell him to come in but not turn on the light. She'd tell him to sit on the bed and they'd talk for a few minutes and then she'd pull him down to lay with her.

Of course she was under the covers and he'd lie on top, knowing her body and his were separated by so little cloth. He'd feel her curves against him and that would drive him to want her more. She might even wrap her arm around him and gently caress his neck. She'd say something like "You make me feel so safe." He'd probably try to kiss her and when he did, she'd allow him a clumsy try and then send him away wanting, telling him that she couldn't as long as she was still a prisoner.

He'd either unlock the doors that kept her in this barn at night, or he'd leave her with that stupid collar locked to her neck to sleep alone, knowing she was here, nearly naked, wanting him to help her.

It would drive the poor unsuspecting Randy to do stupid things. She lay in the darkness waiting for Randy to make up his mind for what seemed to be forever. "Come on you stupid hillbilly, make up your mind!" she thought to herself.

She heard the door to the parlor close very gently. Then she heard the deadbolt slam shut. That could only be done from the other side. She knew Randy had left. "Shit," she whispered to herself in the darkness.

After a few minutes she got up, put on a pair of shorts and slipped on some slippers. She checked the doors to the outside and they were securely locked. The only thing he didn't do was put on her collar. It was a mistake on his part, one she wouldn't have made, but then she wouldn't allow herself to be hooked like Randy had been.

"That boy is the stupidest throwback on this farm," she said as she padded back to her bed.

Chapter Ten

Three-thirty in the morning was early even for Jerry. He slapped the windup alarm clock he'd used for 15 years into silence. He'd gotten six good hours of sleep and he was going to need it today.

He knew Tony was probably more excited that he was. Tony hadn't missed a check-in with the Russian commander on the space station since they'd made contact. The young man had formed a bond with the commander and when the two were not talking about bringing the three others back to earth as safely as possible, the Russian was telling Tony of his homeland, his family, his life. Tony wrote it all down on his computer so someone in the future would remember.

Jerry rolled out of bed, turned on the small lamp between the two beds in the room and started dressing. Kellie, who hadn't wanted to interrupt his sleep, was sleeping in her own bed tonight. The small lamp wasn't very bright, but was light enough he could find the clothes Kellie'd laid out for him. He'd grown fond of the woman and she was a good balance for him. She never demanded anything from him and her advice was a solid guide when he was unsure of the right direction to take the shelter. She had taken her position as caretaker of the shelter seriously and kept meticulous records of the inventory. When Jerry wanted to know if they had some piece of equipment, how much fuel was in the storage tanks, or how much food was in stock, Kellie would access her computer and give him the answer.

Before the fall of the world, Jerry had kept just enough records to keep the IRS off his ass. The farm's equipment and supplies inventory was kept mostly in his head or in the little notebook he'd kept on the coffee table next to his chair in the old farm house. It had been simple record keeping.

Kellie had taken it to an entire new level of organization.

But more than what she could do for the shelter, it was her friendship he cherished most.

Jerry tied his boots and reached over to turn the light off to head down stairs and meet up with the rest of the crew headed to the coast this morning. As he fumbled for the chain on the lamp, Kellie's hand reached up to grasp his without opening her eyes. She pulled it to her and pulled Jerry, who had stood up, down to give him a kiss. "Take care of yourself today," she said sleepily, after the kiss.

"Yes, ma'am," he responded. "You too. Randy'll be here if you need anything. I wish I could've found a good reason to take you with us," he said to her as he knelt beside her, "but with Tia gone with three others, I wanted someone I could trust here with Randy and that woman."

"I know, Jer. Mrs. deJesus is a fun woman, but someone needs to take care of the kids and she can't ride herd on five of them all day. Katie went through a lot yesterday and working in the garden is what she needs, and we need her expertise there.

"And Randy's going to have his hands full with the security system, the cattle and leveling out a place to put the motor home coming in. He's also going to run plumbing and wiring for them if Tia is able to find one." Jerry hadn't thought about the wiring. Even half-asleep Kellie was more organized than he was. "Go back to sleep, Kellie. I'll see you tomorrow night or the next day. I'll try to bring you back a souvenir."

She closed her eyes and smiled. "Yes, dear," she whispered. He kissed her forehead and pulled the blanket up to cover her shoulders better. Molly, Kellie's ever-present dog, slept beside the wall on Kellie's bed and growled softly. The little mutt looked at Jerry with contempt. Kellie pulled her pillow to her and snuggled comfortingly to it. She was content to go back to sleep. Without him even saying it, she knew Jerry loved her, whether he knew it or not, and she knew beyond all doubt that she loved him too.

Jerry slipped out of the room quietly and went downstairs. Tony was awake already, as expected, and Monica and he were eating breakfast. A month ago she would have been eating a stack of waffles drenched in syrup, but this morning she was eating half of a honeydew melon. Tony had his usual bowl of Lucky Charms. Boomer, lying on his mat by the door lifted his head, saw it was Jerry, and put his head back down. It was safe to go back to sleep the dog decided.

"Morning guys," Jerry said softly to both of them. They nodded back, whispering good morning to him so as not to wake the others still sleeping. One of the two had started coffee and Jerry poured himself a cup for now and filled a travel mug for later.

"Eddie's already taken the guns to the truck," Tony told him. "I also got the short wave installed last night too. I had to use the SWAT van instead of your truck because of the size of the transmitter and places to attach the antenna. I hope you don't mind."

"No, that's good. We'll just switch Rusty to my truck and you, Eddie and Monica can follow us." Tony nodded and went back to reading one of the survival magazines someone had left on the table.

There was a soft knock at the door and Jerry opened it to find Rusty smiling at him. The door from the cellar opened at the same time and Juan and Mrs. deJesus came up the steps to join the team. "Good morning," he said to all three. "Coffee's on, cups are in the cupboard."

"I think I will, thank you," said Mr. deJesus. "I used to drink a cup before work, on the way to work and then all morning. I missed it at first when the missus and I took to the road. Then I didn't miss it anymore. Since we've been here, I've remembered how much I love it." His wife and Rusty declined the offer.

"I can make another pot and put it in travel mugs for you guys if you want," offered Mrs. deJesus.

"I've already got one, but if Juan wants, I could always use an extra," Jerry told her.

Juan kissed his wife on the cheek. "Mujer inteligente," he said in Spanish to her and she began making another pot. Jerry looked at his watch. The pot would take about 10 minutes, giving them another five to get everyone to the trucks. They'd all be loaded and ready to leave at 4 a.m. just as he'd hoped.

Jerry heard Randy coming down the spiral stairway. He hadn't expected to see his son this morning. He'd peeked through the door to the boys' room on his way down earlier, but the light had been off and he heard his son's snoring. He decided to let the boy sleep. Randy'd been given a lot of responsibility to handle today, nothing new, but there was the added stress of having Cheryl here.

Jerry decided he didn't like Cheryl at all and he'd be glad when she was gone. He would do as he'd promised his son and talk to the woman again, but he doubted she would be able to say anything to change his mind. If she lied to them once, it was because she was hiding something or trying to convince them she was someone she wasn't. Of course everyone was hiding something and he wasn't basing his judgment of her on just the lies he thought she was telling, but because of the circumstances and circumstantial evidence of the entire situation.

"Morning, dad," his son said, rubbing grit from his eyes. Jerry thought his son looked more tired than usual, which was probably how most everyone was feeling this morning. He lifted his cup in acknowledgment. "Randy. How'd you sleep?"

"M'eh. Laying down, on the bed. Horizontal," he said, repeating a running joke he had with his dad, while sitting down next to Monica. She was finishing her breakfast and favored Jerry's son with a shoulder punch. "Hey jerk" she said, to which he responded with a friendly, "Back atchya, Stay Puff."

"You going to be good today?" Jerry asked his son.

"Yes, dad." He sounded just a little exasperated and a little tired. "Cows, security, tractor driving and don't pick my butt. Got it dad." His son was being just a bit too much of a smart ass this morning and Jerry told him so. "Stop it. This is not time to be flippant."

"Yes, dad," the younger Saunders said, a little more respectfully.

Mrs. deJesus broke the growing silence. "Coffee's ready.

Here're the mugs. Now off with you so we can all go back to bed." She handed an extra travel mug to Jerry and the other to her husband and gave him a peck on the cheek and shoved him toward the door.

Tony, Monica and Randy got up from the table. Randy gave his dad a hug then punched Monica playfully in the shoulder and slapped Tony gently on the back. Monica smiled at him and Tony whacked him in the shin with one of his crutches.

Rusty was already headed out, Boomer escorting him, and there were no more good byes to be said.

Randy stood with Mrs. deJesus and watched the five head over the parapet and down the path. "A good papa you have, Randy. A brave man." Randy couldn't disagree.

~ ~ ~

Eddie had both trucks ready when the rest joined him in the driveway. Jerry didn't have to ask if they'd been topped off and checked. Eddie had matured a great deal over the past two months. The tools the Russian commander said they might need had been loaded into the job box in the bed of the truck.

"Morning everyone," Eddie said as he saw the group. They all bid him the same. There was no need for Jerry to give them a pep talk or re-iterate what they were about to do. He had gone over the basic plan the night before and he was sure they'd talk a lot on the CBs or walkie-talkies on their trip.

"Saddle up. Lock and load," Eddie told them, quoting Mr. Data from a Star Trek movie. He, Monica and Tony climbed aboard the SWAT truck and Jerry, Juan and Rusty loaded up in the Ford.

Both trucks started and radio checks were made. Jerry looked at the clock on the dash and it was just a few minutes after 4 a.m. He put the truck in gear and they were off to rescue some astronauts. How strange the world has become, he thought to himself.

~ ~ ~

The same morning scene repeated itself in the living room and kitchen of the shelter three hours later, but with different players this time. Randy had fallen back to sleep on Tony's couch so he could listen to the CB for as long as his dad and friends were within range. Tony had called three times, the first time when they left the driveway for a radio check and the second when they'd made it to the interstate. Tony told them the rescue team was having no problems and were making good time. The third time he called the team was just getting out of range and Randy heard Tony say things were okay, but everything else was lost to static.

Mrs. deJesus had gone back to the cellar, ostensibly to sleep, but in reality to pray. She was a devout Catholic and had rosary beads and a bible she kept by her bed. She prayed for the safe return of her new friends and the people from space, but mostly she prayed that God watch over her silly husband who she loved so dearly.

Shortly after 7 a.m. Tia tapped lightly on the door. Randy hadn't locked it so she opened it enough to see if anyone was awake. Randy was roused when he heard her call out softly. "Yeah, I'm awake. Come on in," he said, sitting up from the couch. Boomer came racing in with her, probably looking for the little dog. Since Molly was still upstairs, the big dog ran to Randy to lick his face and make a nuisance. He'd been left in the drive when the others had pulled out and decided he'd best go check on Tia and the kids. They were still asleep, so he spent some time wandering around making sure the shelter area was safe before finding a place to sleep under Tia's motor home.

"How'd everything go?" she asked, sitting down beside Randy on the couch as her three girls and one boy sat down at the table in the kitchen. Boomer, pushed away by Randy, finished searching the place for anyone who'd play with him. No one took him up so he decided to lay down by the door on his mat and wait. Time for play would come. He knew it would.

"Everyone got off okay," he told her, rubbing his face and head in an effort to wake up completely. "They made it to the interstate without any problems and the last time I had contact with them, Tony said they were making good time."

"That's good to hear," she said. "I hope our trip goes as well. I figure about two hours to get there, four hours to find something useful and two hours back."

"Sounds about right. We went to Anniston a few times and it took us an hour. Figure twice that now because you can't drive 70 miles per hour anymore and two hours sounds about right."

"I wanted to ask if we should take a trailer on the Escalade when we go in case we see something we could use."

"Might not be a bad idea. You have three guys with you, if you happen to come across another big generator, we could use one, especially for that other wind turbine. Do you know what batteries dad needs for the power grid in the basement?"

"He showed me yesterday."

"We need more of them and you might find them at an RV dealership. If you can't, we can use the regular kind for now. The more the better so the trailer is probably a good idea."

"I'll hook up the trailer," she said, taking out her computer tablet and making notes.

Sade, Josh and Nick all showed up at the door together. Sade and Nick each had their own tents in which they'd been sleeping. Jamal shared a large tent with Danny. They were two strangers who'd met in west Texas and survived long enough to become friends. Josh slept in a camper with his daughter Marissa, and Katie the nursery manager.

"Good morning everyone. Ready for TDY?" Tia asked everyone. They looked at her blankly, having no idea what she was talking about. "Sorry, my husband was Army. TDY stands for going away from the base on temporary duty."

Tia was an enigma of personality. She wasn't very tall and kept her blond hair cut short and just beginning to show grey. She had a slender frame but a wiry musculature and defined features. Her ice-blue eyes were piercing, yet tender and she appeared at first glance to be a frail feminine-type woman. But after a few minutes of conversation, one could tell she was a strong alpha-type who didn't take shit from anyone. She was a very gentle woman, with a streak of hardiness to balance her femininity. In her past, she'd driven semis, worked in a factory, was on a collegiate track team where she threw a javelin, had been an Army wife for 15 years and was a stern and a doting mother to her two kids and the twin girls she'd taken in. She was doing what she could to be both mother and father to them and succeeding well.

The plan was for her to drive to Anniston and look for the RV dealership there and bring back a motor home for the astronauts. She was taking three people with her and if they found an RV that they could get running, she'd drive it back and Nick would drive the Escalade. If they found batteries, they'd load as many as they could onto the trailer.

She planned on an eight hour time-frame so they could get the motor home, if they found it, set up before nightfall. The absolute soonest, and this was if everything with Jerry went off on schedule and with no problems, that the rescue team could be back to the shelter with the astronauts was 5 a.m. the following morning. She was sure they wouldn't be back by then, but she wanted to be ready if they were.

Everyone on the RV team said they were ready once they'd finished breakfast. Kellie came down the spiral staircase with Molly following one step at a time, and Tia smiled. "Morning, Kellie. Sleep okay?" She and Kellie were the same age, but Kellie looked younger with her hair not yet flecked with gray and she didn't seem to have as many wrinkles around her eyes.

But both were still attractive women, but Tia showed her age gracefully while Kellie's was more of elegance and refinement....except for this morning. She was wearing a pair of grey sweatpants and a sweatshirt. Her locks of usually well-brushed dark blonde hair with Viking curls were a tangled mess. Everyone suspected her and Jerry had been sleeping together, no one cared to ask if they had been, and looking at Kellie this morning might have been all the proof anyone needed.

What no one knew was that while they had slept together, they had only slept and held each other.

Boomer saw the little dog and jumped from where he was to greet the littler dog with a nudge of his huge nose. Molly growled which signified to Boomer it was play time so he started running happily around her, egging her on to play. Molly was having nothing to do with the big monster.

"I'm fine. Was just restless all night. Sorry I'm late getting up. Coffee?" She asked looking at everyone. "I need some but don't want to make too much." There were a couple of nods so she made a full pot.

"We're going to be leaving at about 7:30 and want to be back by four this afternoon," Tia reminded Kellie adding in a 30-minute fudge factor. "You have everything covered here?"

"Yeah," she said as she poured the water into the coffee maker and filled the hopper with fresh coffee grounds. "Randy's got a full day ahead and he'll probably be working with Danny. I'm going to work on inventory that was brought in yesterday by Eddie and his crew, and Katie is going to work in the garden with the kids." The kids groaned a little hearing that they had to work in the garden because it wasn't any fun. Katie would find a way to make it less boring for them.

"Mrs. deJesus said she wanted to try her hand at baking, so she'll be in the kitchen on and off most of the day. I think we'll all keep busy while you're gone."

"I'm good without Danny today," Randy said. "Most of what I have to do is a one-man job. He will be on the tractor and a chain saw and clearing a spot on the other side of your motor home."

"Sounds good to me. We'll take care of that once Tia and her crew get on the road. You want to take lunches with you?" Kellie asked Tia.

"We might need something to eat and drink on the road," Tia said. "If it isn't much trouble."

"No trouble at all. I'll have four lunches made by the time these guys are done with breakfast," Kellie said as she opened the refrigerator.

~ ~ ~

Tia and her men got on the road later than expected. The trailer they were taking with them had a tire that needed repairing and it took Randy and Nick 25 minutes to get the tire off, repair it, inflate it and put back on.

Randy waved to them as they pulled out of the driveway then called Kellie, who'd remained in the shelter to feed the kids and begin her work, to let her know they were off safely and that he was starting his morning chores. She told him Danny was awake and that he'd be down in about a half hour for the tractor.

"Roger, Kellie. I'll look for him," Randy said to the walkie-talkie, then "damn" to himself. That gave him almost no time with Cheryl. He had to get the chores started and the tractor out and fueled for Danny, then show him where he wanted the new motor home to be put.

He hurried to the barn to unlock the doors and tell Cheryl about the beer he'd stashed just for her. The barn was about 150 yards away from the driveway and he could see the grated window which was Cheryl's room. He couldn't tell from here if she had her light on because the sun had risen. He hoped she was still asleep so he could wake her up.

He hoped she would be very grateful he hadn't made her wear the collar last night.

~ ~ ~

Cheryl saw Tia and three men leave in the big SUV and Randy turn toward the barn. She knew he was coming to do the morning chores by himself.

Two truck loads of other people had left earlier that morning, so he would be unlocking her door to the outside before he started chores. He believed she liked helping him do the chores when he had to do them by himself, mostly because she told him she did, when in reality she hated it.

If he was by himself this morning, he'd unlock the door, allow her to put on clean clothes, put the leg cuffs on her and then start his chores. She'd "help" where she could, but mostly stood around while he did everything. She'd tell him the leg cuffs kept her from working.

Seeing him heading her way, she jumped back into bed and pulled the covers over her. She was still working on a plan when she heard his key in the door. It startled her, but she settled herself before Randy knocked. He waited and knocked again, just a little louder.

She didn't move.

She heard the door open.

"Good morning, Cheryl. You awake?" he called softly.

"Wake up, sleepy head," he called again playfully and came all the way inside her room.

Cheryl faked a grunt, like she was just coming out of a deep sleep.

Randy reached over and touched her shoulder.

Then the acting began. Cheryl pretended to be startled by the touch and she squealed, not too loudly, but convincingly. She rolled over and pulled the covers up to her neck and pulled away from Randy. "Don't hurt me!" she cried.

"Cheryl, it's me, Randy,' he said as soothingly as he could. "No one is going to hurt you." Cheryl acted like she was just waking from a frightening dream. She added a little bit of fake confusion on her face and her eyes darted around the room. "Where's Billy? Where's Jack?" she asked, picking the names of the two men Kellie shot when they were trying to take over the shelter.

"No, no, no, it's okay," Randy said softly, placing his hand gently on her shoulder. "They're not here. It's just me."

She acted like realization was coming to her and she reached out and hugged Randy. She squeezed him hard, pulling him close to her and allowed the bed sheet to drop into her lap. She had on the same tee shirt he'd seen her put on the previous night, but her lack of a bra meant he could feel her breasts against his chest.

"Oh thank God," she said, not letting him go. "The dream was so real."

"It's okay, Cheryl. It was just a dream. No one's going to hurt you here." She whimpered in his arms for a few moments, allowing him to "hold" and "comfort" her.

"I have some good news for you," he told her, removing the collar. She pulled back from him, smile brightening. "My dad's gone for the day with Monica and I'm working alone. No need for you to have to hide in here or go away whenever Monica comes around."

He said it like it would be a joyous day for her, a day where she didn't have to think about someone coming around and hating her on sight. He thought he was telling her great news about him and her being able to work together without interruption and the associated stress. He really thought he was giving her good news.

She continued to smile the smile she didn't feel. "That's great, Ran!"

"And even better," he added, holding her at arm's length. "I have stashed away a case of beer that Eddie got yesterday. I think after all the chores are done today, I'll bring it down with a TV and DVD and we can watch a movie together."

Cheryl's fake smile widened. This 22-year-old child was making it easy on her. "Won't your dad object? He said I could only have books."

"He won't be back until tomorrow at the earliest. I'll bring the stuff down tonight and when he gets back, I'll tell him you were bored at night and they helped you make it through the night."

"Oh Randy, you're so thoughtful. Oh, and thanks for not putting that collar on me last night. I slept so good." This she meant. He was getting so comfortable with her, he was beginning to disobey his dad.

He looked at his watch. "Hey, we have to hurry. Danny's going to be here in a few minutes and I need to get started on chores."

She released him and threw off the covers. The shorts she was wearing showed an enormous amount of immodesty which included the powder blue panties, which she knew he'd seen again. "Go start your chores and take care of Danny. I'll change into some work clothes and stay here until you get back," she promised, and really meant it. When she was ready to run, she wanted to have as much lead time as she could and take as many weapons with her to defend herself.

Randy couldn't help himself and looked at her long legs. She hugged him quickly and kissed his cheek. In his ear she whispered "Maybe tonight I'll show you how strong these legs are." She then pushed him away. He was smiling like he'd never smiled before and went to through the door leading to the parlor. Half-way through the door he turned to tell her he'd be back shortly, but she'd already begun to take her tee shirt off. He saw her bare breasts and quickly turned back and left the room before she got it over her head and saw him staring.

Cheryl wondered if he'd try to peek at her body again. She just suspected and timed her tee shirt removal to give him a look. Not only had she hooked the young man like a rainbow trout, she was now reeling him in like a master angler.

Randy went back and unlocked the parlor and started morning chores. He was as happy as he'd been in a long time. He had a "date" tonight. Even if it was with a prisoner and even if it was just a movie in her "cell." He knew that all day he'd be a happy man.

~ ~ ~

Jerry and his two-truck convoy had made great time by his reckoning. They'd followed the same route they'd taken to find the motor home for Tia and her girls. Having been that way before, Jerry remembered most of the obstacles and how they worked their way around them.

They made it to I-65 south, passing the exits for Pelham and Alabaster without encountering any real troubles. They'd stopped taking bridges over the local roads when one they were driving on shook uncomfortably when both vehicles were crossing. Now when they came to a bridge, they took the on/off ramp, just like they did when an overpass had fallen onto the highway.

The highway was still littered with debris, wrecked cars, busses and semi-tractor trailer rigs, but not so much that the convoy couldn't keep up an average speed of 40-50 miles per hour. After two hours on the road, Jerry could see the distant capital of Montgomery.

His CB cracked to life. "Are you there, Jerry?"

Jerry took the microphone from Rusty who was riding in the front seat with him. "I'm here. What's up?"

"Just heard from the ISS. Colonel Rustov, the commander, said the rescue capsule will begin it's de-orbit burn at 17:04 our time. There is a 90-second window for the capsule to de-orbit to land within 50 miles east or west of Gulf Shores. How close to shore is an educated guess based on weather conditions and experience."

"Are you still in touch with him?"

"Negative. We were lucky to get him when we did. He said he'd been trying every time he gets near overhead. He said the rescue capsule has already released from the station and is maneuvering away preparing for de-orbit burn. Scheduled splashdown time is 18:47 local time.

"Okay, Tony. Thanks."

Juan, who was in the back seat of the Ford had been sleeping, must have awakened at the call. "They are trusting we'll be there to pick them up, Jerry. I trust we'll be able to be there?"

Jerry looked at the clock and the distance to Montgomery. "We're making very good time. As long as we don't run into any trouble, we'll have three or four hours to get a boat ready and into the Gulf."

Juan didn't want Jerry to have any illusions about the possibilities of the capsule landing within easy reach. "The space station is moving at more than 17,000 miles per hour 230 miles above our heads. A little piece of it is going to pull away and slow down enough so gravity will bring it down unpowered.

"Now the astronauts usually have a building full of computers on earth and thousands of men and women helping them land in the target area. The Russians usually land in the desert and I've heard they can sometimes wait up to three or four hours for rescue.

"The rescue capsule will float for a while, but it's not like the Mercury and Apollo capsules that had flotation bags. We're going to have to get really lucky and so are they," Juan said solemnly. "I think the Russian commander was being generous with 10 percent chances."

"Yeah, I thought he might be exaggerating a little. I don't know if he was giving us hope or giving the other astronauts hope," Jerry admitted.

Jerry picked up the microphone. "Come in Tony."

"Goat head, boss." Tony was enjoying this trip and getting more excited.

"If you reach the commander again, tell him we'll be there

and we'll do our best."

"Will do, Jerry."

Jerry gave the microphone back to Rusty.

"Let's do our best guys," he said to his passengers.

~ ~ ~

Tia and crew made it almost to the Oxford exit before they ran into major obstacles. They had made good time once they got on I-20. There was a lot of debris Tia navigated around. They also encountered the same bridge and overpass issues Jerry and his team were encountering and came up with the same solution. The major issue they ran into had nothing to do with vigilantes or zombies, rather the lack of there being an interstate anymore. They drove past the County Road 109 exit, thinking they had a straight shot to Anniston when they came upon a gully. The gully was 40 feet wide and had taken all of the interstate with it. There was no way the Escalade could navigate through or around the area with the trailer it was hauling.

Tia turned the truck around and headed back to the last exit. She got on County Road 78 and headed east to Anniston again, hoping 78 hadn't been wiped out as well. They saw the same wreckages as they saw on the interstate and the washed out area which had grown to take out the interstate.

They had to drive off the four lane highway to avoid damaged vehicles that had been piled up against a bridge abutment. Tia tried to find the best way around the wreckage but she must have run over something. Just as she was pulling back onto 78 east, she felt the change in the way the trailer was pulling. Looking in her side mirror and saw the trailer had a flat tire.

Tia had Nick remove the flat tire on the two-axel trailer. The tire they'd leave here, but kept the lug nuts. When he was finished, he threw the jack into the back of the SUV and they were back on the road.

She started off slowly, but after a quarter mile the trailer was tracking fine, even with the missing tire. They would have to get a replacement before loading the trailer, but for now, everything was copacetic.

They knew they were entering the outskirts of the city of Oxford from the GPS, but looking out the windows of the Cadillac SUV, they could have been in any town hit by a Class 5 tornado. Modular homes had been thrown around this area of the city. There were entire walls scattered along the sides and middle of the road. Fire places, furniture, bathtubs and other interior fixtures had been scattered as far as the crew could see.

Tia was avoiding most of the garbage when a large piece of debris caught their eye as they drove by what used to be the sign for shopping mall. It was the picture of a RV painted on a large piece of metal that was embedded into the steel post. They were able to just make out a partial address ....way 78, Anni....

"That must be it," Nick said. "Must be ahead somewhere."

Tia agreed but she wasn't pleased with what she'd seen and wasn't too hopeful. The amount of devastation was unreal even though it was right in front of her.

Entire blocks had been wiped away clean to the foundation. What had been a bustling city was dead and destroyed. No light poles remained upright; very few buildings were still standing and none that were not heavily damaged. Fire had ripped through others.

It was looking like the storm had hit this city as hard as anywhere and exacted revenge for some unknown offense.

Even if the world hadn't fallen apart, this city would have been declared a disaster and probably rebuilt from scratch. She passed the street which she would have been on if she could have stayed on the interstate. The interchange was destroyed and the Escalade would have been hard pressed to make it into town. "This reminds me of one of the cities I saw as a child in my homeland," Sade said. "It had been attacked by artillery for days. The only difference is there are no bodies."

"Probably the vultures or zombies got them. Be glad they did," Nick told him. "You don't want to see a month-old dead body."

They continued driving east on 78 passing hotels and motels that had probably been abandoned even before the hurricane because of the virus that killed everyone. Hotels and motels had been closed, along with most common areas, by presidential decree. It was probably the final act of the president.

The brick and steel buildings didn't survive any better than anything else in town. They counted five of the motel-type buildings; all had been heavily damaged to the point of being unlivable. Tia's hope of finding a motor home dropped a little more.

The three men in her SUV were staring open-mouthed at the devastation. They passed what used to be a car dealership that was leveled. Every car still on the lot during the storm had been pushed up against a semi-tractor trailer rig that had been wrapped around concrete pillars in front of another collapsed building. It looked like one of those car recycling depots.

The next parking lot was empty, but at the far end of the lot, a pile of campers were piled up against what appeared to be a long garage. "Campers! This must be it!" exclaimed Sade.

"Settle down, Sade. Look at this damage. I bet not one of them are usable, but let's take a look," Tia said, slowing to pull into the parking lot.

The four climbed out of the Escalade and stretched. They hadn't realized how much their bodies had stiffened up in the tense two-hour drive and seeing the horrific damages to what must have been a beautiful city.

After everyone had stretched and gotten a drink of water, Tia asked the group where they wanted to start. Sade spoke up as the others looked around. "Out back."

"Why out back?" she asked, tossing her sun glasses back into the SUV. Rain clouds had moved in and the bright sun they'd seen rise two hours earlier was now obscured.

"Because everything out front is down there in a pile of scrap. Maybe the back was protected some from the storm," he explained. She nodded, doubting his reasoning but willing to humor the man, and reached back into the SUV and pulled out her shot gun, a 20 gauge with six rounds and one in the chamber. Sade and Jamal had their AR-15s and Nick had opted for a pair of 9mm pistols.

"Stay together, but keep your eyes open," she said.

They began walking along the side of the building. Fully half of the long L-shaped building had collapsed during the storm and been blown away. They saw bits of brand new motor homes the size of Tia's that were wrecked and crushed. They walked around the fallen part of the building and the four of them stopped and stared.

"Jackpot!" Nick hollered.

"Holy Mother," said Sade.

"Sweet Jesus," Josh added.

Tia was speechless.

At the far end of the building were motor homes. All were damaged, some appeared to just have windows knocked out, and others had minor body damaged. But there were at least a dozen of them that looked to be usable.

If they could find keys. If they had fuel. If they could get them started. There were a lot of "ifs" but they were here to get one motor home. Tia was sure they could find at least one that could be drivable.

"Let's go," she said to the men. "Let's find the best one we can for the astronauts."

For the next hour, the four found three motor homes that were in good enough shape to probably be usable. None of them had keys. Sade said they were probably in the sales office. Despite the amount of damage to the building, finding the sales office was not going to be easy. Every door was locked. The garage doors were too large and the man doors were heavy duty. Even though the building was heavily damaged, there wasn't an easy way to get in.

Also, no one wanted to be the first in a dark building and they only had regular flashlights, not the spot lights or thermal imagers the SWAT truck had. The reality was, unless they could get some big garage doors open, no one wanted to go inside.

After walking all the way around the building, Tia finally made a decision. "Let's crash the place,"

The men looked at her. "I'll drive." She smiled mischievously.

They went back to the SUV and drove it around back of the building. Tia's plan was to drive into one of the garage doors that didn't have a vehicle on the inside. Sade stopped her. "Can't we pull the door off?" he asked. They'd surveyed every door. The man doors all opened inward and were set in steel frames. The only thing to strap the tie downs to were door handles and they'd come off before the door did. There were no handles on the garage doors. They started looking for other ways into the building without crashing their only vehicle that they know worked.

Near a line of air conditioners and where the building had started to collapse, Nick found a glass man door that had been covered with part of the fallen roof. "Here we go!" he hollered to the other three. They came running and all agreed this was probably the best way into the building.

Tia and Sade went back to the SUV to drop the trailer while Josh and Nick found a place on the piece of fallen roof they could attach a strap to. Tia backed the SUV up to where they were standing and Nick tied the strap to part of the metal structure and the other end to the hitch on the SUV.

Everyone stood way back as Tia pulled the truck slowly away from the building until the strap was taut. She then gunned the Escalade's big V-8. The structure moved some but not much. Both back tires on the truck began spinning and screeching like a teenager's first car in a high school parking lot.

Tia took her foot off the accelerator and backed the SUV up about six feet. She asked Nick to double check the strap. He did. She smiled wickedly at him and he gave her a look like she'd gone just a little nuts. "Watch this," she said to him and he hurried to where the other men were standing.

This time the SUV was in all-wheel drive and she got a six-foot running start. The strap pulled tight and 4,000 pounds of SUV powered by a 400 horse power motor grunted, hunkered down and pulled with everything it had.

The building's wall, roof and door grudgingly gave up it's

will to the truck and broke free.

The SUV sprung forward with a 16-foot piece of wall and attached insulated roofing. The men cheered and clapped for the little woman for almost a full second before grabbing for their weapons. When the wall came free, a trio of zombies came racing out of the hole at them. Maybe it was their hunger that made them brave the out of doors, or maybe the dark overcast. Whatever it was, the men were glad they were 20 feet from the wall Tia had just pulled down.

Tia saw the men raise their weapons. She was a very bright woman and knew in an instant why they were aiming in her direction. "Oh shit," she said to no one and looked in the rear view mirror. The zombies had just cleared the hole she'd made and were coming straight at her and the men who were on her crew.

"Like hell, you sons of bitches," she hollered and threw the Escalade into reverse. The little woman, whose feet barely reached the floor, pulled on the steering wheel and stomped the accelerator again.

The back window was shattered by the head of one of the zombies as she hit the two coming out first with the rear bumper. She felt the bodies being crushed beneath her truck, and shredded by four spinning tires as she gunned the SUV's 400-horse powerplant.

She briefly recalled how it felt when she drove her old Durango too fast over speed bumps.

The Cadillac felt the same way driving over zombies.

The third had dodged out of the way, its body bouncing off her left rear quarter panel, smashing the lights and denting the steel. The momentum and speed and the strap that was still attached caused the hitch to snap off as she backed over the wall she'd just pulled down.

The truck only stopped when it reached a load-bearing wall eight feet inside the building. The truck stalled and Tia, only slightly panicked, tried restarting the big truck. Nothing happened when she turned the key. "Oh shit again," she said to herself. She saw the zombie, still outside the building, quickly coming at her. She started to scream and reached for the button that would roll up the windows on the truck. She'd given her shotgun to Nick to hold on to while she was pulling down the roof, so she ducked, giving the men time to start shooting.

It was just climbing aboard the hood to come at her through the windshield when parts of its head started coming off. She watched it turn to look toward her men and two more shots hit it. The damn thing was starting to jump toward where the men must have been when the top of its head came apart completely and it flopped to the ground.

Then she saw her men. They had been lying on the ground so their shots were going high above her as they shot the zombie. Waving at her now that the coast was clear, they were giving her the signal to pull out of the building. She tried to start the SUV again but it wouldn't turn over. She realized the truck was still in reverse and slapped herself in the head. She moved the shifter into "Park" and the Escalade started with the turn of the key.

She pulled out of the structure, driving over all three zombie bodies.

Once she was 20 feet away from the building she got out of the truck. She ran to the men and hugged and kissed each one of them. Not one of them minded one little bit, even Josh, who was kissing Katie at night.

The four took their time making sure the building had no more zombies inside. They knew they'd been lucky. For some reason they all believed zombies wouldn't be in a garage for motor homes.

From here on in, they were very careful, with Tia holding three flashlights while the three men had four guns out and ready. It took an hour, but Tia refused to let anyone do anything inside the building until she was sure it was safe. After watching their pretty little Army wife drive over three zombies after pulling down a building, they were inclined not to argue with her.

Once they were absolutely sure the place was clear, they patted themselves on the back. There were six brand new motor homes inside the building, undamaged and with keys in the ignition. The four outside that had been slightly damaged were forgotten.

It took 45 minutes to get the doors open for each of the motor homes. They had been after just one, but they were taking back four motor homes, all longer than 38 feet. Tia found a dolly and would tow the slightly-damaged Escalade on the back of her motor home.

Before they headed back to the shelter, she remembered Randy asking her if she'd look for batteries and she found a room filled with them. It was hot work, but they loaded 20 new motor home batteries into the back of the SUV.

All four motor homes needed fuel, but they'd seen dozens of wrecked semis between here and the shelter. They had siphoning hoses and an electric pump with them. She looked at her watch. It'd take a while, but they'd be home by 6:00 with four new homes.

~ ~ ~

Montgomery was dead. Few buildings, from where they could see from the interstate, were left standing. Massive fires were burning in several areas and other parts of the city had been destroyed by the hurricane.

Jerry was somehow glad that people hadn't been living in the city when the hurricane came through. Thousands would have died. More likely tens of thousands with the amount of destruction the people in the two trucks were seeing.

There would have been long-term suffering and so many slow deaths from disease and the inability of rescue crews to reach those trapped.

But when the hurricane came through, most everyone was dead already, their rotting corpses, if they were in the open or in one of the collapsed buildings, would have been washed away with the deluge, stacking up around drains and in rivers. The few still living were probably out of the city and as far away from the dead and decaying corpses as they could get. He didn't care if the zombies had died.

They had to make two different detours off the highway because of major damage, but they finally had the capital in their rear view mirrors. Jerry wouldn't be happy to have to drive back this way, but they would either tonight or in the morning.

The rest of the drive to Gulf Shores was no less depressing, with the destruction of the countryside easily visible. Jerry began to wonder if they'd even find a boat big enough to take into the gulf.

They made good time on the second half of the trip. They stopped to scavenge fuel from a stack of four semis that had been wrapped around the same bridge abutment. Neither the Ford nor the SWAT truck needed fuel, but both were topped off and every one took a personal rest break. Jerry had allowed for a 10-hour drive, but after looking at the map and the GPS, he figured they'd make it to the gulf in less than eight hours.

The final hundred miles were uneventful and when they passed the Jack Edwards Airport, they had just over four hours to find a boat. Tony suggested parking the SWAT truck on the beach. He would then put a larger antenna onto the truck to better able him to talk with Col. Rustov.

Jerry agreed and told them while they were setting up the antenna, he and his team would begin looking for a boat to take out. Jerry pulled over and let the SWAT truck pass. He'd let Eddie find the spot that would be best for Tony.

Jerry, Juan and Rusty began looking around the little city. It was as wrecked as everything else they'd seen in the past eight hours, even more so maybe because of the ocean swell and waves that had crashed through and flooded the little city. Juan voiced Jerry's doubts about finding a boat because of what they were seeing.

They followed Eddie until he parked the SWAT truck in a vast empty parking lot. Tony told them over the CB that this is where they were going to set up and wished them luck in finding a boat.

Turning parallel to the beach and heading west on State Road 180. Jerry drove slowly, hoping there was a boat anchored somewhere close to shore that had weathered the storm that had destroyed cities between here and Birmingham. He hoped, but didn't expect to get that fortunate.

They reached the end of the peninsula and stopped. They could see Dauphin Island but couldn't reach it so turned around to look back the other way. Every house they passed was wrecked. Most were nothing but the foundation. Eventually they were back to the lot where Eddie had parked his truck.

His next try was closer to the beach. He took State Road 182 west and saw the same destruction he saw on 180. All the buildings on the beach side of the road were wiped off the face of the earth.

The other side of the highway wasn't much better. He had to stop at the place where a bridge used to be. The bridge was gone completely, leaving nothing but the concrete abutments.

Jerry turned the truck around again and Juan saw a building that hadn't been wiped to the ground. It was in from the beach and looked to be heavily damaged, but still part of it was standing. Two blocks from the beach Jerry pulled into the parking lot of what had been called Compass Point.

They got out and walked around the building. There were no usable boats on this side of the building that had survived the storm little better than most others. They could see how high the storm surge had reached from the telltale water marks on the building.

Jerry looked at his watch. They had two hours and a few minutes.

Rusty pulled out his binoculars. He was searching the lagoon's beaches and was looking as hard as Jerry and Juan when he spotted a possibility. "There!" he hollered, pointing westward but on the other side of the lagoon.

Jerry took the binoculars and looked in the direction Rusty was pointing.

"Could be, Russ. Juan, take a look." The older Mexican looked through the binoculars too. "That might work. Let's go look at it."

"We have to hurry," he said looking at his watch. It was five minutes to five which meant an hour and 50 minutes before splashdown. They ran to the Ford and Jerry quickly drove to the other end of the lagoon and circled back. They probably found the one boat that was still floating within 20 miles. It was a 50-foot catamaran. Not what Jerry was thinking for a boat to take out onto the gulf, but he would if it were sea worthy.

"The nose has some damage, but not real bad," Juan said as he started looking it over. "It looks pretty new."

Jerry said it looked like a sail boat, and they were looking for something with speed. Juan shook his head. "It was both. See where the main mast broke off," he said pointing to where a six-inch in diameter pole had been on the boat. "Let me look inside." He climbed aboard and went inside the ship. Jerry heard it rumble and start up and immediately shut off.

The catamaran was one of the newest models of high-end sailing boats. It was made of carbon fiber mostly, strong yet light-weight. Its cabin was centered between the two large pontoons on either side, and was roomy enough for a small gathering. There were decks for and aft of the cabin for swimmers and storing smaller watercraft like jet skis. Aside from the sail and sheets that were no longer on the deck, there were two power plants, each nestled in the middle of each of the pontoons, which propelled the catamaran when there was no wind and supplied electrical power to the rest of the boat.

It really was a rich man's toy.

Juan came out smiling. "She's got fuel and she still runs. Now we have to get it back in the water." The cat had been washed up on shore…25 feet from water. It took all three of them and the Ford to gently get the catamaran back into the water. Jerry looked at his watch. They had 40 minutes.

He got on the CB and called Tony. "What's the latest?"

"The good colonel said the de-orbit burn appeared perfect. We are still expecting an 18:47 splashdown."

"Can he tell how far from shore they'll come down?"

"I asked him that and he didn't know exactly because he can't measure the upper atmospheric winds, but his educated guess is between five and 10 miles," Tony told him.

"Okay. We'll go with what we have. We have a boat. Juan and I will take it out seven miles, straight south.

"Can you move the SWAT truck to the end of this lagoon we're on?" he asked.

"Yeah, shouldn't be a problem if we go slowly. Give us 10

minutes. What do you have planned boss?" Tony asked him.

"Just meet Rusty there and we'll be there in a few minutes," Jerry said and then put the microphone back on the dash. He turned to Rusty. "Juan and I are going to take this down to the end down there," he told him, pointing west. "Meet the others. We're going to take everyone we can. Hurry."

Rusty didn't have to be told twice. He was already headed to the rendezvous location before Jerry got on the boat. Juan hadn't been screwing around. He was familiarizing himself with the cat, warming the engines and testing the controls.

Immediately he pulled away from the beach where they'd push the boat back into the water and spun the boat in the right direction.

"She feels nimble. Quick response. I bet she isn't a year old," Juan said as he maneuvered the 48-foot boat to the end of the lagoon. "I wouldn't usually take this size out to the gulf, but it appears everything, including GPS, works and the water is smooth today. So let's use this."

There were so many dials and switches, computer screens and devices in the window that obviously meant something to Juan, which meant zero to Jerry. He just nodded. Jerry's idea of a nice boat was a 12-foot flat bottom with a six-horse Evinrude. By the time they reached the shore Jerry had indicated, the others were there.

"Eddie, grab any ropes you can, Monica grab all the binoculars." Eddie opened the back of the SWAT truck and pulled out two ropes that were neatly rolled and tossed them on the fore deck. Monica grabbed the binoculars from both trucks. "Great, now you, Monica and Rusty get aboard. We might need you." Jerry was glad none of the three hesitated. "Let's go Juan."

He pulled the walkie-talkie out of his pocket and called Tony in the truck. "Sorry Tony, but we have got to go and we would have had to work around you too much," he told the radio man.

"No sweat boss. I get sea sick just looking at the ocean," he radioed back.

Juan expertly moved the boat out of the lagoon and into

open water. Jerry could tell this man had experience with watercraft. He used the GPS and the depth finders to keep from running aground. Once clear, he opened up the throttles and the cat climbed up on the water nice and smooth.

It took 20 minutes to reach the area Jerry had suggested. Juan shut the boat's two motors off and let the cat drift in silence. There was a slight breeze under the now clear skies and the boat barely rocked on the choppy waves.

Jerry pulled out his walkie-talkie after looking at his watch. They'd cut it pretty close. It was 18:43 by his watch. He called Tony. "We're here. You got anything?"

"No sir. The station is out of range. I have the frequency of the capsule but chances are I won't hear from them until the chute pops."

"Roger that, let us know if you hear anything."

Everyone on the boat began looking skyward through binoculars.

Jerry looked at his watch. It was 18:44.

Tony came on the radio to say something at the exact same time Monica screamed. Everyone swept their binoculars to where she pointed: about two miles out and aft of the boat, they saw a huge red and white parachute high in the sky. "Go Juan!" Jerry almost pushed the man below deck. He then climbed up to the front of the boat, in front of the windscreen and pointed in the direction of the falling capsule. Juan pushed the catamaran for all it was worth. They would reach the space craft minutes after it hit the water. He hoped the people inside were ok.

"Call Tony!" he hollered back to Rusty.

"I already did. He has them on the radio and is talking to them," Rusty hollered back over the roar of the catamaran and 25-knot wind in their face. They all witnessed the space capsule splash down. Jerry hoped they got to them before the capsule sank.

They arrived and Eddie and Rusty, who had tied life jackets to ropes, threw them to the capsule as the catamaran coasted up to the bobbing Soyuz life boat. "Monica, call Tony and tell them we're here!"

A moment later the hatch on side of the craft blew off. Fortunately, it blew away from the catamaran and just winged the port pontoon as it blew away. Jerry ran forward with another life jacket as the three astronauts crawled out. They were wearing standard ISS work clothes and smiling and waving and yelling congratulatory things to their rescuers.

There were several tense minutes as the three crawled aboard the little catamaran. They found it easier to go into the water first then be hauled up by the life jacket. The boat's ladder had been missing. Eventually all three, two American men and one Canadian woman were lying down in the comfort of the cabin.

"Thank you," the woman, who was the senior specialist of the three, said to Jerry and Juan. "Thank you so much." Jerry felt there were very few things in life that would make him feel as good as he did with those words.

"You're welcome, ma'am," he replied. "We're now going to get you home."

~ ~ ~

Randy spent the day wondering between how his dad's rescue mission was going and how his date with Cheryl would go later tonight. He finished the chores in the barn then showed Danny where to clear a spot for the motor home.

When he was ready to start on the security system he went back to Cheryl's room. His dad had told him that if she wanted to be outside the room, she had to wear leg cuffs. When he knocked she told him to come in.

Her smile told him she was glad to see him. He didn't know how fake it was.

"Ready to go?"

She nodded and put her legs straight out for him to put the leg cuffs on her like she did every morning. Her smile went away. Randy saw her smile go away. Her lower lip pouted and she clasped her hands on her lap. Randy picked the cuffs up from the corner he'd put them in the night before. "I want to spend the day with you, but I hate those damn things," she whimpered. "They hurt so bad."

"I know," Randy said, "but my dad said if you don't wear

them, you can't go outside."

"But I want to go outside because you're outside." She was getting into the act of being petulant. "I won't tell him if you won't."

Randy hesitated but kneeled down in front of her and opened the cuff. "Please," she begged and placed her feet flat on the floor. "I promise I won't run away before our date to-night," she teased, spreading and closing her knees, right in his eye level.

Randy loved the looks of those legs and knew she was teasing him. He was naïve, but he wasn't stupid. He thought she just didn't want to wear the cuffs because they hurt her ankles. What he didn't realize was the real reason she didn't want to wear them. He knew it was a risk, but he believed she was a good person and he could trust her. He really believed she wouldn't run.

He also thought if he allowed her this favor, even after what his dad had told him, maybe he'd be allowed a favor during their date.

"Okay, I won't put them on," he said, putting the cuffs on her bed. "But I'm going to work your cute little butt off today because I have a lot to get done."

He stood up, thinking she would give him a hug and maybe a kiss for not making her wear the cuffs, but instead she gave him a smile and thanked him. She reached around him for another shirt to put over her tee shirt.

"Let's get started then," she said, nearly bouncing out the door.

They spent just part of the day together with Randy doing the work and Cheryl asking questions about his life. Randy thought she was interested in him so he told her freely of his life, what he liked to do and things he'd done. Randy made witty comments and she obligingly laughed every time.

She really was interested in him and the story he told about the death of Jeff. She asked a lot of questions about Eddie and his part and Jerry's reaction. Randy thought she was just curi-ous so he told all he could remember. He talked about the guns they'd found on their trip to Trussville and how close Monica had come to being killed. He embellished just a little and she seemed awed by his fearlessness.

They worked their way around every area of the farm except the buildings. Randy kept her away from the kids and the other people. He suggested sharing a lunch with her in her room, but she talked him out of it, saying a picnic-like setting would be nicer. He accepted her reasoning, but it was just another lie.

Cheryl listened to Randy ramble on through the day. She thought he was boring and uninteresting. He talked a lot about video games, the internet and playing online. These all bored her, but she feigned interest to keep him talking. When he talked about the layout of the farm and the people on it, that's when she paid attention.

She made sure he told her all of what had happened since her capture. Her injuries had mostly healed and she was ready to blow this taco stand. She was surprised she hadn't been executed that day. That's what she would have done if their situations had been reversed. Law and order were gone. The law of the land was kill or be killed. She learned a lot about the lay out of the property and the people who lived here. She couldn't understand how this untrained bunch of yokels had gotten the better of her and her team.

Cheryl let Randy talk and kept memorizing important facts she would need.

At lunchtime, Randy left her in her room, foul-smelling hole she'd had to live in for the past 11 days. She hated the place, but hadn't come up with a good plan to escape until Randy began showing interest in her. There were always too many people around or she was wearing those damned leg irons like a prisoner at a military correctional facility.

He came back to her room with sandwiches, fruit and two juice boxes. He wanted to sit in the room, out of the possible sight of everyone, maybe to get intimate, but Cheryl had other plans. First, she wanted to get out of the foul-smelling barn, and second, she wanted Randy teased into doing something very stupid. She wanted him trusting her completely. He was already violating at least one of his dad's rules which was a good start.

During their lunch she found out most of the people who lived here at the shelter were gone. Randy mentioned that Tia and a crew were gone. She also knew from Randy's ramblings that Jerry was gone with four or five others, including that fat ass Monica, who had put the final bullets into her Army friend's head.

That left the two older women and some kids on the property and one other man. She guessed the one called Danny who was running the tractor and chainsaw today was one of the newest people on the farm. She'd caught a glimpse of him and he was tall, sandy-haired, well-built and carried two revolvers all the time. He was also someone Cheryl would like to have on her side, and if he was new here, and not part of the two crews out on the road, maybe he was ripe for being recruited.

The afternoon dragged. Cheryl begged off mid afternoon, saying she needed a nap because she wanted to "be fresh" for their date this evening. Her real reason was because she really was tired, both physically because she hadn't slept well the night before even without the collar, but also she was tired of Randy's compliments. He seemed to pepper every conversation with something nice to say about her looks or her eyes or her hair.

Cheryl also tired of his attempts at showing how deep he was by using big words and spouting some diatribe about his faith, almost like he was trying to convert her.

What really gnawed at her gut was his constant fawning. He was always smiling at her and her smile was beginning to wear thin. There was only so much she could take before she felt should would lose it and begin punching him in the face.

She went back to her room to sleep for an hour. She was going to be busy this evening. Her plan had a lot of holes and a number of unknowns, but it was her best chance to get free of these weirdos. She wasn't going to let them hand her off to some other encampment where she'd have to work her way back to the top. They weren't going to let them drop her on some island somewhere where she would have to live alone.

Most of all, she sure as hell wasn't going to be some love interest for an immature 22-year-old.

She put together a kit she would need of items she'd lifted off the farm the past three days. She'd had to be very careful not to raise suspicions of Randy and took care to hide them in the bathroom of the barn. The bathroom was disgusting and no one but she used it. She had an iron bar about eight-inches long, a blade from a piece of farm machinery she'd made into a knife, and several lengths of wire long enough to tie someone up. The garage, she knew, was still unlocked and it was where the deJesus minivan was parked. Randy'd had to move the van out of the garage to do repairs and she saw he left the keys in it.

She heard Randy in the barn late in the afternoon, so she pretended to be asleep. She figured he was doing the evening milking which would take him about 45 minutes. Danny brought the tractor back and she watched through her little window as he drove it into the far side of the barn. He was dirty and tired she could tell and didn't look at all happy being made to do the shit work on the farm. He closed and locked the barn door and then walked around the barn, probably to get a hot shower and a hot meal then back to his tent to sleep before another day of working for Randy and his dad.

Cheryl thought about going after him to try recruiting him, but the timing was bad.

She heard the equipment in the parlor shutting down. Randy would be visiting her for their date soon. She had to be ready.

~ ~ ~

Randy shut down the equipment in the milking parlor. He went out the back door and over the hill. Cheryl, he believed, wanted their date to go well. He pictured her cleaning herself up in the bathroom in the barn. It was the only bathroom his dad would allow her to use.

Throughout the day he had talked and worked with her. She always was ready to help if he asked and she had such a wonderful smile. She didn't talk a lot about herself, but he figured that was to be expected after the hell she'd been through.

He talked about how happy, all things considered, the group here was.

For lunch he'd brought a blanket that he spread out on the ground beside the large maple tree that had fallen during the storm. They talked a little and she asked more about the people in the group. He told her about how Kellie and her dad were becoming close, how Monica and Eddie were his best friends and the rescue of the astronauts and Tony making contact with the Smith Compound in Kentucky.

The afternoon went slow for him. After he'd finished the security system and the repairs to the garage, he helped Danny move some brush after Cheryl said she wanted to get a nap.

Danny had been doing good work today and had a large area cleaned out. The older man helped Randy run some wires from the shelter to the clearing.

The man from Texas was working with a chip on his shoulder. After a while of working in silence, Randy asked why. Danny, never afraid to speak his mind asked Randy why he hadn't got to go on one of the crews but was left here to do manual labor.

Randy was straight with him and didn't think to lie. "That's probably my fault, Danny. You told Jamal you had been in jail for auto theft. I told dad because he is in charge here."

"You mean your old man doesn't trust me? After the shit we went through yesterday to get your food, you told your dad not to trust me? You son of a…." Danny's face became red and his anger boiled. Randy backed off from the larger man because he was afraid.

"No, no, no," Randy told him quickly. He knew the large man was in better shape and had a ton more experience than him and his hands looked like they'd seen a lot of fights. "I told him if you knew how to steal cars, you were probably good at driving things. I wanted you to use the tractor because I'm not real good at it," he admitted, somewhat embarrassed.

Danny looked at Randy. His anger level dropped like a rock in a fish tank.

"You're shitting me? You wanted me here because you can't drive a tractor and you're a farmer's son?" Danny asked incredulously. "Dude, what is wrong with you."

"I can drive one," Randy admitted, seeing that he wasn't going to get the shit beat out of him. "But you must be really good at driving things. Dad wanted this clearing done before Tia got back and I told him you'd probably be the best person for it. I don't care that you were in jail. That was before. You're a nice guy and Jamal likes you, and what happened before you came here is none of my business.

"If you want to be mad at someone, be mad at me."

Danny was still mad about being left out, but now he understood more. "Well shit. If that ain't the shit. Here I was pissed at your dad and it was you I should have been pissed at."

Randy, still a little afraid of the big man, said "sorry," and walked away, leaving Danny to think about what had been said. Danny was nearly finished with the clearing and Randy had to get the milking chores done, and now Danny felt like hell for thinking bad about Jerry.

Randy finished his evening chores and went to the shelter. He didn't give his conversation with Danny another thought. He wanted to clean up before going to meet with Cheryl.

Kellie was still out in the garden with Mrs. deJesus, Katie and the kids so he had the shelter to himself. He showered quickly and changed into clean clothes. It took all of 10 minutes.

Randy was just about to leave the shelter to pick up the brand new TV and DVD he had stored in the garage with the beer and a movie. He'd also put together a meal of shaved ham sandwiches, dill pickles, and chocolate chip cookies. He was so excited about the date and nothing else mattered until he heard Kellie's walkie-talkie. "Are you there, Kellie?"

Randy reached for the walkie-talkie. "This is Randy. What's up Tia?"

"We ran into some problems and we won't be back for about an hour. But have we got a present for you!" She sounded excited and happy, and he wanted to know what the present was, but more about what problems they were having. "What happened?" he asked.

"We blew a tire on the car hauler, but we'll get it changed and be there in about an hour. Just get something for us to eat because we've had a busy day," she told him, not answering his question completely. He really liked Tia and her attitude. "Tell the kids to be good and I'll see them in about an hour.

"Roger, Tia. I'll tell them." He took the walkie-talkie to Kellie out in the garden. Katie was finishing cleaning up the weeds they had pulled and Jamal was pushing the smaller kids in the wheelbarrow.

He walked out of the shelter, into a cool breeze and found Kellie. Randy passed on the message to Tia had asked him to and handed her the walkie-talkie. "I'm taking Cheryl supper and will watch for Tia," he told her. She didn't comment about his clean clothes, but did furrow her brow. That was okay with him. She'd come around when his dad did that Cheryl was a good person and should be welcome into the clan they were building.

The big downside to the message was that as much as he wanted to be with Cheryl the rest of the night, he knew at some point in the next hour or so, he was going to have to help her and her crew when they got home. He hoped the TV and DVD for Cheryl would make her less upset that they couldn't have an entire date.

"Okay. We're going to feed this bunch of hooligans so they can help when their mom gets here," he heard Kellie say as he headed to the barn. The twins squealed because Jamal pushed them over a bump. Hannah was helping Katie rake up the last of the weeds and Josh and his daughter, who still looked frail even after a week, sat on a blanket husking sweet corn. Randy left them to what they were doing and headed for the garage. He gathered up the TV and DVD from the garage and went to his date.

He knocked and she opened the door. She had cleaned up, but had dressed a lot more conservatively than he'd hoped. "Hey you!" she said, acting like she was genuinely pleased to see him. "Come on in."

He brought the boxes in and handed her their supper meal. "I know it isn't a meal fit for a queen, but it's fresh made bread and the ham is good." She took the meal and he started unpacking the TV. "Where's the beer?" she asked.

"Oh, that's the bad news," he said, standing back up. "Tia's running late, but will be here in less than an hour. I am going to have to help her when they get here, so I thought maybe we'd hold off on drinking until later tonight?" he formed it into a question, hoping she'd see the logic of waiting.

She grimaced and sat the food down on her bed, not saying anything. "But we can get the DVD and TV set up," he said, bending back over to open the boxes of new electronics. "That'll give you something to do while...."

Randy's world then went dark. He never saw the short piece of steel bar Cheryl had stashed under her pillow. She hadn't thought she'd need it. Her plan was to get Randy drunk until he passed out, something she knew she could do as she'd done something similar in her life.

~ ~ ~

Randy's bad news of Tia showing up in an hour would mean at least four more people would be at the shelter and less of a chance of her escaping. She needed to move now or she might lose her chance to get away altogether.

She slugged him as hard as she could in the back of the head and he dropped like dead man. He fell face first onto the floor and blood started flowing from his nose and mouth. She looked at the young man with absolutely no pity for what she'd done to him.

"Sorry my little friend, but I can't be your princess and I ain't staying in this rotten hole one more minute." She kicked him hard in the crotch, fortunately missing his jewels, to make sure he was not faking. He didn't move.

She picked up the knife she'd made and looked out the barn door. She needed some weapons and Randy had told her they kept them next to the door in the shelter. She didn't want to go up there, but was pretty sure if she ran into anyone, she could talk her way out of it.

She ran up the path to the shelter entrance. She saw Josh's daughter walking back to their camper, so that accounted for two people. She worked her way closer to the shelter doors, which were open, and where she'd been shot almost two weeks earlier. She heard kids talking and laughing and instructions by an adult. She assumed it was Mrs. deJesus by the accent. Randy had told her she was an older woman. The kids, regretfully, would have to be frightened into doing what they were told, but life wasn't fair.

She listened for a minute, making sure she had a good idea where everyone was located in the shelter. She didn't hear any men in the building so she assumed Danny was back in his tent, at the far end of the clearing. It was another piece of information Randy had passed on. She hoped he was too tired after his hard day of work and sleeping in his tent and out of her way.

She didn't hear any other older women, so she wasn't sure where Kellie or Katie was in the shelter. She wanted to know where Kellie was most of all. She was the one who'd shot her and on whom she wanted to exact the most revenge. All Cheryl had was a knife and she didn't want to have to face a gun with just this make-shift weapon. She didn't have a lot of time either.

Randy had said Tia would be here in less than an hour and that had been 10 – 15 minutes earlier, and the little girl who had just gone in the camper might be back any time and see Cheryl lurking outside the shelter. Cheryl wasn't sure how much time she had available to her.

She looked past the shelter to make sure no one else could see her. She heard the closing of an oven and the sounds of pots and spoons and the smell of hot food. The shelter got quieter. They must be eating. That would be good. It meant everyone must be at the table and focused on their meal. The guns would be in the safe by the door or at least down and not cradled in someone's hands.

The table they ate at was beyond the gun safe, which was next to the door on the left. Randy had described the entire layout of the shelter to her over the course of two days of careful questioning.

She'd hoped to be able to get in when no one was there, but she couldn't wait. Time was wasting before more people would soon be here.

She heard the distinctive sounds of people eating and figured this was the best time to move. She ran through the door of the shelter and grabbed the first person she could reach. It was a young girl, maybe seven or eight years old. In the heartbeat it took her to choose, the little girl kicked and screamed as Cheryl puller her by the hair.

Kellie lunged to protect the little girl, ignoring her own safety as Cheryl swung the knife at her. She was able to get herself between the attacker and young Hannah and pushed the little girl to the far side of the table.

Cheryl grabbed at the older woman who stumbled as she pushed the little girl away. What good luck it was for her that it was Kellie. Using her training, she dragged Kellie away from the table by the simple expedient of throwing her arm around her neck and pulling back. The surprise at the table was complete and more of the kids started screaming.

Katie, who killed two or three zombies the previous day, stood up from the end of the table to reach for her .38 in its holster. Cheryl put the knife to Kellie's throat. "Sit down hero or I start cutting." Mrs. deJesus reached up, put her hand on the woman's shoulder and whispered something to her Cheryl couldn't hear.

Katie sat down slowly but the other kids were still screaming. "Shut 'em up grandma or I will," she warned Mrs. deJesus. The older woman encouraged the kids to a quieter crying and fear. Katie pulled John and one of the twin girls so she was between them and Cheryl. She motioned Hannah, who had been sitting next to Kellie to move back behind Katie.

"No one has to be hurt, I just need a couple of things before I leave," Cheryl said, still choking Kellie, who was struggling for breath. Cheryl's forearm across her neck felt like it was crushing her throat.

Cheryl backed up, pulling Kellie with her, until the gun safe was beside her. She was making up her plan as she went. Keeping an eye on the kids and not letting go of Kellie, she told the woman she had in the stranglehold to pull out a rifle and load it.

"Can't…breathe," Kellie was able to get out and Cheryl loosened her grip slightly, but kept the knife right up to her throat.

"Not that one. One with a scope," Cheryl ordered. Kellie loaded it. "Set it down." Kellie did as she was told. "Now a pistol. Fill the magazine. Hurry." When Kellie looked as if she might aim the gun over her head and try to shoot Cheryl in the face, she pushed the knife deep enough in her neck to draw blood. "Don't try it lady or your neck will have a new hole and then I'll grab one of your kids."

Cheryl told Kellie to hold the pistol by the barrel right in front of her own face which she did carefully. She then tightened her grip on Kellie's neck until the older woman started to struggle. Cheryl dropped the knife and grabbed the gun in a smooth motion. She then released and pushed Kellie away and Kellie fell to the floor, hitting her head on the corner of the table. Molly started barking in earnest.

"Just leave," Mrs. deJesus pleaded. "These children do nothing to you. You have what you want. Please don't hurt these poor babies."

Feeling better and in more control with a loaded pistol in one hand and a rifle in the other, Cheryl looked at the frightened children who were crying or hiding their faces in the folds of Mrs. deJesus' clothes or behind Katie. Both adults were looking with pure hate at the intruder. The black Cajun Jamal looked ready to leap at her, which he might have done, had Katie not had her hand on his shoulder.

"You're right, they didn't. But she did," at which time as she aimed the pistol at the woman bleeding on the floor. "This is for my brother. You never met him, but you killed him in cold blood." Kellie recalled how she'd shot through the door, in fear of her and her friends' life 11 days earlier.

She saw the pistol in Cheryl's hand aiming down at her and the woman's finger looked like it was about to twitch so she rolled, but the bullet got her anyhow. Kellie groaned and doubled over in pain.

Danny came running into the shelter hell bent for leather with his .45 caliber revolver out less than a second after the gunshot. He didn't see Cheryl, hidden as she was by the door of the gun safe, and when he realized he'd run right by the gunman he turned quickly.

It was too late. Cheryl pulled the trigger two more times and Danny didn't have a chance with the first round going into his gun arm and the second grazing his skull, knocking him out cold. He fell onto Kellie's prone and bleeding body.

The children were all screaming and crying again. She heard another voice from outside calling for Danny and the big dog barking. Someone was coming, and they were coming fast, maybe more than one. She had the upper hand now, but if there were more people with guns, she couldn't kill them all. She didn't know it was Marissa, just heard the voice calling and decided it was time to run. Boomer, who had been sleeping under Tia's motor home, was racing to the shelter too.

Cheryl saw the spiral staircase Randy had told her about. She ran up the stairs two at a time. The top hatch was open and she climbed out, accidentally dropping her handgun. She was about the reach for it when she noticed the big dog Boomer, who was standing with the little girl by the door of the shelter, had seen her. He went from looking into the shelter with the girl to breaking into a full gallop, working his way up the hill to get at her.

Cheryl ran. She'd gotten a gun and also the woman who'd shot her. Now she needed to get away. She wasn't done with this bunch of yokels. She didn't think the dog would catch up with her but she wasn't taking a chance. The stupid animal did follow her, but she was able to get off a shot in his direction.

The dog wasn't running in a straight line which was fortunate because she would have killed the dog without remorse. He was scared off his straight-on attack, giving her enough time to get to the garage.

The van was where Randy had left it in the garage. She looked over at the barn where she'd been held prisoner and saw the door of the barn still closed. She was sure she'd killed Randy as she drove as fast as she could down the driveway. She'd hit him hard and he'd dropped face first onto the concrete floor. There had been blood immediately. Kicking him in the groin felt good to her too. If he wasn't dead, she hoped she broke what he'd been thinking with for the past two weeks.

Cheryl thought about the blood that flowed from Randy's mouth. She thought she might have cracked his skull with how much blood there'd been. Yeah, she thought to herself, that boy was as dead as the major who had her court martialed her and ended her military career.

Driving wildly, she raced away from the farm. She knew she'd be back to take this farm from that hillbilly. She didn't know how and she didn't know when, but she knew she'd come back. Considering the living conditions she'd been made to live in for the past weeks, they'd been living in comfort.

It wasn't fair.

She'd make them pay for treating her unfairly, but right now, she was free. There was no one from the farm who could catch her. She had gotten away and there was no way she'd ever let anyone control her again.

Cheryl looked at the gas guage and it read full. She knew could go a long way in the minivan, but she needed to go somewhere where she wasn't living on some farm, digging in the dirt to subsist.

"No," she said to herself as she gunned the little van onto the interstate. "I've had enough of that farming bullshit. Time for me to take bull by the balls and get what should rightfully be mine."

~ ~ ~

The spacemen were uncomfortable. They had been in space for more than three months. They'd exercised for more than an hour every day to maintain muscle tone and bone density, but still, the return to gravity wore on them. It'd be weeks before they felt back to normal again.

Something Jerry hadn't foreseen was the seating for the return trip to his shelter. There was plenty of room in the two vehicles, but none of it was that comfortable for the people who'd been in space.

A solution presented itself when the two-truck convoy was 30 minutes north of Gulf Shores. They had to leave the interstate because of the collapse of the I-10 interchange. Jerry weaved through the wrecks and concrete, circumvented the rebar and broken street lamp foundations.

They'd come through here early this afternoon, but then they were excited about reaching the coast. Now they were thinking about the long drive home. All three astronauts were both tired and uncomfortable and it was difficult to engage them in conversation while they were in such shape.

Juan saw it first. The sun was going down and a half hour from now, they would have missed it. Sitting between a stack of crushed semis at a truck stop and a brick garage was a tour bus.

"That's a Prevost," Juan said, a little bit of aw in his voice. "I bet the spacemen would be comfortable in that thing. Jerry didn't know what a "Prevost" was, but he saw the bus, protected from the storm by the 18-wheelers and the brick and steel building that had only partially collapsed.

Jerry called Eddie on the walkie-talkie and told him they were stopping to take a look at the bus.

Jerry, Rusty and Juan walked up to the 45-foot bus. Rusty had his 9mm in his hand and Juan had a shot gun under one arm. Jerry had the Desert Eagle his son had given him out and ready. They weren't taking any chances.

All three walked around the bus. It must have been here for repainting because it was covered in a primer gray basecoat. All 10 tires were inflated which was good. The men had to remove some wood and sheet metal debris from beneath the bus if they were going to move it.

"Prevost makes the best tour busses for celebrities," Juan told them. "I saw Allan Jackson's in Houston and these are rolling mansions." He pulled on the door handle and surprisingly, it opened. The keys were in the ignition.

Juan turned it over and after cranking for a few revolutions, it started up with a plume of black smoke from the pipes. He pulled it out of where it was parked and drove beside the SWAT truck. Jerry and Rusty were looking in wonder at the comfort someone who rode in this bus enjoyed.

"Full tanks," Juan told him, "if the gauges are correct.

They probably are. I bet this was here to be refurbished and painted. I bet it was sold to someone new."

"Damned if it don't look new," Jerry said, sitting on the six-foot long leather couch. "This is better than the house I owned."

"Probably cost more, too," Juan said. "These can go for more than 300 grand." The bus was decked out with twin sinks, a shower, beds, stove and refrigerator, empty as Juan found out, and a well appointed living area. Everything in the bus was brand new, including the linens. "I'd live in this if we weren't giving it to the spacemen. It's got to be 45-feet long if its inch."

"If we find another, Juan, it's yours. Or maybe Tia found something for you and the missus," Jerry told him, patting him on the shoulder." The old man shook his head and walked back to the front of the bus. "I get to drive it though. Better than the passenger seat of your old truck," he said lightly.

Jerry grinned at the man's comment and walked through the very well-appointed bus. Eddie and Monica joined him. When they got to the back of the bus, where the master bedroom was located, Eddie poked Monica in her side with his elbow. "Wanna test out the bed?" he asked with a wicked smile.

Jerry, who'd thought Monica and Tony would eventually hook up, or probably already had with them sleeping in the same room back at the shelter, thought Eddie was being rather tactless. The blush that turned Monica's face and neck red told another story. "Oh my God, Eddie. Not in front of the children," she replied, punching him in the shoulder and pointing at Jerry.

Jerry could tell the young lady was not offended, but just embarrassed at the timing of the comment with Jerry in the room. They must have been talking some real trash in the SWAT truck. He left the two to whatever they were going to talk about and walked back to the front.

This bus might be primer gray on the outside, but inside, it was immaculate with no expense spared on the cupboards, counters, seating, entertainment center and other living arrangements. It made what he'd done with his shelter look like a six-year-old with Lincoln Logs. "Have you ever driven something like this, Juan?" Jerry asked the elderly Mexican-American (not just Mexican, not just American, but Mexican-American as Jerry had been told). "I used to drive a corrections bus. This is a little longer, a little nicer on the inside, but I think I can handle it," he said with a smile.

"Let's get the spacemen over here. There's plenty of room and it's a lot more comfortable than the SWAT truck," Jerry told him, again looking over how nice the whole bus looked on the inside.

Twenty minutes later, the astronauts were relaxing in the back of the bus. They told Juan and Jerry it was better than the transfer bus NASA made them ride in from the prep room to the shuttle. The two Americans took the queen bed, the female Canadian took the single couch/bed.

~ ~ ~

Back on the road, Jerry was in the lead by himself. Rusty and Monica had decided to ride in the bus with the astronauts to get some sleep on the twin bed that folded out of a wall. They'd take over driving duties at the next rest break in three hours.

With his headlights on bright and speeding along at 45 miles per hour, Jerry felt good. He could see the bus between him and the SWAT truck that was bringing up the rear of their little convoy.

Without anyone else in the truck, he had time to think.

He thought about Tia and the crew she'd taken with her to Anniston. She might be a little pissed when they drive in with a bus because that'd mean she hadn't needed to go to Anniston under-manned. He prayed no one had been hurt. The bus would be helpful because they needed more living space. Danny and Jamal were still living in a tent and so was Rusty.

The deJesus's were sleeping in the cellar of the shelter so they were also one step up from sleeping on the ground. Katie, Josh and his daughter Marissa were sleeping in a camper on the back of a Chevy truck that was so crowded, it wasn't funny.

No, he decided. Tia would understand they needed the

room and a motor home was the quickest and easiest way to provide good shelter. The bus would be a bonus.

Jerry thought about his relationship with Kellie. He liked her a lot and she made him feel like he could be who he was. He didn't have to impress her or be someone he wasn't. He never intended to start a relationship with her. Things just developed and he wasn't going to complain. This morning, he almost told her that he loved her, but he held back. If he had, and she'd said nothing, or something like "How sweet," things would have been uncomfortable and awkward in the shelter.

Jerry spent a lot of time thinking about his son. He loved his boy unconditionally and was always worried he didn't do a very good job raising the boy. He hadn't been a firm father, like Tia was, and maybe Randy would have been a different person, more independent and have a better work ethic if Jerry had been harder on him.

No matter how things turned out in this new world and with new people now living on his farm, Jerry was going to make sure Randy knew how important he was to his dad.

"Hey, let's pull over. I gotta piss," The call from Juan over the CB nearly scared the piss out of him, so he thought he might better pull over.

"Roger," Jerry responded and pulled on to the shoulder of the highway to switch drivers, stretch the muscles and take care of other personal needs. The bathroom in the bus worked, but no one knew if the septic tank had solution in it, so that was off limits for now.

Everyone who was awake got out of the vehicles and took care of business wherever they found convenient.

Jerry, feeling like what he'd done today was possibly one of the best things he'd done in his life, looked skyward. The world of his yesterday was so gone.

But seeing the Milky Way with a clarity like he'd never seen before the fall of civilization, he believed the world he was helping put back together would be okay.

He would be home in a little more than two hours.

He was looking forward to a peaceful sleep in his own bed.

Coming Soon:

Hell Revisited

Look for availability date at www.ramblingdad.com

Exerpt from Hell Revisited:

They were losing the farm to soldiers with training and experience. Jerry knew the odds were against them before the first HUMVEE crashed through the fence across the driveway.

He only wanted to live here in peace with his son and friends and they were trying to defend themselves. Chances were slim and not getting better with at least one of his friends already dead, one of their vehicles being shot up by fire from the .50 caliber machine gun, and now three more HUMVEEs coming through the back gate.

"I got an idea, dad," Randy told his father over the radio. Jerry looked to where he knew his son was positioned and he could just see the berm through the trees. "It's not a very good one, in fact it's a real bad idea, but I think Kellie's in trouble." Jerry could hear a little bit of fear in his son's voice, something he hoped he never had to hear again.

Jerry watched as Randy did something really stupid. He thought quickly. "Eddie, Monica, cover Randy, he going to do something stupid!" he hollered over the other radio to the kids in the Strykers parked on the far hill.

Eddie saw the third heavily-armed vehicle that had entered the rear of the farm crash into the shelter's escape trench. He also saw Randy running toward the crashed HUMVEE. "You're right Jerry. Your son's an idiot, but God love him, look at his fat ass run."

About the Authors

Terry Stenzelbarton is the author of two other books, neither of which has been best-selling, but not bad for someone who is not part of the "in" crowd of authors.

He spent 16 years in the military as a photojournalist, newspaper editor, combat engineer and military policeman.

As a civilian, he has been a sports editor, photographer, traveling salesman, carpenter, computer expert, grave digger, Director of Marketing & Advertising, Information Tech and Software. and most recently started a consulting business called "Rubber Chicken Consulting, LLC."

Jordan Stenzelbarton, lone son and eldest child of Terry is the loving brother to Amanda Stenzelbarton, and exchange students Norwegian Stefan Jenssen and Hungarian Richárd "Rizzo" Seres. He's a fan of video games and reading. He is also an unemployed factory worker.

Together they live, with their little dog, TwiLight's Child, in the same town in which Terry grew up and where they try to scratch out a living, play a little tennis, some softball, a round or two of golf and volunteer their time to Thornapple Valley Church.

Made in the USA
Charleston, SC
10 November 2012